BOURBON HARMONY

A BOURBON CANYON NOVEL

WALKER ROSE

LE Publishing

Rhys Kinkade was my everything. Then he was nothing. Now he's the only thing that can save my career.

Fifteen years ago, I was eighteen and Nashville-bound. I thought Rhys would follow; he knew he wouldn't. Now, I'm one album shy of headlining my own world tour and the words have dried up. Too much betrayal. Not enough fresh mountain air. It's time to come home to Bourbon Canyon.

After Rhys plucks me off the side of the road in the middle of a thunderstorm, it's clear the now-divorced single dad isn't the boy I once loved. For one, his daughters don't know he broke their favorite country singer's heart after high school. For another, he's grumpy. He stress bakes. And he can't put space between us fast enough. And yet, one kiss later and I'm four songs deep into my new album.

With Rhys as inspiration, I can achieve my dream. But when it's time to go, that'll be the end of us. He's never leaving Bourbon Canyon, while the whole world will be my stage. If he can't set aside the past and see what's waiting for us, then the biggest love of my life will be nothing but a bourbon harmony.

CHAPTER ONE

Rhys

Fifteen years ago . . .

June popped out of the cabin when I pulled up. Her jean cutoff shorts framed the top of her curvy legs. She wore an orange Copper Summit T-shirt tied at the waist, and her sandals smacked the floorboards of the porch as she jumped up and down and waved. The long light-brown hair I loved to run my hands through hung loose. The excitement on her face blazed brighter than the summer Montana sun.

I swallowed hard. She was my world, and that world was coming to an end. I'd been through it once before, but I didn't want to shatter hers.

I'd do anything to make sure June Kerrigan got to live out her dreams, and that wouldn't happen for her in tiny Bourbon Canyon, Montana.

I got out of my pickup, my limbs heavy with dread. I was dressed for ranch work in my worn jeans, my beat-up boots, and an old T-shirt. Not for the trip June thought we were taking.

"Hey, babe." She gestured to her car. The back seat was full of boxes and a guitar case. "You can toss your stuff right in. I left you half the trunk space but not as much of the back seat as I promised."

My heart hung heavy at her grin. "I don't have anything."

Her smile dipped. "Oh. Okay. Is your dad dropping your luggage off when he grabs the pickup?"

That would've been the plan. We'd drive together to Nashville. June would work on becoming country music's next rising star. I'd start college at Tennessee State University. We'd live together in a little apartment she'd found and she'd work as a server until someone discovered how fucking amazing she was.

June was my songbird, but she needed the world to hear her songs. She wanted to share her talent, and she should be able to. I wouldn't be the one to stop her. "I'm not going."

Her smile vanished. "What?"

"Dad's leukemia . . ."

She ran down the stairs, her hair streaming behind her. "Oh my god. Did something happen? Did he get worse?"

"No." Just thinking about Dad's illness was making my throat close up. I stepped back from June and the comfort she'd offer. I had to stay strong. "It could be five years, it could be ten." Dad's leukemia diagnosis was fresh and so was the fear that came with it. He'd been tired for months, and I'd been picking up more of the slack. We had answers now, but I wished for sweet ignorance. "They need me. My place is in Bourbon Canyon."

Relief flared, followed quickly by guilt. I wouldn't have to move. I wouldn't have to leave my dad and stepmom to handle a sweeping ranch that had grown to be too much for them too soon. I wouldn't have to worry about stifling June's rise.

Confusion played across her expression. "You're . . . You're not coming?"

"I canceled my enrollment at Tennessee State." I had quit college before I'd even started. I shook my head and stuffed my hands into my jeans before I could capture a strand of her hair and tell her I was kidding, I'd absolutely be there with her every step of the way. If only I wouldn't trip her up. "Dad needs me. Wren's so damn stressed about the ranch."

"He's hiring someone to help, Rhys. So you can go."

"He's hiring me."

Her expression remained bemused. "Your dad *wants* you to go."

"He'd never tell me he needed me to stay." I'd seen Dad's stark relief. He'd have me to run the ranch. My stepmother would have me as support and to help with Dad if he . . . I bit back tears. As he got weaker.

"But he said he wanted you to go more than anything. He said he didn't want to be the one ever holding you back. I was there, Rhys."

"He was lying."

"Jonathon Kinkade does not lie." She folded her arms. "Your daddy wants you to go almost as much as me."

"June . . . He might be dying."

She blinked and a big tear rolled down her cheek. "I —I know. I'm sorry." Another tear.

This time, I didn't hold back. I captured the second drop with my thumb, wishing I could change it into a diamond. I'd wear it on a chain around my neck. A piece of June would be with me every day.

I rubbed the moisture between my thumb and forefinger. It was best I didn't have a trinket to remind me of her. The task of forgetting the girl I'd loved since eighth grade would be impossible enough as it was.

"I am so damn excited for everyone to discover June Bailey." I cupped her face. My determination to tell her I wasn't going was dwindling. I needed to leave, but my boots were stuck in place. She was hurting and it was my fault. "But my place is at the ranch."

"I don't want you to think I'm not worried about your dad. I am." She shook her face out of my grip and started pacing. She swiped her hands under her eyes. "I'm supposed to start work in a week. The lease needs to be signed in three days."

"I'll send money for the rent."

She barked out a laugh. "You're going to pay for a place you're not living in?"

"I'll be a ranch manager."

She quit pacing, her sandals skidding in the dirt. "We've been together since eighth grade. This will be our first time apart." Her lips quivered. "I'm scared."

Tell her it's over. Tell the only girl you've ever loved that you're done. She's going to Tennessee single. Because you're letting your songbird go.

Instead, all I said was, "I know."

The girl had been my everything since I was the new kid in middle school. She'd been my first friend and my first and only girlfriend. Panic filled my chest. This couldn't be the end.

No. It had to be. Dad needed me, and June would do better without me. "I love you, June, but I gotta do this." My voice was strangled at the end.

She sniffled and her eyes welled with more tears. She sucked in a long breath and lifted her chin. "What about tonight? We were supposed to finally have a night together. The first of many."

I wanted that more than fucking anything. To go to sleep with June. To wake up to her. We were adults now. We could be together. Her brothers and sisters thought we were moving in together. Until tomorrow, when June would tell them she had to leave without me.

I'd let her go. She'd tell them I broke her heart. I'd endure the looks and whatever retaliation her brothers thought fit. I'd do it all while nursing my own shattered heart.

"We're going to be across the country from each other." I steeled myself for the task. "I won't be able to visit. It's better for us to see this for what it is. It's the end, June. I'm sorry."

More tears rolled down her cheeks. "Long distance doesn't have to mean the end."

"It's best for us each to take our own path—"

"I know you won't be able to travel, but I can still come home." Her voice wavered and she sniffled, but determination grew in the amber depths of her eyes. "I'll still be doing work for the distillery."

"June—"

"I'll work and save some money, but I'll still come home. It won't be a stressor for you, trying to figure out time away from the ranch and your dad's treatments.

When your dad is better, then you can move out. I'll be there. College will still be there."

"We don't know the timeline on any of this." I didn't know if Dad would even make it through treatment.

She took both my hands in hers. "We can talk every day and see each other over the phone. There are lots of ways two people in love can stay connected."

I loved her with everything I had, and that was why I had to let her go. I couldn't be the reason she suffered. She didn't want to give up on us because she had no idea how much better for her goals that would be. But I did.

"It'll be fine," she continued, her face filling with color again. "I can commute a little more often than planned. Daddy wanted me to do a few voice-overs for some radio promos anyway. Since you won't be in Tennessee, I'll use my time off to keep writing songs. "

My temples throbbed. She wasn't listening. I could barely fathom life without her, but I'd had more time to prepare myself. "June—"

"I can probably even sell some songs. I mean, I think they're pretty good—"

"*June.*"

She stopped, snapping her mouth closed. Hope lit her eyes, then wavered, hanging on to what I would say next. I could tell her we were over again. I could leave to punctuate it. But my stubborn little songbird would follow me. She'd stay with me, and she'd ruin her chances. For me.

My stomach lurched. "What about if you go, and then I'll join you? Just like you said."

"Really?" The light in her eyes brightened. "I know you can't promise me when, but I really think it's the right choice. You'll get to be in Bourbon Canyon with your dad, and I'll get a record deal."

"I want you to get everything." I gripped her shoulders and ducked my head to look her straight in the eyes. "I'll come down, okay? Just, not now." Bile rose in my throat. I'd never lied to June. Until now. "I need you to go ahead without me. When Dad is better or after he —" My voice caught. "If the worst happens, then I'll join you."

A tremulous smile graced her lips. "I'll be waiting." Her gaze was earnest. "Long distance isn't the end. We can't give up on each other."

"I know." I'd never give up on her. But I would give her up. I wrapped my arms around her. She buried her face in my shoulder. "I'm sorry."

She squeezed her hands in my shirt. "You scared me."

"I am scared. About everything."

"I know." She rose on her toes and pressed a kiss to my lips. "Come on. Let's go inside. Can you stay over?" She looked over her shoulder, her big eyes almost pleading.

Goddammit. "Yeah." I pulled her back to me and cupped her cheek in one hand. "Then you're gonna go. Just like Mama Starr would've wanted—you on that stage for everyone to hear."

June's birth mom had nurtured her gift, encouraged her, especially during the hardest of times.

"I wish she could see me. Both of them," she said.

"They'll be with you everywhere you go. When you take the Grand Ole Opry stage, they'll be right here." I tapped a finger over her heart. "And Mae and Darin will absolutely be filling the Opry seats for them." June's adoptive parents had nurtured her talent too.

"I want you there. I want you in the audience."

I lifted her chin and captured her mouth. My dick, half-awake since June had been jumping up and down, paid even more attention. When I'd arrived, I had thought I'd never get to touch her again. This would be my last night. Our last night.

I released her and touched my forehead to hers. "Let's go inside."

"Promise me you won't give up on us."

"Promise me you'll go and be a star," I countered.

"What if no one likes me?"

"Everyone's going to love you. Just like me."

A wide smile graced her face. "You're biased. What if they only let me on the county fair stage because of Daddy and the distillery?"

It was a legitimate concern. Her parents had a ranch much larger than ours, but more impressively, they owned Copper Summit Bourbon Distillery. The distillery invited a lot of tourism and employed many locals. Without Copper Summit, a town as small as Bourbon Canyon might've faded into nothingness, businesses slowly shutting as people moved to larger towns like Bozeman and Lewiston for work and play. Instead, the town thrived, thanks in no small part to the distillery.

But none of that had gotten June up on that stage. It was all her.

"You earned your way onto those stages, just like you'll earn each and every show you perform in Nashville." I tugged her inside the cabin. I was giving myself one last night with her, and suddenly, I was a greedy man. I pushed any thoughts of the future out of my head and concentrated on now. "Now, let's quit wasting time. We don't know when we're going to be together again."

We spent the night in each other's arms. June fell asleep, her soft breathing wafting across my chest, but I stared at the ceiling. I didn't get a damn bit of rest, my mind tumbling until dawn.

When it came time to say goodbye, I didn't fess up and tell her it would be for forever. I hugged her instead, long and hard, trying to communicate how much she meant to me. How much she'd *always* mean to me.

We stood on the porch, her head buried in my chest. The car was loaded with the last of her luggage. Birds chirped like they didn't know or care that it was one of the worst days of my life.

"I can't wait to see you again," she murmured. "I'll make sure to get back as soon as I can."

I'd do my best to make sure she didn't have a reason to, outside of her family.

She rose to her tiptoes and placed a kiss on my lips. "I'll wait for you."

"Be safe, and be yourself. Everyone will love you. But never as much as me."

I finally got her loaded. Her eyes glistened when she drove away.

My gaze wavered and I sniffed. Her car disappeared, and just like that, June Kerrigan was out of my life.

∞

June

Eleven years ago . . .

. . .

I dabbed at my eyes. The gloomy, cold fall weather fit the mood of those gathered at the graveside for Rhys's dad. Wren was destroyed, leaning on Rhys and weeping with a heartbroken sound that made it hard to keep my tears at bay. Only years of performing helped me control my features.

Jonathon Kinkade had been a kind man. I was grateful I had been able to say goodbye to Rhys's dad before I'd moved away.

The church had been packed and I had stayed in the back with my family. My gaze lingered on Rhys, and my heart skittered across my chest wall. He'd never looked so good. Beyond the fatigue and sadness in his eyes was a sexy man where last I'd seen a good-looking kid.

He hadn't met my gaze yet, and honestly, I hadn't tried hard to capture it.

Don't wait for me. The last text I ever got from him.

During my first year away, he'd been "too busy" for phone calls, "too absentminded" to text, and "too broke" to visit Tennessee. After he'd sent that text, my calls and messages had gone unanswered. The very few times I'd returned to Bourbon Canyon, Rhys couldn't be found. I'd finally given up. My sisters occasionally saw him around town. He was congenial, but he never asked about me.

Three years after I had moved, my next oldest sister, Autumn, had hesitantly revealed that she'd seen him at Curly's Canyon Bar and Grill with a woman who'd recently moved to town. He'd started dating. Someone else.

Maybe a lot of someone elses.

So, I'd started dating again too, but I still wasn't convinced our story had ended.

The service wrapped up and an especially chilly wind cut through my pants. I'd worn the cowboy boots Rhys's dad used to say were my CMT Music Award–winning boots. They had teal and pink embroidery on the shaft and toe, and I'd put streaks in my hair to match.

I hadn't been to the CMT Music Awards. Nor had I been to any other award show. I waitressed a lot, nannied a little, and sang on precious few stages.

There'd been a few bright moments, times when I'd thought maybe I was finally crossing the starting line, but when I'd left Nashville yesterday, I'd had one lingering thought: After the funeral, after I caught up with my family . . . should I return to Tennessee? Could I take another four years of toiling away in the slush pile? And another four after that?

I was tired, and coming home only showed me how far everyone else had moved on. Many of my classmates were done with college, living on their own, and working on their careers. Some even had families.

The only reason I didn't have a roommate was because I received some income from the family's bourbon distillery. Daddy had asked me to lend my voice and face to our advertising. I was happy to, and the pay was enough to support me while I sang to half-empty coffeehouses and got my ass grabbed in rowdy bars after a set. But I didn't delude myself. A nepo-baby opportunity wasn't going to make me a country star.

People broke away from the group graveside. Some hurried to their cars to get out of the chill. Others swarmed Wren to offer their support.

My youngest sister, Wynter, squeezed my hand. "Want to ride back to the church with me?"

She'd driven in from Bozeman and met us at the church. I'd ridden with Daddy and Mama.

"Sure. I'd like to talk to Wren first," I said. "Give my condolences."

Wynter linked her arm through mine like she sensed I needed the moral support. My oldest sister, Summer, was already waiting in the group around Wren, but she broke free to join us. Autumn, the next oldest, followed her.

When there was an opening around Wren, I approached, hesitant. We'd exchanged short texts in the time I'd been away, but hers had been sweet and supportive. She hadn't elaborated on Jonathon's condition and she definitely hadn't mentioned Rhys.

Her face crumpled when she saw me, and she held her arms out. I returned her embrace and we hugged for a long time. The pain rolled off her in waves, but she rubbed my back. "It's good to see you, honey."

"I missed you," I murmured into her shoulder. Between Mama's house and Wren's hug, my will to return to Nashville was crumbling. "I'm so sorry."

She released me only to put her hands on my shoulders. Her eyes were red and puffy, but somehow she managed to smile. "I know. Jonathon was proud of you. You should've seen how he beamed when he heard your song on the radio."

Jonathon must have been listening to the right station at the right moment. I wasn't on mainstream radio, but I'd been featured in a Sunday night program of select up-and-comers that maybe a hundred people in the whole country had heard. Since then, my phone and inbox had stayed pretty quiet.

My mama Starr was dead and buried, but each time I trudged into the bar for a shift, I felt like I was letting her down.

Wren let me go and swiped at her eyes. "You have a manager and everything now?"

If she wanted to steal a moment that wasn't about loss and funerals, I'd comply. "Yes. My manager, Lucy, found me at a coffee shop a couple of years ago, but I officially started working with her last year." Lucy was almost the only reason I hadn't run home yet. The other reason was that I didn't know if I had someone to run home to. My family, yes.

Was Rhys seeing anyone?

"It won't be long now before everyone knows your name. You're not going by June Bailey anymore, right?"

"Lucy thought June Bee was catchier." A little sweeter and more innocent, just how people liked their country starlets. But it was also another separation between June the singer and June Kerrigan, the orphaned girl whose parents were homeless, the girl who'd survived the same car crash that had killed her parents. That girl wrote songs about the high school sweetheart who'd let her go. I hadn't shared those songs yet. June Bee wrote about young love and bright futures. Of course, no one was interested.

"June Bee. That is catchy." Her smile dipped when more gatherers approached. A reminder that she was at the burial of the man she loved. She gave my hand a squeeze. "Thank you for coming. It means a lot. I wish you all the best."

Then she was giving my sisters hugs and newcomers were wedging in. I backed out.

Rhys stood ten feet away, his back to me. A few guys lingered around him. I recognized a couple as hired guys at the Kinkade ranch.

I should give Rhys my condolences. We were adults and this funeral wasn't about us. I walked over, my steps slow and dragging. One of the guys saw me, recognition flaring in his eyes. He tapped another guy and cocked his head toward the line of cars parked down the road winding through the cemetery. They walked off and the third guy followed, leaving Rhys alone.

His head was tipped down and he'd shoved his hands in the pockets of a black sports coat. "Rhys."

He turned and my pulse stuttered. Being confronted with a fully grown Rhys was a new experience. One I should have grown into with him.

"June." If he was pleased to see me, he didn't show it. Grief lined his handsome face and darkened his blue eyes. The short, trimmed beard was new and it fit the more solid, more grown-up Rhys. Made him even more ruggedly good-looking.

"I'm so sorry about your dad." I adjusted the lapels of my coat lest I reach out and touch him. "How are you doing?"

His expression softened. "You can imagine. How 'bout you?"

"It's been . . ." Demoralizing? Pointless? Slow? I shrugged. "One step forward and two steps back."

"You knew it might take time."

The way he spoke, alluding to our history, made my chest ache. The light sear of tears touched the backs of my eyes. "Yeah. I just didn't know how lonely it would be, I guess."

He looked away. The muscles in his jaw popped, then his denim-blue gaze cooled. "I'm sure you've made friends. You always do."

Confusion mingled with the hurt and the hope. Had I thought he'd open his arms to me like Wren? That he'd welcome me back and apologize for ghosting me after five years of constantly being by my side?

Yes. I had. "I have, but it's not like home."

"Home isn't like home anymore." He glanced around us. We were attracting the attention of the visitors who lingered in the chill. The burn of their collective gazes seeped through my wool coat, yet I shivered and the movement caught his attention. "Did you get acclimated to Southern weather that fast?"

Like with Wren, I'd take the change of topic and run with it. I was also grateful to be on friendlier ground again. "You should see me walk around in a T-shirt when everyone else is wearing winter coats."

"Your cowboy boots the only ones that've seen some real manure in that town?"

"Not this pair, cowboy." I grinned. He flashed me a smile. The grief briefly vanished from his expression, and the guy I'd fallen in love with stared back at me. The air between us crackled. Then a vacuum opened. The sizzle was gone, leaving only the cold.

His jaw flexed hard. "Thanks for coming."

The changes in his demeanor were giving me whiplash, but he was going through a hard time. "I was thinking of staying for a few days, if you want to talk at all."

The corner of his jaw popped again. "You know that high school stuff is over, right?"

That high school stuff? Another fissure in my heart opened. "I was offering out of concern for you. I still care about you, Rhys."

"You don't need to be concerned for me." His tone softened but only slightly. "We're over. We've been over for a long time."

"You lied to me that day." I winced. I had not meant to bring up the past here. The heartbroken eighteen-year-old in me wanted answers, but she should've waited for a better time and place.

"You didn't want to hear the truth," he said flatly.

I reared back, then caught myself before onlookers could notice. "You spent the night with me knowing you weren't going to Tennessee." My mouth needed to stay shut. *Not the time or place, Junie!* But why? He didn't have to go through any of this alone. I would've been there for him.

His gaze skated away. "Like I said—"

"I didn't want to hear the truth. Right." I swallowed the hard lump of questions I wanted to ask. Why had he lied? Why had he led me on that last night? Why had he given up? All I said was, "I waited."

His hard stare met mine. "I told you not to."

"You *texted* it."

The sound of his sharp inhale cut between us. "You didn't come to my dad's funeral hoping to rekindle something, did you? Because I have to say that was a waste of a plane ticket."

I sucked in cold air. Hurt ignited a blaze in my stomach. How could he go from the love of my life to a jackass? The last four years had to have been hard, but the old Rhys would've never been harsh like this. "I came to pay my respects. I didn't mean . . ." I let out a long exhale. "I didn't mean to bring any of this up. I'm sorry."

"Thank you." He relaxed only slightly. "But you have to know that whatever we had, we were just kids, and I'm not a kid anymore. I have responsibilities, and I can't just leave."

"Your text made that clear."

His wince was subtle. "At least it got you to listen."

My gasp slipped out.

Regret flashed through his eyes and he opened his mouth. But then resolve filled his features once again and he pressed his lips into a line. He yanked his gaze off me, pivoted on a heel, and stalked away.

I swallowed and my raw throat burned. I blinked back tears. I hadn't gotten any answers, but I had gotten clarification. Rhys had never planned to leave Bourbon Canyon. *Never.* I was the fool who'd ignored his words and held on.

Wynter veered away from the group around Wren, her gaze jumping from Rhys's rigid back to me.

"Are you okay?" she asked, searching my eyes.

No. I was wrecked. For only a moment, I'd seen the boy I'd been madly in love with. But he was gone. In his place was a hard man who wanted nothing to do with me. I hadn't been ready to hear him years ago, but I was now. He'd get his wish. "I'm done here. Can we leave?"

Surprise flitted through her eyes, but she nodded. "You can send Mama a message and let her know you're coming with me."

We walked in the opposite direction of the dispersing crowd. Cars lined the narrow roadway that cut through the headstones. I didn't bother to look back.

"Are you leaving tonight?" she asked.

I hugged my arms around myself. "Yes." There was no reason to stay in Bourbon Canyon anymore.

CHAPTER TWO

Rhys

Present day . . .

Darkness had fallen. Big, juicy raindrops splattered the windshield. I turned the wipers up a notch and squinted out the window. I wasn't usually out this late, but Bethany and Hannah had each been in the school play. Afterward, Wren had invited us to her house for ice cream.

The treat was innocuous enough, but Wren loved to indulge the girls. Whipped cream, caramel, fudge, sprinkles, cherries. They'd wanted to plan all the activities for their annual school's-out Grandma visit too. Wren took the girls for two weeks each summer, starting the weekend after the last day of school. It had started with an overnight, and the length grew each year, especially after my divorce.

"Dad, my tummy's upset," nine-year-old Bethany groaned.

Shit. "Is there a bag or something back there?" I glanced at the back seat of my pickup. She was pale and grimacing. "Why don't you have your glasses on?"

"I don't need them," she said with the weakness of someone on their deathbed.

I suppressed my heavy sigh. "It's dark, Bethany. No one can see you."

"Here they are." Hannah yanked out the motion sickness goggles. The opaque white frames were filled with blue liquid. Giant circles on the sides gave her four googly eyes. She looked cute in them, but she'd rather puke up copious amounts of ice cream than be caught with them on her face.

"Put 'em back. I'm already sick." But not too sick to argue with her younger sister, apparently.

"Can you just wear them and see if they'll help?" We lived out of town, and I was still on the highway.

"But it's raining," she argued. "Isn't that liquid enough?"

I checked the rearview mirror. Bethany was shoving at the glasses. The fluid inside of them was supposed to signal her brain that we were moving or some shit. Would rain imitate the effect? "I don't want to find out it's not enough after you throw up."

"Ugh, fine." Bethany stuffed them on. "I still don't feel good."

Maybe it was the rich food her stomach wasn't used to.

Up ahead, blinking lights caught my eye. I slowed. Our turnoff was soon, but I could make out the dark outline of a car about a hundred yards beyond it. The hood was open. Someone was stranded.

I didn't want to be a Good Samaritan today. I wanted to get home before pukefest began and get the girls to bed.

A figure crossed in front of the hazards. Shapely legs. Most likely a woman. My inner chivalrous man reared up, the bastard. Whoever it was likely had a phone. They were probably local and had someone to call. I didn't need to rush in to save the day.

Although tourists took random roads all the time and got more than they bargained for in the Montana wilderness.

The rain grew heavier and a crooked flash of lightning lit the sky.

Shit. I had to at least make sure they had everything they needed. The girls were with me, so it wasn't like I would be giving a stranger a ride, but I could ensure all was well. "Someone needs help up ahead. I'm gonna check on them. You two stay in the car with the doors locked."

Both perked up, unbothered by my warning.

"Remember—stay in the car." I eased to the side of the road and turned my hazards on but stopped twenty yards behind the stranded motorist.

I kept the engine running. Who knew what kind of person I was helping? "I'll lock the doors. Watch for me and unlock them."

I got out. Rain pelted me in the face. I tucked my chin down and jogged toward the car. Whoever the girl was, she wasn't by the trunk. I couldn't see a blown-out tire. Must mean engine issues. I blinked water out of my eyes and made a wide arc around the front. If this lady wasn't stable, or if I surprised her, I didn't want to be close if she lashed out.

But I didn't want to terrify the poor girl, so I called, "Need a hand?"

The woman was bending over the engine, barely sheltered by the open hood. Her top hung down and I caught nice cleavage and the shadow of her bra.

I swallowed hard and looked away, but my gaze landed on long legs. I jerked my attention to her face and found large amber eyes blinking at me and ripe pink lips opened in shock.

"Rhys?" Her voice rolled over me just as a crack of thunder rent the air. An uncomfortable heat filled my veins that had nothing to do with the storm. Because I knew that voice.

Everyone knew that goddamn voice. Her songs played every hour on the radio, and her face was splashed across every screen. Everywhere I turned, I heard her voice or read her name.

A guy shouldn't have to avoid his past in his own goddamn house, but the high school sweetheart who'd left me behind for fame and fortune sure as fuck made it happen every damn day.

"June."

June

Anxiety fled just having Rhys Kinkade so close. Irritation filled its place. Why did he have to be the one to come to my rescue in this storm?

Why had I decided to go to the hunting cabin tonight?

It was my refuge, and I'd been seeking a hiding place. Somewhere no one but my family knew about. I had a lot of homes. The press liked to make a big deal out of it whenever I bought one, but they didn't know about the cabin Daddy had given me.

And miracle of all miracles, they didn't know about Rhys. He was my before, and my fans didn't care about my before. They thought my life had been nothing but bourbon and small-town Montana. My present-day relationships were of more interest than my past.

It'd been ten years since I'd seen more than a passing glance of him. For a guy so unbothered about our breakup, he sure did go out of his way to avoid me when I was in town. But then, I did the same.

Now I was facing him. His dark hair was plastered against his forehead and his short beard glistened from the rain. His scar bisected his upper lip to the left of his nose. His soaked shirt was plastered against his hard chest. My mouth watered.

He had changed so much since we were kids. How much wider his shoulders had become. How burly he'd gotten. I couldn't answer why the darkness in his expression sent tingles right down my spine to between my legs, but here I was, soaked to the bone, cold, and wishing he'd make me feel as good as he once used to.

Don't wait for me.

Well, that doused the lust effectively.

"What are you doing out here?" His incredulity hadn't dissipated.

What was I doing here? Wasn't that a story the media would want? "The engine just died."

He raked his irritated gaze over the car. It was dark and the glare of the headlights from his pickup made it impossibly hard to see the deep blue of his irises. "Have you called anyone?"

God, no.

Thunder split the night. I jumped and squeezed my eyes shut. I was safe. The car was fine. I was fine.

"Shit." Rhys's eyes flashed, ripe with indignation, then he turned and beckoned me to follow him. "Come on. We'll talk in the pickup."

I was tired of being told what to do and, most of all, wary of being manipulated, but when Rhys ordered me to do something, my brain shut off and my body listened.

My only other choices were to walk the six miles to the cabin or to get into my dead, brand-new car and call one of my siblings. Then I'd have to explain who, what, when, where, and why I was back in Montana.

I had just . . . needed to leave it all for a few days. But that explanation wouldn't satisfy my family.

He jogged around the passenger side and knocked on the door. Someone moved inside and then the locks thunked. Who was with him? He opened the door for me.

I smiled my thanks at him, but he refused to look at me. He stepped out of my way and opened the back door. "Get that blanket and pass it up to the front, please."

His voice had turned kinder, impossibly gentle. He'd said please. I was no longer a recipient of that tone.

I peered into the back seat before I crawled in.

Oh my god. Of course he had his daughters along. "Hey," I said timidly. I'd seen him with them around town, but they hadn't seen me. My big floppy hat and sunglasses might be over the top, but they allowed me a surprising amount of anonymity. The getup had given me moments to spy on a version of Rhys who doted on his adorable little girls.

One audible gasp sounded, followed by another. Two sets of big eyes pinned me.

There it was. The recognition. I scrambled into the pickup and was surrounded by his cedar-and-soap scent. That part hadn't changed.

He got in on the other side. Droplets cascaded from his hair and down his face.

"You're June Bee," one of the girls said.

"I am. What's your name?"

Both girls giggled.

"I'm Bethany."

"Hannah."

They each spoke so fast I couldn't tell who said what.

"I can't believe it," the one with odd goggles gushed. "I heard you were from Bourbon Canyon, but I've never seen you. I almost didn't believe it."

I frowned at their dad. He wouldn't look at me. He just shoved a fluffy red-plaid blanket toward me. He hadn't told the girls we'd been friends? Of course he wouldn't have told them about the women before their mom, but these two had no idea I even *knew* their dad, much less how intimately well.

At least he hadn't told them he hated me. Because he'd acted like it at his dad's funeral.

"Yes, I was born and raised in Bourbon Canyon." I stared at Rhys. A muscle in his jaw was popping. I draped the blanket over my lap. I hated to get it soaked, but shivers were racing up and down my body. I'd be shaking soon. "Your dad and I used to go to school together."

The first day he'd shown up in my class, he'd cringed when the teacher had announced he'd been living in New York City and he'd also lived in LA. All the kids had peppered him with questions about the big city, but during lunch I had set my tray next to his and asked what his favorite song was.

The relief and gratitude in his eyes were something I still treasured despite everything.

A high-pitched squeal came out of the oldest. "Really? You know our dad?"

"Really." I grinned back at her. Whatever those goggles were for, they were supercute on her. When she spotted me eyeing them, she groaned and clawed at her face to get them off.

"Don't take them off," I said. "They look good."

She stopped and slowly pushed them back into place. "Really?"

"Absolutely. What do you wear them for?" They didn't have lenses.

"I get motion sickness."

"Ah. May I try them on?"

The girl thrust them at me. I put them on and vogued. "Who wore them better?"

Giggles erupted from them.

The youngest squealed, "June Bee's wearing Bethany's glasses!"

"I'm just a girl like you." I winked at Bethany as I handed them back. "Can I trust you both with a secret?"

Rhys cut his head toward me, a furrow bisecting his brow, one I itched to outline with my finger. The line was new, but it fit him. He'd always been a serious kid.

The girls were quiet, waiting for me to continue. I had their rapt attention, but their dad had half of mine.

"I don't want anyone to know I'm here for a while," I confessed. "I just need some time to relax." To lick my wounds. To repair my pride. To figure out why the hell I'd been so gullible. "Can you keep seeing me to yourselves?"

"It'll be our secret," Hannah said. She had her dad's dark-blue eyes and chestnut hair.

"Thanks." I clutched the blanket as a shiver racked my body.

Rhys punched the heater on and turned it up to high. "Girls, you don't keep secrets when a stranger asks you to, even when that stranger's a *celebrity*."

I bristled at his tone. I was more than a media puppet. I was more than a caricature of a singer. I wrote my own music and I sang to my strengths. My talent was real.

I just had to figure out what else was. "Are we strangers, Rhys?"

His eyes narrowed. This man was not used to being challenged. But he had a point. He had daughters to keep safe and I was a stranger to them. And to him too.

I sighed. "I shouldn't have asked you guys to keep a secret, but if it's okay with your dad"—I lifted a brow at the brooding man behind the wheel—"I'd appreciate it if you kept my visit quiet."

"Daddy?" one of the girls said.

He worked his jaw. "Yeah, that's fine." Without looking at me, he said, "Do you need to call Tate or one of your other siblings?"

I shook my head. "Can you just take me to the cabin? I'll deal with the car on Monday."

He slanted a quick glance toward me like he wanted to ask more questions, but there were two sets of ears in the back seat. "Do you have some luggage you need to bring?"

"I can get it later."

"With what?"

Good point. My new car was the only set of wheels I had. "I'll go grab it."

He shook his head and kicked the pickup into gear. He pulled up next to my defunct car. I put my hand on the door handle.

"Don't." He twisted in his seat. The position made his chest broader, and those abs . . . I bet he still looked good with his shirt off. "Stay here and don't bombard Miss Kerrigan with questions."

Miss Kerrigan? I was highly insulted he, of all people, had addressed me so formally but also soothed because how blissfully normal did it sound? "Junie is fine. And I'm okay with questions." I loved chatting with kids. But he shot me a disgruntled look. I held my hands up. "But your dad said no questions, so no questions."

His headshake was barely perceptible as he got out. The rain muffled the thunk of the tailgate and then he moved my two suitcases and my guitar case to the bed of the pickup. He had a bed cover. My items would be protected.

"Why'd he call you Miss Kerrigan?" Hannah asked.

A smile tugged at my lips. Little rebels. No parental injunction would stop them. "It's my name. The Baileys adopted me and my sisters a long time ago, but we kept our birth name to remember our other parents by." I winked at them. "I also like being able to come home and just be Junie Kerrigan."

They smiled, but nothing more came from the back seat. If they didn't ask more questions, then I'd stare at their dad's powerful body as he rescued my luggage, and Rhys had made it clear I was not welcome to him or his body.

So I would be the one pestering them with questions. The one I really wanted to ask was *Did your dad really not mention me?* "So . . . how old are you two?"

"I'm almost ten," Bethany said.

"And I'm almost nine," Hannah said in a singsong voice. "We were just at our play tonight."

I perked up. "Oh yeah? Who's your teacher?"

"Mrs. Ellison."

"Oh, I know her. She's so nice."

Rhys climbed back into the truck. He was soaked again. I lifted the corner of the blanket to dab at his face.

He pulled back, his expression aghast. "What are you doing?"

Trying to touch him. I dropped my hand to my lap. The move had been instinctive, but embarrassment chased some of the chill away. "You're soaked."

His gaze dipped to my chest and shot back to meet mine. "You need to cover up more. You're the one who's drenched."

I straightened in my seat and glanced down. My gauzy cream shirt was plastered to my boobs and the outline and color of my yellow bra was plainly visible. So were my hard nipples, and there were kids in the car. Abashed, I tugged the blanket up.

Yesterday, I had wanted to get away. To figure my life out. Why did my car have to die? Why did it have to be so close to the turnoff to where Rhys now lived?

Why did he have to be the one to find me?

Because I hadn't called my brothers. They lived for coming to their sisters' aid. Instead, I'd gotten Rhys. The ex who wanted nothing to do with me and hadn't even told his daughters he used to date the country singer they seemed to be fans of.

I'd done what he'd told me to. I hadn't waited for him. I'd made a name for myself. Once I found some peace and finished the album my record label was waiting on, I'd be gone again.

His jaw was tight as he kicked the pickup in gear and took off toward the cabin.

CHAPTER THREE

Rhys

Why wasn't she calling her family? Why was her brand-new car a lemon? Why was she in Bourbon Canyon anyway?

My windshield wipers were going fast and furious. How could a rain-soaked June Kerrigan smell so damn good? Like fresh blooming peonies during the month she was named after. The month that was my favorite time of the year.

I'd have some explaining to do with my girls when we got home. The town was protective of their singing Kerrigan. People spoke among themselves about her but otherwise kept her privacy right where it needed to be. My history with her was not forgotten but had been brushed off as insignificant. If someone tried to bring up me and June, I changed the subject real damn fast. Most of the teachers in the girls' school were transplants who didn't know how hot and heavy it'd been between us back in the day. Though June's sister Autumn and her sister-in-law, Scarlett, were also teachers in town, they seemed to know I didn't want the gossip spreading to the girls.

I'd skated through it all for years until tonight.

I navigated the narrow road to the goddamn cabin. Of all places, why did we have to return there?

The girls and I had lived at the old Dunn ranch for a few years, and of course I'd known the cabin was only six miles away, but it seemed like a hundred miles when June wasn't within state lines.

I'd spent plenty of time at that place with June. More than her parents probably knew or wanted to know. Those memories had been shoved back into the recesses of my brain since I last walked out the door.

The road wound through the foothills and just where the trees started growing thicker, there was a flat landing and an outline of a dark building.

The Baileys kept the place up, but how long had it sat empty? Was it ready for someone to seek refuge there during a storm?

Uneasiness settled in my gut. "You're staying here?"

"Yeah. Tenor makes sure the power and water are still good. He said he was out last month after most of the snow melted and checked on everything."

She had both vents aimed at her, but she continued to shiver. I slowed as I approached. The dirt path to the door was now mud. June was wearing strappy sandals.

I remembered when those long legs had disappeared into cowboy boots. Did she save those for the camera to keep her country persona alive?

The next strike of lightning showed me how thin her shirt was, as if I hadn't been noticing already. Her satiny skin was covered in goose bumps, and worse, there was fear in her eyes. She wasn't comfortable staying out here alone in a storm.

Of course she wasn't. How much of her shivering was from being stranded in a car in a rainstorm? She'd been in the car with her sisters when her parents had crashed and died. She might be an adult, but that shit stayed with a person.

Fuck me. "Is there bedding and a TV or something?"

Her bark of laughter was full of scorn. "I'm staying away from TV and social media. I just want to crawl into bed and sleep for five days."

"You're only here for five days?" I could gut out that length of time.

"Uh, a little longer." A low, growly noise filled the air. She pressed her hands to her stomach and her cheeks flushed pink. She gave me a forced smile that I hated. "Thanks for the ride."

"Do you have food in there?"

"Um . . ." She studied the house. "There might be some canned food?"

Was she asking me or telling me?

"She can stay with us, Daddy," Bethany offered.

My stomach bottomed out. No fucking way. June under my roof? The house was my safe place, the only location I could go that didn't have memories of June.

June shot her a kind smile. "Thanks for the offer, but it's late and I've intruded enough."

She was cold and likely had no food. And she was alone when something was clearly wrong.

Stay out of it. I'd been strong for fifteen years, I couldn't break now.

Fuck me.

Instead of pulling closer to the house and gouging the muddy land with my tire tracks, I swung around and backed up.

June whipped her head toward me. "What are you doing?"

"Like Bethany said, you can stay with us."

"N-no. It's fine."

I didn't glance over to see if she looked as alarmed as she sounded. "We have a guest room with a bed already made up and we have food."

"Daddy stress bakes," Hannah said proudly. "We have muffins and strudel and cookies."

"You bake?" June asked.

I kept my gaze out the window. The brush of her astonishment licked over my damp skin. "I've learned a few things since you left town."

If she heard the bitterness in my tone, she ignored it. "I bet you have."

June

Rhys drove to the old Dunn place. Summer's husband had grown up on this ranch. She'd dated Jonah's younger brother in high school and college, so my sisters and I had visited this place before. Jonah's brother had gotten killed drinking and driving, almost taking Jonah out with him. Due to the injuries, Jonah had stopped helping his dad ranch. A couple of years ago, I'd heard Jonah's parents were moving and that Rhys had bought the place.

"This is our new ranch," Hannah said.

"It's not new," Bethany said, sounding exactly like Summer used to when we were kids and she'd barely tolerated her sisters' helpful comments. "We've lived here since I was seven."

Rhys parked by the back door. The garage was detached—for now. Support beams were erected between the house and garage. He was enclosing them. Was he doing the work himself?

What'd he look like all sweaty? If it was hot, did he work with his shirt off? I used to love catching him with his shirt off.

But that was then. I'd seen lots of men without their shirts since. Professional athletes. Country singers. Random men at the bar who thought their muscles were tip enough. Muscles didn't affect me.

Would he wear a really tight shirt or take it off entirely?

Nope. I was done with men for more than a little while. I wanted a guy who wanted me, and only me. Two standards that had been lacking in my dating history.

"Girls," Rhys said, "it's way past your bedtime. I know we have a guest, but you both need to brush your teeth, get into pajamas, and crawl into bed. I'll be there to tuck you in after I get Miss Kerrigan settled."

"Junie," I said on a sigh.

He didn't acknowledge me and got out. I folded the blanket and left it on the seat when I climbed out. The girls took off inside, screeching about the cold rain.

I ducked through the downpour and went to the back of the pickup to get my stuff.

"I got it," he said through gritted teeth. We were

getting pelted with fast, tiny drops. The storm had grown in strength.

Grateful I didn't have to spend the night waiting for an empty cabin to heat up while I was starving, I lifted my guitar case. "I'm already here."

We carried my stuff in.

Inside the door, I set the case down on a long rug, and he put my luggage next to it and ran back out, probably to park in the garage.

I wiped rain off my face and inhaled. The place had a homey smell. Baked goods. A hint of cedar and fresh linen from the laundry room behind me. The kitchen was square, with a squat dining room at one end. Modern cabinet doors updated the whole look. Either Rhys or Jonah's parents must've switched them out.

If Rhys had done it, had he been shirtless?

I was tired. Policing my thoughts was too hard right now.

At my feet, polished hardwood stretched through the kitchen and into the living room on the other side of the wall. A square table butted against the far wall and a tiny island on wheels sat in the middle.

I peered into the living room. I could make out pictures of the girls, furniture upholstered in earth tones, and more blankets than I had in the whole cabin.

Footsteps pounded down the stairs on the other side of the living room wall.

Bethany peeked out. "Do you know where your room is?"

I didn't know a whole lot about my life at this point. "No. Is it upstairs or down?"

"Daddy's room and the guest room are downstairs.

Me and Hannah sleep upstairs." She beamed. "We each get our own room."

I smiled. I had been terrified at first to have my own room when my sisters and I had gone to live with the Baileys. "Awesome."

Bethany straightened and swept her arm toward the kitchen. "Help yourself to a muffin."

My stomach clenched at the mention of food. "Thank you."

I toed off my sandals and crossed to the counter. A round serving plate of muffins was piled high under a clear plastic dome. Stress baking. Rhys had barely ever turned an oven on when we dated.

The muffin was full of shredded carrots and coconut. The thing was like a ripe orange, much heavier than it looked. I continued to inspect the handiwork of a man I no longer knew as I leaned against the counter and kicked the heel of one foot against the ankle of my other leg.

I took a mouthful and groaned. My eyes rolled back in my head. So decadent.

The back door opened. I opened my eyes and found Rhys staring at me. His shirt was plastered to his barrel chest and his hooded blue gaze was unreadable. He'd packed muscle onto every inch of his frame, and he'd been a sturdy guy when we'd dated.

The beard changed him the most from the boy I'd planned my life with. When I'd seen him around, I'd done little more than note how good it looked on him. But this close?

Heat seeped in, curling through my belly and lighting up places that should be locked up solid while I got my life back on track. I'd get on top of those feelings once I got some sleep.

I dropped my gaze first. "Bethany offered me a muffin."

He jerked like he was snapping out of a trance. "I can heat up some leftover spaghetti."

My stomach twisted. I was so fucking hungry. My body knew I was home. The stress had rolled off my shoulders and I could just . . . be. I could forget what I'd left behind. The expectations. The obligations. The betrayal.

But Rhys was still dripping on the rug by the door like he was afraid to enter any farther into the same room as me.

"No, thanks. The muffin will be enough." When everyone was asleep, I could sneak a second one. I took another bite.

His gaze grew more intense, then he looked away. "I'll make sure your bedroom's ready."

He took his boots off. His jeans curved under his heels when he walked, just like before. I used to tease him about fraying the bottoms of his jeans like that.

An unexpected ache in my chest made me wince. I took another bite of muffin. "God, this is good," I said around my mouthful. A delight to my taste buds. I missed home-cooked food.

"It's got shredded carrots and zucchini. Sometimes it's the only vegetables I get into the girls."

My mouth went dry. He was a family man. I gulped the bolus of muffin down. "They're adorable."

"The muffins?"

"No, the—" I caught the twinkle in his eye. Years

melted away between us and I laughed. "The muffins. Absolutely adorable."

He cleared his throat, his gaze skating away. "The girls are the best. I'm a lucky guy."

"What's Kirstin doing these days?" I stuffed the rest of my muffin in my mouth before I asked more questions like a jealous ex-lover.

"She's in Costa Rica, shooting the scarlet macaw and the great green macaw."

"Wow." Rhys hadn't moved on from me to a slouch. "Why macaws?"

"Why not?" His flat tone said everything. Why not photograph macaws when you could've stayed with a man like Rhys? Why not travel to fabulous places for your job? Why not do whatever the hell you wanted to do, even if it meant leaving your own children behind?

I tried to swallow my giant mouthful, but a crumb caught in my throat and I coughed. Shit. I turned my back on him. My irritated throat ignited more coughing.

Was this how I would go? Choking on his homemade goodies while talking about his ex-wife?

His heat surrounded me and a glass of water appeared next to me. "Drink."

I took a long pull. A few more small coughs came out. I gulped another mouthful.

"Thanks," I wheezed.

He didn't move away. I didn't want him to.

"Take it easy, June Bug. I've been told my baked goods are to die for, but you don't have to prove it."

I smiled weakly up at him. "They're seriously good though. When did you start baking?"

A crease formed in his brow. "Why are you back and don't want your family to know?"

I chewed on the inside of my cheek. I'd stuff another muffin in my mouth if I hadn't just choked myself. "Baking's a touchy subject. Noted."

"No." He sighed and ruffled his damp hair. "It was a way to take my mind off Dad being sick and . . . Anyway. I kept doing it and the girls were born, so I had to keep cooking and baking."

A way to take his mind off his dad and me. "Why don't your girls know about us?" I bit the inside of my cheek, but it was pointless. The question was out.

As close as we were, I could see the deeper-blue striations in his irises. He clenched his jaw and looked away. "Why would I talk about my ex with my girls?"

"I get that, Rhys, but come on. I'm not just any ex." And he'd been divorced for years.

"You want to know why I didn't brag about dating country music darling June Bee?"

When he said it like that, I sounded arrogant. *Country music darling.* That was me. My next album was supposed to catapult me all the way to the top. If I could write it. "I just thought since Bethany and Hannah are fans . . ."

"All girls their age are," he said flatly. "But my ex isn't."

"Gotcha." His ex probably wasn't the only reason he'd stayed quiet on the subject of June Bee. I doubt he wanted to talk about me with anyone. Was it the stress of staying behind that had turned him off me so hard? Did he resent me for leaving? Or did he resent me for hanging on when he'd wanted a clean break?

I'd never know, and I'd moved on.

I looked around his kitchen. Somehow I hadn't moved far.

He strode to my luggage and lifted my bags. "The guest room is down the hallway off the living room. You can bring your water."

I lifted the glass in a salute. When he disappeared, I refilled the cup. Then I went for my guitar. I sucked in a deep breath and followed Rhys deeper into the house.

Fifteen years after our one night in the cabin, I was sleeping under the same roof as him again. In different beds, in different rooms. Only this time I would go to sleep knowing there wasn't a future for us.

CHAPTER FOUR

Rhys

My night of sleep had been really fucking fitful. A woman I'd never thought I'd interact with again slept across the hallway. Last night, I'd dropped her bags in the guest room and checked on the girls. By the time I'd retreated to my room, June's door had been closed.

After years of changing the radio station when the first notes of her songs played, averting my eyes at Copper Summit bourbon billboards plastered with her smiling face, and avoiding anything related to her family's distillery in case I ran into her, June Kerrigan was right across the hall.

I needed to piss, but this old house didn't have a bathroom in the main bedroom.

Was she awake?

I hadn't heard a peep. The girls were sleeping in after their late night. Otherwise, they'd be knocking down my door, excited *the* June Bee was under their roof.

Rolling up, I suppressed a groan. I was fucking tired, but I had to get some chores done.

Since there hadn't been a single floorboard creaking, I put on a pair of sweats and tiptoed to the bathroom. The reflection staring back at me was of a thirty-four-year-old guy with messy hair, bloodshot eyes, and a couple of gray strands in his beard that had appeared in the last couple of years.

I shoved a hand through my hair. Now it was messy but going in the same direction.

When I was done, I swung open the door and faced wide amber eyes.

"Oh." Her gaze dropped to my shirtless chest and her pink lips parted. "*Oh*. Sorry."

What did the second "Oh" mean? Was she impressed? I hadn't been a scrawny kid, but years of helping my parents on their ranch and then building my own, plus a hobby farm, had packed on some muscle.

I wasn't the clean, manufactured country boy she'd been dating lately.

Irritation itched along the back of my neck. "It's all yours."

She didn't move. Her long light-brown hair with gentle blue highlights billowed around her face. She wore a tank top, and one strap hung off her shoulder. I fought a worthy battle against checking if the front of her top was dipping because of that damn strap.

Her gaze danced from my left shoulder to my right and brushed over the dark hair on my chest. I rocked a faint farmer's tan on my biceps and at the base of my neck. Some of the recent spring days had been warm while I cleaned up the flower beds and gardens, and the sun had left its print.

The interest in her eyes was like a time machine, transporting me back to when we'd hole up in that cabin of hers and do very adult things to each other. Warmth coiled through my gut and further south until it threatened to give me an erection that wouldn't go away.

"June," I barked. "You're in the way."

Embarrassment flooded her expression, and she hopped to the side. "Sorry. It's just— It's not— It's been a while since I've seen you shirtless."

Fifteen goddamn years. "Yep." I brushed past her and stalked to my room. Inside, I could take my first full breath in several minutes. My blood was boiling for a reason other than anger.

Long fucking legs. So damn curvy. I wasn't the only one who'd filled out.

I scrubbed a hand down my face. "Fuck."

I dressed in jeans and a black T-shirt. When I left my bedroom, I was shrugging into a red flannel shirt when the bathroom door opened and June breezed out.

She ran into my chest. Thankfully, my arms were trapped half in the sleeves or I might've done something idiotic like wrap them around her.

"Jesus, June Bug. It's a small house, not one of your presidential suites."

Her face went from stunned to mutinous. "You're right. My chalet in the Alps has a kitchen the size of this entire house." Sarcasm dripped from every word.

"You have a chalet?" Bethany's excited voice broke between us.

June spun, the soft strands of her hair tickling my skin. "No, I was kidding. I have a place in Nashville."

I lost the battle with my eye muscles. My gaze dropped to her ass. Fuck.

Two round globes were right in front of me. If I stepped forward, we'd be flush. We'd always fit together so damn perfectly.

"I travel a lot, so I don't see the need for a big house," June continued when I needed her to put a lot of distance between us real quick. "But I have stayed in some presidential suites."

"Cool." Bethany grinned. "Daddy, can I have a muffin?"

"Yeah. I'll be right there." I took one more look at a billboard-worthy ass. "When someone gets out of my way."

Bethany giggled like I was kidding around. June shot a scowl over her shoulder. She stepped aside with a saccharine smile. "Excuse me, Mr. Kinkade."

I grunted and passed her, adjusting my shirt, and when I turned the corner and no one could see, I palmed my unruly dick back in place.

In the kitchen, Bethany was staring at the muffins and worrying her lower lip between her teeth. "Daddy, I feel like we should have something better for June Bee for breakfast."

"Why?"

"She's famous."

Fuck me. I pressed a palm against my forehead. "She puts her pants on one leg at a time like the rest of us." That wasn't the imagery I needed right now.

"Can you make her pancakes and eggs?"

"I'll make you and Hannah pancakes and eggs, and she's welcome to have some."

Bethany's relieved grin was my answer. "Thank you, Daddy."

I started digging ingredients out. Bethany got the griddle for me.

Hannah entered the kitchen, rubbing her eyes. Her little feet stuck out from her pajama pants. Clarity wiped out the sleep in her expression. "She's here!"

She darted upstairs, presumably to change.

I shook my head and continued cooking. Soon, the kitchen smelled of sausage and sweet buttermilk pancakes.

"Morning, Kinkade crew," June's voice rang out. I kept my back to her.

"Morning, June Bee," Hannah said.

"Aw, you can call me Junie like everyone else."

"Daddy doesn't call you Junie," Bethany said.

"Your daddy has called me a lot of things over the years."

I stiffened. I had used all the endearments on her once upon a time. I steeled myself and faced her. She wore black leggings and a long, multicolored sweater. Thank fuck she wasn't wearing her cowboy boots, so I could stay in the present where I belonged. "You gonna eat?"

"Sure. Do you need a hand?"

God, no. I didn't need to be dancing around her. "Nope." The girls had already set the table. They'd taken extra care with June's spot and argued over what side the napkin should go on. "Have a seat."

"Right here." Hannah did a little curtsy by the chair.

Everything was done cooking. I loaded the sausage, eggs, and cakes onto a rectangular serving plate and turned. The wall I'd built for fifteen years and fortified with steel cracked. Longing rammed into my chest so hard I almost staggered back.

June was smiling, her hair cascading down her back. She was listening attentively to the girls, nodding and laughing at all the right places. Even worse, none of it was for show. I knew her too well. I could tell when she was putting on a performance, during an interview or on stage.

Of course, I had avoided watching all those.

She glanced over at me and her happiness faltered. Her gaze landed on the food heaped on the plate and a light brow lifted. The corner of her mouth tipped up. She found my domestic skills amusing. At my glower, that smirk turned into a full grin.

The girls were watching us.

"Did you know," June started in an *I've got a secret* tone that had my girls on full alert, "that when I knew your dad, he didn't even know how to turn on an oven?"

Hannah's scandalized gasp rang through the kitchen. "He didn't?"

"Of course I did." I stomped to the table and dropped the food in the middle. "Sit and eat up." I sat in my chair and scooted forward with extra force. "Wren made sure I knew how to cook, but I spent all my free time and then some with you."

The kitchen went silent. Two pairs of owlish eyes gawked at me, and I ignored the pair of shocked amber ones.

How could I save my epic fuckup? I did not need my girls knowing their celebrity idol had been like my other half and I'd felt half-empty since she'd left. "We used to hang out."

"And do what?" Bethany asked.

June speared a sausage link. "Yeah, Rhys. What did we do?" She took a bite off the tip.

Lust rammed into my gut. "Talked about knitting."

"You don't knit!" Hannah said.

"Well"—I shrugged—"you can see why we lost touch, then. Eat up."

June's gaze turned introspective, but I worried about loading plates.

"Where's your guitar?" Bethany asked.

June flipped some stray strands of hair over her shoulder, half of them blue. "In the guest room."

Excitement lit Bethany's eyes. "I want to learn to play."

"Me too," Hannah said. "And piano."

"I can do a mean 'Chopsticks' on piano," June said with a smile. "But I can teach you how to play guitar."

Alarm sent my fork skidding across my plate until a pile of eggs landed on the table. June did not need to be in my house, cozied up with my kids any more than she already was. She was too easy to fall in love with, and the girls were already halfway there with her entertainment persona.

June was hard as hell to fall *out* of love with. Proximity was not a good thing. "You can't just make offers without talking to me. I know you're used to planning everything around you, but I have others to think about."

The blaring silence made a return.

"I'm sorry," June said quietly. "It'd have to be okay with your dad."

The girls shrank in on themselves.

Guilt replaced my flare of irritation. It wasn't June's fault I wanted her far away from me. Just like it wasn't her fault I'd been an ass the last time we talked. But neither of us could do the things we needed to do in life if we were in each other's orbit.

I flipped the eggs back onto my plate. "I've gotta get outside. I'm already late and the animals are hungry. Girls, feed the cats and dog when you're done." I rose and stuffed an entire pancake in my mouth on the way to the sink.

Then I shoved my feet into my boots, grabbed my cowboy hat, and stormed outside. The girls would be fine in the house with June. I'd trust June with my kids' lives, but I couldn't trust myself not to unearth all those feelings that had taken me years to bury.

⁂•

June

"Honestly, you don't have to help." I lugged a suitcase after Bethany. She was carrying my other one with both hands instead of rolling it. Hannah was struggling with the guitar case. She'd run it into the wall once and almost died of fright until I adamantly reassured her the guitar was fine, that was why it was in a case.

"I wish you didn't have to go," Hannah said, huffing through her haul.

"I wish you could give us lessons," Bethany said with so much disgruntlement I almost felt sorry for Rhys. He was going to *get it* from her.

"I'm sure your dad has a good reason."

Bethany's stomps grew louder. "He never yelled when I asked to raise a goat for 4-H."

"I got a chicken," Hannah added.

Finally, my luggage was at the door. I stuffed my sandals into one of my bags. I'd already dug out my most comfortable pair of cowboy boots that I didn't keep at Mama's place.

Tenor pulled up in a pickup. Clumps of mud from last night's rain caked the sides until I could hardly see the blue underneath. Tenor was the mellowest of my brothers and the youngest. He was also the most likely to stay out of my business if I asked.

The girls grabbed what they'd been carrying before. Tenor got out and dropped the tailgate. He grinned and waved. He didn't rush to help Bethany or Hannah, ever the mentor for teaching kids how to handle themselves. It was a hazard of the household we'd been raised in, with its multitude of foster kids. Everyone had to pull their share.

I stepped out, ready to leave this ranch behind and forget Rhys's cutting comment about how selfish I was.

"Tenor." Rhys's voice cut through the day. He was walking toward us from the barn. Goats roamed a large pen next to the red building, and red-feathered chickens darted in and out of the open barn door.

"Hey, Rhys," Tenor replied. "Thanks for rescuing Junie last night. Hell of a thing. Brand-new car just dying."

That was what I got for buying the first one I found. I hadn't even test-driven it. "I'll call the dealership today."

"Lane and Cruz are going to tow it to the shop at Mama's place," Tenor said.

Lane and Cruz were Wynter's brothers-in-law. They'd been young adults when we'd met them, but Mama had taken them in like me and my sisters and so many other kids over the years. Even Wynter's husband, Myles, had been one of her fosters.

"Thanks." I loaded my guitar case in the back and shut the tailgate. "It was nice meeting you two," I said to the girls.

They rushed me for hugs, and I soaked up the attention. I'd run into a ton of adoring fans over the years, but many of them only knew me as June Bee. Bethany and Hannah had seen me irritate their dad and wash dishes and wipe sticky syrup off the table. I'd put them to work too. When it came down to it, I was a Bailey, and every Bailey did their part around the house. Good thing Rhys hadn't been in the house to get upset again.

"Bye," they said in unison.

I lifted my gaze to meet Rhys's stormy blue eyes. "Goodbye." I'd never gotten to say it before, not since he'd snuck out of the cabin and all.

"Got everything?" he asked.

Yes, including the imprint of his gravelly voice in my head so it could keep me awake for another night.

Both sets of my parents had taught me manners and I would use them to keep Tenor from connecting any dots to Rhys. "Thanks for the ride and the food. Sorry to intrude."

Rhys's jaw turned to granite and he gave me a curt nod.

I took a mental snapshot of the rugged, bearded man who looked like sex in flannel and got into the pickup.

Tenor chatted for a couple of moments with Rhys and then hopped in.

When we were on the road, he slid his deep-brown gaze toward me. "So that was awkward."

Busted. "You should've seen the rest of the time. He yelled at me during breakfast."

Tenor's eyes narrowed. "How bad?"

"Okay, he didn't yell. He . . . snapped. I kept doing stuff that interfered with his parenting style, so, I mean, that's on me. He's their dad, and I'm no one." That thought clawed against the divide in my heart. Rhys had never talked to me the way he'd done today. Except for at the funeral. "I offered to give the girls guitar lessons, and he called me selfish."

I got another side-eye.

"In so many words," I clarified.

"I see," he said in a way that meant he didn't but that he understood I might be sensitive about Rhys and his tones.

He turned down the highway. In front of my dead car was a large truck. Cruz and Lane were hooking my dud to a tow rope. Tenor pulled to a stop next to them.

I rolled down the window and handed my fob to Cruz.

He was almost as big as Tenor now. Mama's cooking and sunshine were having the same effect on him as whatever had happened to Rhys after I'd moved away. Cruz's dark hair was long but pushed off his face.

Lane was only a few years older than his brother, but his eyes were more guarded and he was the more cynical of the two. Both he and Myles were wary of the world. Lane was in his midtwenties, but he acted like someone approaching forty.

Cruz behaved exactly like a guy in his early twenties.

"Thank you," I said to them.

Lane stopped behind his brother. "I'll take a look at it, but we're going to have words with that dealer."

"You're the mechanic." Why hadn't I thought of calling Lane? Mama wouldn't have questioned him if he'd left late last night. If he'd even been home. "Thank you. I owe you guys."

Lane winked. "Never saw ya."

Good. Tenor had talked to them.

"Don't lie for me," I said. "But thank you. I just want to lie low for a while. The spotlight was getting too bright." I said it in a joking tone, but I was dead serious. I'd been burned. Hard.

Tenor rolled the window up and pulled away. "I got a few bags of groceries in the back."

"I owe you."

"No, you don't. We're family." He draped his wrist over the wheel. "Unless I need you to keep something quiet. Then you owe me."

I grinned. The only thing Tenor would hide was a calculation error in one of his coveted spreadsheets. He was too by the book to mess up much.

I propped my elbow by the window and put my head in my hand. Closing my eyes, I sighed.

"You ready to talk about why you left Nashville?"

No. The fatigue flooding every cell of my body wasn't just from crappy sleep in a perfectly comfortable bed. I finally had the silence I'd been craving while on my last tour. Silence I hadn't found in a big city. "Just found out that everyone who was supposed to have my back was just stabbing it, in a way."

"Sorry."

"Yeah. Me too."

"How long are you staying?"

So much was unknown until I had a hearty talk with

my lawyer. "I don't know. I have to return in time to record my next album."

"When's that release?"

I bit my lower lip. "End of July."

He huffed out a shocked breath. "Shit. You can record that quick?"

"I'll have to." I'd have to write the damn thing almost as quickly.

"Wasn't there talk of a headlining tour? Sold-out stadiums?"

My stomach twisted and the pancakes—which had been as delicious as the fluffy muffins—threatened to make a resurgence. "After the album release, Lu—my manager will finish working with the tour promoter and I'll hit the road."

He regarded me. Tenor was too sharp to have missed my slipup. In addition to writing a new album, I'd have to find a new manager.

"Mama's pleased as punch, but she's worried about you," he said.

"She's always worried about us."

"She knows when to be."

She was correct. I loved singing. I loved music. I loved playing with the melody and the lyrics and I treasured having something I was proud of at the end. But what did it matter when I was nothing but a dollar sign to everyone around me?

"Remember what Daddy used to say?" I asked.

" 'Bourbon's making a comeback one Kerrigan at a time.' "

I laughed. "No. Well, he said that too."

Tenor's lopsided grin was easy on my sore eyes. "Then you'll have to be more specific."

Daddy had a lot of sayings. " 'It's the story that sells.' " Daddy used to tell us that bourbon wasn't just a drink. It had a history. We didn't call liquor *spirits* for nothing. Alcohol had the flavor of the land from the grain. It possessed the essence of the oak barrels. The concentration was dependent on time and weather. He said people didn't buy bourbon because they wanted bourbon. They bought the story that went with it. "I love my job, but I don't know my story anymore."

"Gotcha."

He probably did. But he also didn't.

My birth mom used to tell me that I came out of the womb singing. When my parents ended up homeless and drove us from campsite to campsite to sleep under the stars, she used to say, "Let me hear you sing, Junie."

One day, she hadn't been there to hear me anymore, and hitting my goals had become more important than ever. Mae and Darin Bailey's support had made it possible for me to achieve them. Only now I was faltering.

I wanted to honor both sets of parents. Mama Starr and Daddy Bjorn. Mama and Daddy Bailey. But also . . . Was this what I wanted? Navigating the minefield of people and politics and money and sometimes getting burned?

"Want me to bring out the Ranger or something for you?" he asked when the cabin came into view.

"I don't anticipate having to go anywhere." Though I'd need some sister time soon. "I won't hole up for too long." My wounds were in terrible need of being licked, and after this morning, I had one more scar that had split open.

He parked and helped me haul everything in.

I let out a long breath once I was in the cabin. The floor plan wasn't much smaller than the main floor of Rhys's house. There was no basement or upper level. Stacked logs made up the walls, and beams crossed the ceiling. This was no rustic hunting cabin. Daddy had joked that it was his man cave, but I thought he'd built it just for me. He'd known he was giving each of his kids a tract of land. Daddy was the type who'd want his wandering daughter to have a place to hang her hat. He'd known how important having a home was to me.

"Thank you, Tenor."

He gave me a one-armed hug. "Anytime, Junie."

When he was gone, I closed the door and leaned against it. I slid down to my butt and stared at the quiet, empty space in front of me. The cabin was tidy. My life was a mess.

I'd never allowed myself to regret leaving Bourbon Canyon the summer after graduation. I had prided myself on not looking back. Yet the heartbreak had followed me everywhere. At one time, I would've returned had Rhys asked.

I had used those emotions. I'd poured them into writing and singing. Because of them, I'd done what I'd set out to do. I was almost at my final goal. My own tour.

And yet, I was right back where I had started. Rhys hadn't waited for me to return. And the heartbreak was still here.

CHAPTER FIVE

Rhys

I stared out the kitchen window at the barn. The sun was bright and the sky was clear like it hadn't dumped loads of rain on us last night.

June had left again. Why was I surprised? I'd bitten her head off.

I rubbed my sternum. She'd been her normal, generous self. But the thought of her having a reason to come to the house and teach the girls, to continually tease my brain with thoughts of *what if?* I couldn't handle it.

When I'd seen Tenor pulling up, I'd known. She'd called him because I'd hurt her feelings. I had said exactly what would make her run, and it had been for self-serving reasons.

"Dad?" Bethany tugged on my sleeve. "*Dad.*"

"I'm right here, hon."

She gave me a look that came right from her mother.

The *I'm talking and you're not listening* stare. "Do you think she's okay?"

"Who?" As if I didn't know.

"Junie."

"She's fine. She always lands on her feet."

"You were rude." Hannah sat at the table, kicking her feet in her chair.

I was supposed to be making lunch. They'd gotten all the sandwich materials out, but I'd spaced at the sink when I should've been rinsing grapes. "I was not rude."

Both girls leveled me with stares. More and more like their mom every day. *You're so set in your ways you're like cold concrete. One change and you think you'd crack.*

"How was I rude?" I knew exactly how.

"You hurt her feelings." Bethany was relentless. "I was afraid she was going to cry."

June hated crying. She hated people seeing her cry. The only time she'd felt comfortable sobbing was around me.

Shit. "I'll apologize the next time I see her."

"You should call her," Hannah said helpfully.

"I don't have her number." If social media was to be believed, she'd switched her number several times over the years, thanks to hacks and overly enthusiastic fans. She was a social media darling, but she'd had to work twice as hard to get taken seriously in the country music arena.

Or so they said. Since I didn't keep up on anything June related.

"Dad." Bethany sounded distraught. "What if she doesn't have food?"

"She'll get groceries." But how? Had she told Tenor she needed supplies?

She'd said there was canned stuff in the cabin. There had to be a can opener too.

"Can we bring her some?" Hannah asked.

I didn't answer. I rinsed the grapes and put them on the table.

They each sat, still watching me.

"Why can't I take guitar lessons?" Bethany asked.

She'd brought up the subject before. I could say I was too busy, she was too young, they were too expensive. But she was old enough to dig deeper. Not long ago, Wren and I had sold the Kinkade farming and ranching operation to one of my old classmates. I hadn't wanted to give up the life, but she'd seen that after the divorce, I couldn't balance the workload with being a single dad. She'd worried. She'd already lost her dream of retiring with Dad. I had to give her something to look forward to.

I'd bought the old Dunn place. It was smaller, more manageable, and I didn't need employees. One wise investment took the pressure off production. I could relax and raise my kids.

Thanks to the sale, I could afford a lot of goddamn guitar lessons.

"I'll have to think about it," I finally said.

She grinned. I'd said maybe and they'd inferred yes.

"What should we bring her?" Hannah asked. "Can you make her cookies?"

"What about some sandwiches?" Bethany added.

"Fine. Whatever." Guess we were going to the cabin.

My mood lifted and the day felt less dour.

No fucking way was I excited to be around June again. But I could gut through one more time seeing her before we went our separate ways for another fifteen years.

The girls threw themselves into making cookies. I monitored their progress, but as I helped them with each pan that came out of the oven, pressure built behind my skull. What if June was vegan or some shit? What if she'd cut out all sugar? Wasn't she just interviewed about how she didn't eat dairy or something?

My *maybe* should've been a *no*. I was staying out of June's life.

But what if she didn't have food and was too stubborn to tell her family?

Irritated, I made some sandwiches, going off what I used to know about June. Details from high school. She liked real mayonnaise, lots of lettuce, a shitload of lunch meat, and one slice of cheese. I prepared two and shoved them in a Ziploc bag.

"I'll get some fruit, Daddy." Bethany grabbed a baggie.

"A basket!" Hannah sprinted up the stairs and came down with a wicker basket that they usually hauled their dolls in. Bethany was growing out of playing with dolls, much to Hannah's heartbreak.

"We need something at the bottom." Bethany ditched the grapes and rummaged through the drawers. She withdrew a cornflower-blue dish towel my ex had detested because it hadn't matched the rest of our decor.

Once the towel lined the basket, the girls loaded their cooled cookies into baggies. They arranged the cookies, sandwiches, and fruit. Hannah got a can of sparkling juice and added it too.

A picnic basket. This would be a romantic gesture if I didn't have two kids with me.

Whatever. It was their idea.

"Load up."

They darted out the door and left me to carry the food. I set it on the front seat and started for the cabin.

Tension threaded through my back and shoulders. June's car was gone from where it had broken down. Tenor had said they were towing it. One of the guys working for their ranch was a mechanic.

By the time we reached the cabin, my shoulder was cramping. My posture was too rigid. I rolled my arm and parked. Tracks from Tenor's pickup were in the mud, but the dirt had dried quite a bit. The cabin was quiet and it was a couple of hours until dark. Was June inside?

The girls didn't hesitate. They ran up the few steps of the porch and knocked. I hefted the basket and dragged my feet toward the door.

"Is she home?" Bethany went to the window and peered inside.

"Bethany, don't spy." Did she see anything?

Hannah ignored me and ran to her sister. They both stared in.

We were being creepy. "Come on, guys. You can't—"

"Hey," June said from behind us.

We all spun. June was dressed the same as this morning. She'd braided her hair and it hung over one shoulder. Her cheeks were pink from the crisp air, and she wore cowboy boots. Normal ones that weren't dyed different colors. These boots were more like her hair. Some light blue lined their seams.

She was so fucking beautiful and, at the moment, attainable.

"It was their idea," I blurted. I held up the basket. I

would not be another one of those men commenting on June's legs and her looks and how fuckable she was.

The black leggings only teased how muscled and curvy her legs were. She'd always had an ethereal beauty that left me speechless, and I remembered too well how the night before she'd left went. Fuckable.

Men were assholes.

Interest lined her face, and she walked around the porch. Her steps weren't loud like mine had been.

"We brought you food!" Bethany announced.

Hannah rattled off the items they'd packed.

With each one listed, June's smile grew. "That's so sweet of you. I'm afraid to confess that Tenor got me some groceries, but they aren't nearly as good as what you brought."

Tenor might be a bachelor, but a guy raised on Mae Bailey's food knew good eats. I gave June a dubious look and her eyes danced.

"You can go on in," she said.

I was standing in front of the door, and she probably didn't want to push past me. I didn't move. "You were out, and you left your door unlocked?"

"I was in the back, checking the trail to the creek. It was too muddy to trek, but I was enjoying the fresh air and I found a couple of birds' nests." She looked around at the sloping valleys to where the creek cut through. Farther out, the land flattened and was turning green. By the end of May, it'd be a brilliant emerald. Her dad, Darin, had never wished to farm or ranch in this area. He'd said he was lucky to be able to preserve its natural beauty.

I opened the door. Memories unlocked as I looked inside. The plush furniture, at odds with the polished wood floor and the log-beam walls, lent a posh air to the exposed wood. The couch and fluffy chair told a person to sit down and stay awhile. The fireplace still had a family picture hanging above it. A framed image of June's parents and her brothers and sisters before Tate had graduated and left for college.

Stepping inside was like trudging through three feet of mud. Nostalgia might choke me. We used to talk and laugh and make out for hours. The night before she'd left, I'd finally gotten to hold her all night.

The girls shoved past me, shattering the memory like a popped bubble.

Bethany took the basket from me. "Where should I put it?"

"Anywhere on the counter," June said, coming in behind me and stepping out of her boots. "Y'all hungry? I've got a frozen pizza to throw in the oven."

The *y'all* was another pop in my mental balloon. A sign that her time in Nashville meant we'd been apart for so many damn years. I shouldn't be this twisted inside when it came to her.

I'd grown up and so had she. I was a different man, and the sandwiches were a sign that I only knew the girl June used to be. I didn't know the woman she was now. So why did I feel hung up on her?

"I'm *starving*," Hannah said as if she didn't have a belly full of cookies.

June folded her hands in front of her. "You're welcome to stay."

"Can we, Dad?" Bethany rose to her tiptoes, her face full of hope.

Dammit. I was just thinking that I had to get over the past. "We've already intruded," I said hesitantly.

"The pizza will go to waste if I eat what you brought. I have to admit, I wasn't looking forward to it. My tastes have gotten a little snobbish and the quality of frozen pizza has dwindled over the years."

"I love pizza," Hannah said.

"I guess that's it, then," I conceded. "They'll devour your pizza."

"What about you?" she asked.

I dropped my gaze down her body, brushing over the swell of her breasts, along the curve of her hips, and then along those long legs. She wore thick socks that covered the bottom of her pants. I'd devour whatever she wanted me to.

My lungs froze. I was checking her out. I spun toward my kids. "Whatever. I'm not picky." I winced. Would she take that the wrong way? She'd made the pizza comment almost sheepishly.

"Sometimes, that's a good thing," she said, walking past me. "But I've learned the hard way that having high standards isn't always bad." Just when I was about to chafe over her censure, she shot me a smile over her shoulder. "Unless it comes to pizza."

"Can we go look for the nests?" Bethany asked.

"Yes! Please?" Hannah clasped her hands together to beg.

If they went outside, I'd be alone with June. Everything but the logical part of my brain liked the idea, yet I couldn't come up with a valid reason why they couldn't without insulting June again. "Go ahead."

"They're on the big pine at the farthest edge of the backyard," June called after them as they ran out the door.

She pushed the pizza tray into the oven. I ripped my

gaze off her backside and wandered to the mantel over the fireplace. A couple of the awards June had won over the years lined the top. Did she keep a few in each house she owned? Was her New Female Artist of the Year in the Nashville home? The Single of the Year in her Florida condo? What about her Country Kids' Choice Award, was it in her LA apartment?

The girl needed a lot of homes. I would've only been able to give her one.

Laughter from outside preceded the shadows of the girls running by the kitchen windows. June leaned against the island with her arms folded, her eyes downcast.

My presence used to comfort her. Now it was the opposite. I had myself to blame. "I'm sorry. About this morning."

She pushed her hair behind her ear. "I understand. I was overstepping my bounds." Her pink lips curved up. "As celebrities do."

Couldn't she hold my behavior against me so I could stay hardened against her? "I shouldn't have reacted the way I did."

She fiddled with the mixed brown and blue ends of her hair. "I imagine being a single parent is a challenge."

"Being a parent is a challenge, period." I shrugged. "I don't feel like some struggling single dad. I have Wren, and the girls have friends' parents who help me run them around if I get tied up."

"And Kirstin?"

Hearing my wife's name out of June's mouth sent my world sideways. Which reality was I living in? I had fought harder to keep June off my mind when I'd been with my wife. "She calls. Between assignments, she'll come back and stay with me or Wren."

June kicked up a brow. A lot of people did, but usually I didn't care, and I didn't feel the urge to explain myself. Yet today, an explanation tumbled onto my tongue. "There's nothing between us. She just needs a place to stay, and she gets more time with the girls."

"I'm glad it's amicable."

It was that. "It's good for the kids to see their mom living her dream."

The way June peered at me sent my defenses crashing into place.

"Anyway, I'm sorry."

There was a beat of silence. Was she going to continue pushing? Not many people agreed with Kirstin's decision to take her wildlife photography overseas, but she was good at her job. I'd held her back long enough.

"Well, if you think a sandwich is going to make up for it, you're wrong," June said, thankfully moving on from the subject. "Now that I've tasted your muffins, I might need an apology dozen."

June

The girls were playing outside. I'd eaten the sandwich they revealed their dad had made. He still ate simple white bread, my favorite, and he'd used the perfect amount of mayo.

He finished washing the dishes. I was drying and

putting them away while trying not to lust after his veiny, muscled forearms. When he'd unbuttoned his cuffs and rolled the sleeves up, I'd about melted in a pile of arousal.

When was the last time that lust had been slaked hard and dirty?

Right. Never. I'd been with too many selfish men. And before that, way before, Rhys and I had been too young to really understand what we wanted. That was what I'd told myself anyway.

Teenage lovemaking was exploratory but hurried. Innocent, yet at the time so naughty.

What did adult Rhys like—

Not going there. At all.

"Want me to check on the girls?" I offered and hung the dish towel up.

He was peering out the window over the sink. "No, I just saw them run by."

I leaned against the counter. He'd apologized and I should drop it, but he had to know I hadn't meant to blow into his life and create conflict between him and his kids. "I really am sorry about overstepping earlier. I shouldn't have offered without talking to you."

"Been surrounded by a bunch of yes-men?"

His teasing lacked bite, but he didn't realize how wrong he was. "If I had been, I wouldn't be here."

"Why are you?" His soft tone and the genuine concern in his eyes made me want to do nothing but spill my guts. I used to talk to him about everything and anything. He'd been my rock.

My family would listen, but also, they weren't Rhys.

I chewed the inside of my cheek and pushed off the counter. I had my arms wrapped around myself as I wandered into the living area. The corner of the couch beckoned me. I wanted to burrow into the cushions and pretend I wasn't some foolish girl who'd thought she'd known what she'd been getting into.

"Six months ago, I broke up with the guy I was seeing." I peeked at him from under my lashes. He was still looking at the window. "Finn Calhoun."

Finally, he turned, pinning me with a dark gaze. There was a spark of recognition in his eyes, but he remained silent.

Was I really going to tell him the story? I had planned to ruminate over it for a couple more days and then call my sisters. They'd be righteously angry. I'd feel validated.

Rhys wasn't a neutral third party, but I needed to talk about why I'd left Nashville. I needed to handle my own emotions about it and not someone else's.

"Finn was cheating on me. Big surprise." I licked my lower lip and dropped my attention to my twisting fingers. "It was actually. A surprise. We have the same manager, Lucy, and she said he was a changed man. He wanted a real relationship with someone who knew the life, who knew what it was like to get bitten by the writing bug and want to hole up in some house with nothing but takeout for days. He wanted a true connection. So, she introduced us at a party. I fell for him. I fell for it."

He cocked his head at the last part. "What do you mean?"

He crossed to the chair that faced the end of the couch I was on and sat on the edge. His sleeves were still rolled up, and he propped his elbows on his knees and clasped his hands.

Words evaporated. I was not telling this mature, virile, handsome-as-hell man that I'd been an idiot for man-children over and over, was I?

But I'd already started. "Before him was Toby. He plays hockey for the—"

"I've heard of him," he said curtly.

"You can't imagine how many women he slept with when I was gone playing for shows." My laugh dripped with bitterness. "Maybe you can. I didn't. I don't know how he stayed upright on skates when he was horizontal so often." I shook my head. "I fell for it again. And before him was Clinton. He ran a recording studio. A normal guy, Lucy said. She introduced us, and we started working together. He liked to fuck other women in the studio. I got to see for myself." I looked up at the ceiling before I could start crying. "Lucy came with me that day, and we walked in on Clinton and some young thing who thought he was her key to making it big." I swiped at my eyes. I didn't miss a single one of those guys. I missed the girl who'd thought she could trust people. "Lucy was my support then too. She encouraged me to pour my feelings out in words. That's how I started with my songs, so why not use it now? My album *Hush* came from that breakup. Then I met Toby and I got more inspiration. Happier songs. Then he broke my heart and I was back to writing my angst. 'A good balance' was how my record label described that album. In fact, that's what we named it. *Good Balance*."

The girls' laughter filtered into the cabin. This place hadn't heard that sound in far too long.

"When I was with Finn," I continued, "I was opening on tour, but we were working on songs together. Nothing was really clicking—he can be a little set in his ways—and my record company has been on my ass about a new album. After the tour, I was tired, you know? I wanted to just enjoy the breather and not have to hustle so much. But my record label wants a new album. Lucy said I was ready for my own big tour. My numbers were high enough that I could book stadiums and arenas and have my own opening acts. I asked for time. That was when Lucy called to meet me at a bistro in Nashville, and lo and behold, guess who was in a booth kissing a girl who's still in college?"

More tears tracked down my cheeks. Not for Finn. By then, I had expected him to hurt me. I'd been waiting for it.

"That fucker." Rhys moved to the couch, sitting in the middle. He put a big, hot hand on my knee. "Fuck him."

I snorted. "She sure did." I couldn't look into those deep-blue eyes and keep going. I stared at my fingers and willed his hand to stay on me. "I was devastated. Again. My manager kept pressuring me to pour my emotions into writing. 'You know how it is with you. You turn pain into art.' Her words, not mine."

"True though."

Surprised, I glanced up at him.

The corner of his mouth tilted up. "So I've heard."

Warmth seeped into my bones, chasing away the chill of betrayal. Rhys did listen to my music. He might not want to, but he did. Bolstered, I continued. "This time, I wanted to go home. I'd been sneaking back to see my family. Trips that were nothing more than turnin' and burnin'. My manager always insisted they be quick trips. My team needs me in Nashville, she'd say." I let out a long breath. "The day before yesterday, I went to her office to tell her I needed a break. I had a big plan to foster my social media and release teasers and maybe we could push the album a few months. When I got to her office, one of the receptionists told me Lucy was in her office and I could just walk in."

My pulse kicked up and my breathing shorted. I was back in that hallway, listening to Lucy plot my life.

"I heard her telling her assistant about our conversations. They were brainstorming men to introduce me to because she might have to set me up with another loser and entice him to cheat again. The assistant laughed. 'It's worked all the other times you've done it.' "

"No fucking way." His fingers tightened on my leg. The pressure felt so good, so reassuring. "Am I understanding this correctly?"

I nodded slowly. "She introduced me to guys with reputations, some I knew, some I didn't, and then threw women at them until I caught them cheating. And I'd take those feelings and I'd write songs." I wiped at my cheeks and sniffled. "I trusted her. With everything. And she was only using and manipulating me."

The tears flowed fully now. I had thought Lucy was a friend.

"I'd forgotten what Daddy told me. 'Never consider it a true friendship if one makes money off the other.' " I shook my head. "I was so stupid."

His hand was still on me, strong and comforting. "Don't blame yourself for someone else's selfishness. You know your dad would say that too."

Rhys always knew what to say. If Daddy were alive and I had run straight to him, he'd have said the same thing. *Never be sorry you were a good person.*

"I had to get away. I walked out without talking to

her, packed my shit, and caught a flight the next day. Though not before calling my lawyer to fire Lucy for me."

"Your daddy would've been proud. Your mom will be too."

I had to drop my gaze back to my lap. His hand was in my view, so damn big on my leg. "I know. She'll worry though, and she shouldn't have to worry about me. I'm a grown woman." Who had trusted the wrong people.

"I can tell you that it won't matter how old you are, she'll worry. It's what parents do." He shook his head, a line forming between his brows. "This Lucy isn't going to cause trouble, is she? She can't sue you or anything?"

"I don't care about the money, Rhys. You know I never did."

"I don't know what you care about anymore, June Bug."

Fresh, hot tears filled my eyes. That was the real heartbreak right there. The breakups with those exes had reopened a scar that had never fully healed. A wound that cracked right open when Rhys pointed out how much time and distance was between us now.

"I meant other than your friends and family," he clarified. "I know your family will always be the most important."

"But they haven't always been." To get to where I was, I'd had to put my family life on the back burner. I'd had to play the game. And I'd lost. I had traded myself for fame and a fortune that left me empty. "I have four homes, Rhys. Five with the cabin. I wanted a stable place in each corner of the country, but I remember feeling more secure in a tent with my sisters and my birth parents. I try to write and nothing comes anymore."

I had it all. But I had nothing.

The tears continued to fall. "I just had to come home. I have to figure out what I really want to do with my life."

The door banged open.

Rhys didn't jerk away from me. His back was to the girls, and I ducked my head to keep them from seeing my tear-streaked face. He looked over his shoulder. "You two wanna go outside for a little longer? I've gotta discuss practice times with June for guitar lessons."

"Lessons?" Bethany's question was full of disbelief.

"If you play outside for a little longer."

"Yay!" they cried in unison and rushed back out the door.

He was too generous. I'd love to give lessons, but he didn't want to deal with me. "You don't have to—"

"I can't take it back, June Bug, so I hope to hell you were serious about teaching them."

A wave of excitement cooled the heat of my emotions. "Yes, I'd love to. I miss teaching kids. I used to do that when I first moved to Nashville. Well, music tutors grow on trees out there. I was a nanny who taught music lessons."

"I thought you worked at a restaurant."

"I did both. Until I met Lucy."

"Fuck Lucy. She's your lawyer's problem now."

I smiled. "Lucy made sure everyone else fucked."

His pupils darkened and his gaze dipped to his hand. He yanked it off like he'd been burned and rose. Pacing in front of the couch, he shoved that hand through his hair and swallowed, his Adam's apple bobbing. "You want to write. That's what's bothering you, right?"

I nibbled the inside of my cheek. "I do love to write music."

"And that album will get you a tour?"

Not *a* tour, *my* tour. I nodded.

He dropped to a squat in front of me and rested his arms on his powerful thighs. "You still want that tour, don't you?"

Did I want the tour? Or did I want to please the memories of my birth parents? Was I afraid to let down the family who'd supported me along the way?

Or did I want to share my music, songs I'd written and performed, with others who shared those same emotions with me? The same hopes and dreams?

More importantly, did my reasons have to be exclusive?

"I want it," I said hoarsely, finally able to verbalize what had been twisting inside me. The *do I or don't I*. Yes, I wanted that fucking tour. I'd worked for it. Lucy might've manipulated me, but it was my pain in the words I sang. My heart. I would complete this album and go on tour to show her that I didn't need manufactured heartbreak to be good at what I do.

And because I had nothing else.

"I want my songs to be there when people feel like they have nothing else."

"Like the accident."

"Like the accident." I ran my thumb over a fingernail, memories of the crash that took my parents going through my mind. The terror. The crying. The darkness. Mama Starr and Daddy Bjorn hadn't been able to tell us everything would be okay. So I'd sang. My little voice had shaken, but my efforts had quieted the sobs. "And because it's been such a long road. I want to be the one with opening acts. I want to be the one that tens of thousands of people buy tickets for. Because that means I have a voice. Not for the audience but in my career. I can be the one telling promoters who my opening acts will be. I can be the hand up for others instead of having doors shut in my face."

I wasn't in it for the fame and money, but I needed those two things to get the freedom to be an artist and not just a puppet. If I'd let someone shove their hand up my ass years ago and control me, I would've been so much further in my career by now. But then it wouldn't have been *my* career. I needed to connect with my fans on my own terms.

"When do you have to be in Nashville again?" he asked.

"If the timeline isn't changing, I have to be back by the end of June." Two months to write ten songs? Just thinking about it made the words dry up.

But I'd do it. I was home, breathing fresh Montana air and surrounded by people who really cared about me. Rhys included.

He rose, one knee cracking. "Weekends work the best until school's out, except for the two weeks they get with Wren. So unless their mother comes back for a surprise visit, pick your time."

He didn't make it sound like Kirstin planned to return anytime soon. "Want me to start next weekend?"

He leveled a steady gaze on me. Deep in his eyes, I saw the resistance. He didn't want me to start *ever*. He probably regretted picking me up on the side of the road. But he wouldn't go back on his word. This time.

CHAPTER SIX

June

Mama poured four glasses of Copper Summit Original. I soaked in the familiarity of her Keds sandals and simple blue top with capri-length jeans. She had her salt-and-pepper black hair pulled back in her usual bun. I had planned to wait until Monday to tell my family I was home, but school was still in session. Time was more limited to get the four seasons together—Summer, Autumn, me, and Wynter. Fitting that I'd come home now since it was almost June and most of June was technically spring. Hence my name.

Both Autumn and my sister-in-law, Scarlett, would have to work, while Summer and Wynter could be more flexible with their jobs at the original distillery in town. So on Sunday morning, I'd sent a quick text explaining that I had returned home to write my new album in peace, my car had broken down, Lane was working on it at the shop, and I was at the cabin.

Mama had arrived first, sensing there was more to my story. In fifteen years, I hadn't come home for work. Wynter was with her in a lilac-colored sundress, large sunglasses, and her white-blond hair cascading from a clip. Then Summer and Scarlett had ridden in together. Autumn had driven herself. She still lived in town with her husband, Gideon, while Gideon's old family home—and his and Autumn's future home—underwent a major remodel. They all had brought some cookies, crackers, cheese, and olives.

The snacks were needed. The cabin might not have been stocked with much for food, but I had two bottles of unopened wine on the counter and at least five different bottles of bourbon. I liked craft beer, but I wasn't home enough to stock it. By the time I could drink it all, it'd be skunked.

Summer took the glasses of bourbon from Mama and distributed them while Mama mixed virgin mimosas for Wynter, who was nursing, and Summer, who was pregnant.

"I can't imagine what it's like to find out people were tampering with your life and profession." Summer sat and smoothed her pink sundress on her lap. It wasn't loose enough to hide her rounded belly. She was due in September. I'd be starting my tour around then, but I'd tell my new manager to ensure the first show was well after Summer's due date. "I'm glad you found out about it. Lucy would've kept setting up emotional wringers for you until you burned out."

Burnout. Was that what I was feeling? The heavy weight of responsibility. The pressure of producing. I had a team counting on me. If I didn't ride the high of falling for someone and then crashing to the ground, would I be able to write quality material? I had a band who worked with me. A record label. A manager. An agent. Promoters. I wasn't the only artist these people worked with, but as I'd risen in fame, and my revenue with it, I'd become a cornerstone to their individual careers.

I had thought that was why I'd stalled out on inspiration, that the pressure had gotten to me. I had almost accomplished my dream, but everything hinged on my next album not flopping. In the end, it had been the serial betrayals.

"Overhearing that conversation answered a lot of questions." I took a drink and let the bourbon warm my tongue and throat. Hints of caramel and vanilla danced on my taste buds and the comfort of home sank into my bones.

I needed the reset.

"So now what?" Wynter asked. "You're just going to write and let your lawyer deal with Lucy?"

"That's the plan." Lucy had quit blowing up my phone. "I guess I have to find a new manager. I have some contacts."

"Give yourself time," Mama said. "Everything's in motion. You don't have to rush. The other parts of your team are doing their job, so you can do yours."

"Thanks, Mama." Her calm, matter-of-fact tone alleviated the building stress from thinking about Lucy and hiring a replacement. I folded my legs under me and tugged the hem of my shorts down. "I've been thinking a lot about you and Mama Starr."

My sisters' expressions softened. Scarlett's face filled with sympathy. Mama nodded, always encouraging us to talk about our other parents.

"I remember how you used to sing for us." Wynter ran her finger over the ring of her glass.

Summer nodded. "Daddy Bjorn would always ask you to sing when we'd start asking when we could go home."

We'd no longer had a home. "I was a full-on adult before I realized they used me to distract us from being homeless and packing all our things in that cramped car."

"It worked too because I got jealous from all the attention," Wynter said, giggling. "I used to get so mad."

"And then I would get upset because no one wanted to run through times tables with me." Autumn chortled. "Us two middle kids used to argue so much because we always felt overlooked."

Summer laughed. "I sometimes wondered if the way we dissolved into bickering was half the distraction."

"I wasn't mad when you sang that night," Wynter said. The room fell quiet.

The night of our parents' crash, an eternity had come and gone before help arrived. I'd performed for my parents and sisters countless times, but that was the first time I'd felt like we'd *connected* because of my music.

"Speaking of musical kids," I said to lighten the mood, "I'm going to give Rhys's girls guitar lessons."

They all stared at me.

Except Scarlett, who looked at everyone like she was interpreting their reactions. Her glass of bourbon was mostly full. She wasn't as avid a bourbon lover as us. "I know I wasn't here then, but Rhys Kinkade is your ex, right? It's all good?"

My sisters studied me. Mama took a drink, her expression neutral. She liked Rhys, and she adored his girls. She'd never tell me; I just knew. That was who

Mama was. And she'd never let me know if the news of guitar lessons made her happy or worried.

To everyone, including her, I'd left and shattered Rhys's heart. No one knew that I hadn't left him behind. He'd never planned to leave Bourbon Canyon.

"It's fine. He's had a whole other life since we were kids. And he never told them about me."

"What?" Summer frowned.

"They were surprised to find out we were friends," I said. Were Rhys and I friends? We'd have to be for the sake of the girls. "He never even told them we knew each other."

"Seriously?" Wynter's eyes were wide. "How did they not know? You two were together longer than he was married."

Did that thought make me feel better or worse? "I can't imagine people care to tell kids about a woman who's not their mom and her history with their dad."

"True, but you're not a normal case," Autumn said. "I'm surprised other kids haven't brought it up."

"They will." Scarlett could seem timid, but she knew elementary-aged children. "They're getting to the age where they'll hear about it once another kid, or that kid's parents, piece things together. Not every parent is going to care that it might step over bounds with the girls' mother."

"Some will delight in it," Autumn added. "But that's for Rhys to deal with. He didn't tell them for a reason."

I lifted a shoulder. The hurt from feeling like his dirty secret still lingered. I took another sip and let the bourbon burn the ache away. "I'll just be there to teach them how to play guitar."

"Bethany loves to sing," Scarlett said. "You should've heard her at the school play. Loudest one in the bunch."

"I've heard her singing your songs all the time." Autumn's murmur sounded more like a warning.

His kids were fans. I couldn't forget that. The rift between me and Rhys hadn't been repaired just because I'd opened up to him. He wanted to keep his kids buffered from our history, and I'd have to respect that. They had their own mother and maybe . . . Maybe Rhys was dating.

My stomach clenched around the few sips of alcohol I'd had. Was he seeing someone? Was that why he was so uptight about my presence? "Is he dating?" I held up my hands as five sets of eyebrows rose. "I'm not interested, but I need to know if gossip's going to spread."

"Oh, it's going to spread." Wynter snorted. "First, he shocks the town by marrying Kirstin and moving her to Bourbon Canyon. Now he's been single how long and hasn't seriously dated? But his high school sweetheart is suddenly teaching his kids guitar?"

"He won't even volunteer to be a bachelor in the fundraising auction," Scarlett added.

Summer stirred her juice and sparkling water with a tiny straw Mama had produced from the tote bag she'd brought. "I'm sure after what he saw happen with Tate, he'll always stay far away."

Mama nodded. "More than a few bachelors have found their partners with that auction." She aimed her fond smile at Scarlett. "And I'm very grateful Tate did too, with the help of his meddling sisters."

"Money well spent," Summer muttered. "The point is —Rhys doesn't date. I think I heard him actually growl at a woman once."

Autumn's red ponytail bobbed with her nod. "When he came for a mystery reader event for Bethany last year, our admin tried to show him to the classroom and he snapped at her. Said that he'd gone to school there and could find his own way."

I chuckled. "He's not technically wrong." He'd moved in with his dad during our middle school years, but Bourbon was so small the elementary school and high school were practically the same building, linked by the playground. I used to hang out on the playground with Rhys when school was out. He'd push me in the swing.

"It was the tone," Autumn said pointedly. "So when people hear that you're giving the girls guitar lessons, it's going to burn through town like a July wildfire. People's memories are going to suddenly be real clear."

"Ugh." I downed the rest of my bourbon. "It's just lessons. He offered because he felt sorry for me after I told him what had happened."

I flopped against the couch cushions and stared at one of the beams crossing the ceiling. The room got quiet. If I lifted my head, would I find them exchanging loaded looks?

"Rhys has always been a nice boy," Mama said. "The lessons might be an olive branch. A lot of time has passed between you two. But he's still the same Rhys. He's still not dazzled by the limelight, and you're still drawn to it like a moth to a flame."

"Yeah," I sighed. "I am." I didn't know why I was driven to share my art. Why did painters spend hours and hours on a portrait and hope someone displayed it on a prominent wall for others to enjoy? Why did people write books and hope others read them? Why did I pen a song and need to hear it come from someone's mouth, preferably mine?

The limelight allowed me to share my work and that made me happy. I could be heard. Which was more and more important when I went home to my empty house.

I sat up and ignored their curious yet concerned expressions. I was done talking about Rhys. There would be enough of that from everyone else. My family was my safe place. Always had been. As soon as I had been introduced to Mae Bailey, everything in my world had quit spinning. She was solid and secure.

There would be no Copper Summit without the Baileys, and it was why I'd kept my work with them separate from my music career. Lucy and other agents had tried to limit my exposure with Copper Summit and set parameters, but I'd only hired better lawyers. Thankfully, Daddy had suggested I ask around and go with legal representation other than who my manager and record label had recommended.

Copper Summit gave me freedom, and I'd seek refuge there now. And inspiration. Something had to get my creative juices flowing again. "Since I'm only tutoring on the weekends, I have my weeks free. What can I do?"

Wynter set her empty glass down. Mama immediately retrieved it to refill. Wynter didn't stop her. Mama didn't like to sit still for long, and she loved doting on her grandkids and on us as adults. Didn't mean she wouldn't put us to work.

"I'm working on the Christmas campaigns," Wynter said. "Stop by and we'll brainstorm some shoots."

Excitement sparked in my chest for the first time in months. "Need a jingle?" A short verse shouldn't be hard to come up with. Wynter usually worked with me on brainstorming the tagline and I put it to music. Perhaps I'd just found my starting point.

She smiled. "You know I never turn down a tune from you."

Grateful to have something to do instead of hiking through my regrets, I grinned. Working with Wynter at Copper Summit would keep me occupied most of the week, and I wouldn't keep longing for the end of the week when I could see Rhys again.

Rhys

The day I'd been dreading since I'd accepted the offer of guitar lessons was here. It was Sunday.

June had shown up in her repaired car with three goddamn guitars, and I knew she hadn't had those when I'd found her on the side of the road. Perhaps Mae had stored some of her old music equipment, but the two unfamiliar guitars looked brand fucking new.

I'd been outside since I'd left my kids in the care of June, sitting on my couch in her tight jeans. My two excited daughters had sat on the floor in front of her as if June were on stage.

I paced the shop. I had to run to town, but the lesson was almost done, and I didn't want June to be in the house any longer than necessary, if only for my sanity. I kept walking out of the bathroom and picturing her in the hallway, barely dressed with tousled hair.

Checking the time, I pivoted toward the door. Close enough. I stepped outside and Caramel, the orange tabby barn cat we'd inherited with the place, mewed at me. He was sunning himself against the side of the building.

"Catch any mice today, freeloader?"

He blinked at me.

"That's what I thought." The girls fed him too damn much. He had no need to hunt, but he loved their cuddles. So he could freeload all he wanted as long as he let them love on him.

Goldie trotted next to me. I sank my fingers into the dog's fur. She'd been our first addition to this little home we'd built since we'd moved. Her wilder years were behind her, and hopefully that included her urge to eat anything inedible and toxic. I still had the vet's emergency number as a top contact in my phone.

A wad of knots in my stomach turned to lead the closer I got to the house. Staying away for an hour had been torture. The urge to peek through the windows wasn't because I had to check on the girls. They were fine.

Seeing June with her guitar again was an addicting hit of nostalgia. It was also necessary to remind myself that she had talent that was wasted in the middle of Montana. In two months, she'd be back in Nashville and, soon after, conquering the world stage. It was what she was made for.

But sometimes she needed a little push. The scared little girl inside of her was afraid of the unknown, but she wanted to be heard. I'm sure some psychiatrist could tie her need to be visible and financially successful to her parents' accident, but it didn't matter. She was who she was.

I quietly stepped inside the house. June's soft voice mixed with mellow guitar notes.

"He wasn't the guy who got away, he was the one who let me go."

I stopped in the kitchen, my heart slamming against my ribs. I hated this song. I couldn't change the station fast enough when it came on. Only now there was no knob. I was getting a live performance, but I couldn't make myself walk right back out the door.

Two smaller Yamaha acoustic guitars were propped on the couch and the girls were on the floor, a rapt audience. June's gaze flipped up to meet mine. She continued to strum the strings, her left hand moving along the fretboard, but she didn't sing. She didn't have to. I knew the words.

And I'm the girl with all the freedom in the world . . .

I hated the rest.

. . . but I only wish he'd asked me to stay.

That song haunted me through the streets of town. In my car. Even while I worked outside and had the radio on. Whenever June had a new song or album releasing, the hardware store loved to play her songs. Something always broke on the ranch, and I'd be in the damn store, her voice chasing me down the aisles.

A heartbeat of anguish filled her eyes, then she blinked. I shook myself out of my trance.

She flattened her left hand on the strings. "That's it for today, but I have homework."

"What?" Hannah said, aghast. "Homework?"

Bethany's mouth hung open.

"It's easy. Quiz each other on counting." June held up a hand. "First finger—"

"Index finger!" both girls yelled.

June nodded and tapped her middle finger with her thumb.

"Second finger." Another answer in unison.

She wiggled her ring finger.

"Third," they answered.

"The pinkie is the fourth," Bethany added.

"Quiz each other on the frets and the strings. And if it's okay with your dad, practice your downstrokes while counting." June carefully set her guitar aside. The wood on this one was a deep mahogany brown. I hadn't seen it before. My favorite was her denim-blue Dreadnought.

"I wanna practice now!" Bethany jumped up and grabbed one of the guitars. Hannah followed her lead.

I hovered at the edge of the carpet in the living room. The girls were critiquing each other on their posture and how to hold the guitar. The authority in Bethany's voice made it sound like she'd been playing for years.

June packed her instrument. Her hair hung over her shoulder, and the front of her loose top gaped. I yanked my gaze away. She clicked the case shut and straightened. A cacophony of strumming filled the air.

"Sounds like music," June said and stepped over her guitar. She grinned when she approached and my heart skipped a damn beat.

"How'd it go?" I was only interested in lessons, dammit.

"Good. They're so curious and they had a lot of questions." Her white teeth bit into her bottom lip. I stopped my groan before it was audible. "I hope you don't mind that I took some time to answer them."

"About June Bee?"

"Well, I am her."

She certainly was. Did I need to be sitting to learn what they'd asked? I'd rather not hear at all. "Want a snack before you go?"

Her gaze brushed over the counters behind me. A plate of sugar cookies was pushed into the corner by the fridge, a pan of homemade granola bars was on the table, and a coffee cake I'd made for no damn reason was untouched by the oven. Good thing she couldn't see the inside of the fridge. I'd made an oatmeal bake for breakfast and the girls were still toasting my homemade waffles like their own private Eggo stash.

I'd been a little stressed this week.

"I'm sure you have work to do," she said.

There was always work to do. "I came in for a break and to check on how things went. Have a seat."

I went for the counter but I caught her hesitation before pulling out a chair at the table. Was she remembering the crappy way I had snapped at her?

The song I'd walked in on evened the score.

He wasn't the guy who got away, he was the one who let me go.

I'd had to let her go. For her own good.

"I like your new house," she said.

"It's not new." The old farmhouse had needed a lot of work in the early days. I took out four plates, forks, and a knife and started cutting the coffee cake.

"It's easier."

When I looked over my shoulder, she was nibbling on that lower lip again. "What do you mean?"

"Being in the cabin was weird. With you."

A walk down memory lane. It'd seemed wrong not to pull her into my lap while she cried. The first tear had gutted me, but that she still trusted me enough to open up had humbled me. "Would you have told me what had happened if we'd been anywhere else?"

"Probably not."

I put a square piece of dessert on two plates and carried them to the table. "If I lived at my old place, I wouldn't have found you."

A tiny furrow formed along her forehead. "Is this Wren's recipe?"

I was okay with a subject change. My old place was the house I'd shared with my ex-wife and kids. "Yep."

"How is she?"

"Good. She's in a condo in town."

Her nod was slow. "I never thought you'd move."

"Me either." I shoveled a forkful into my mouth. I could bake three more coffee cakes instead of having this conversation. My dad had passed and that was when we had planned I'd go to her. There was never a good time to lose my dad, but both June and I had been single. Yet I'd chased her off at the funeral because otherwise, I'd have gotten in her way. Or worse, she would've stayed. Only that time, I'd known I had to be deliberate. I couldn't have left her doubting what I was saying. "When this place came on the market, I thought I might expand. I could manage the ranch and have a quiet home away from work."

She chuckled. "If only that was how it worked." She knew the life and had grown up doing everything I'd done. When it came to managing a few hundred head of cattle and a handful of horses, there were too many unpredictables that would take me away from home. The plan might've worked if I hadn't lived in city limits, but it would have been impossible to sit out vet emergencies and equipment breakdowns and weather events when I was only miles away.

"I didn't think we'd ever sell, but Wren tentatively brought it up, then felt awful. But I understood. She lived in the old house and it needed work. She got stranded during storms. She was left with nothing but memories. She couldn't move or retire when all the assets were tied up in the ranch. Selling just made sense."

"You miss it." The crease graced her forehead again, and it only made her more approachable. She wasn't an airbrushed image in an ad. Couldn't she have gotten more superficial during her time away? Instead, she was tangible. Touchable. Her satiny skin ready to be stroked.

My mouth turned dry. "No," I lied. "I don't miss it."

She delicately cut off a chunk of coffee cake. "I hope she has no hard feelings. I didn't call, and then life got busy . . ."

"You got all the freedom in the world."

She pushed her plate away. "I should go."

"Shit, I'm sorry." I slapped my fork down. I had no business referencing lyrics even when they had to do with us. Those songs were nothing but a historical account from her perspective. "No. I didn't mean to bring up all that." I hadn't meant to point out that her lyrics made me feel like shit either. "Come on. Finish your snack. Unless you don't do gluten."

"It can make me a bit phlegmy before performances." She accepted my small olive branch.

"Is that a thing?"

The corner of her mouth tipped up. "Celebrities have their quirks for reasons sometimes."

We ate our coffee cake to the accompaniment of

erratic strumming from the other room. As June chewed, I locked on to her lips. Were they still soft pillows that could nibble and suck with—

I shifted in my chair. I wasn't a perpetually horny teen anymore, but my mind was going back in time.

"Wren would love it if you called her or even stopped in. I can tell you where she lives."

Her smile lit up the damn room. "She wouldn't mind?"

"I caught her humming along to one of your songs."

"No way." Her back thumped against her chair and her expression was stunned. "She swore by the classics."

"She still does. But she'll make an exception for you. She always has."

"She's a wonderful person. I'm really glad you had her."

A chill circulated through my blood. June was merely alluding to my mother, and I wanted to shut down. I was more successful at forgetting my mom than I was at pushing June out of my head. "Yeah, Wren is special."

She pressed her fork into the plate to pick up the last of the crumbs. "She and your dad were really there for you when you needed it."

"It wasn't like they had a choice. I made it too hard for Mom to take care of me and herself."

She tilted her head, her crumbs forgotten. "What do you mean?"

Ah, hell. Why had I brought that up? I never discussed Mom or why I'd come to live in Bourbon Canyon with my dad. Whenever anyone asked, including June, I'd said my mom had died. It was the truth. I was a one-night-stand baby from before Dad had met Wren, and I had changed the life of Angela Craft. I had ruined it. "I was an asshole kid," I said gruffly. "You know, the usual young-boy-acting-out stuff. Want another slice of cake?"

She didn't reply right away. I willed her to drop the subject. Finally, she pushed her plate away. "Thank you, but no. I should get going. I have a jingle to work on for Wynter."

"Did you get your muse back?"

"Not really. Marketing music is different. I need some creativity, but it's also very technical." She tapped the center of her chest. "It still comes from here, but the music isn't for me and it's not from me. But the song is for a product and company I love, so in a way, it's opened up a trickle. Maybe ten more songs will follow." She let out a nervous laugh.

"I don't want to pressure you, I'm just curious, but can you really write ten songs in two months?"

Alarm darkened the amber of her eyes. "Yes, it's possible. I can get struck by a huge wave of inspiration and just write until I can't anymore. It's happened with others. I'm not ruling it out."

"Would you sing someone else's songs?"

She smiled sadly. "Then I wouldn't be June Bee. My fans love my lyrics as much as my voice."

Funny. I hated her lyrics. Each verse was like a paper cut to my soul. She was a songbird, though, and I'd never tire of her voice.

She rose and took her plate to the sink. Goddamn, her ass looked good in those jeans. "I'm also worried about the quality. I don't want to go on tour with duds, but if the album's delayed, the tour will be delayed and then it might just go away." She stared out the window above the sink for a few moments. "These kinds of things can be so dependent on popularity and perception. I have to strike while the iron is hot."

"You'll knock it out of the park, June Bug. You always do."

She smiled over her shoulder. Longing slammed into my chest and stole my breath. What would it be like to see her like this every day? To wake up to her half-naked in my hallway like last week? To talk to her when the girls were preoccupied?

It'd be heaven. I'd always known that. Just like I'd always known her needs came before mine. And that was why, in two months, I would walk her to the door and make sure she left town.

CHAPTER SEVEN

June

I leaned over Wynter's shoulder. She was clicking through the mock-ups she'd made for the Christmas campaign. My smiling face shone back at me from several snapshots. Me with a stocking hat and a glass in my hand. Me holding a frosted metal cup with a mound of whipped cream overflowing the top, a candy cane in my other hand as I laughed. Me in a snug red velvet dress Wynter had worn last year to the Christmas party for Myles's distillery in Denver.

The smiles were real. My second-oldest brother, Teller, liked to make smart ass comments while I was modeling to keep me real—his words, not mine.

The image that kept drawing my eye didn't include a smile. A simple stemmed glass with a candied cherry at the bottom was on the floor. Inside the glass, bourbon was mixed with sparkling apple cider and a dash of cinnamon. It was a lovely and fresh cocktail, but I had set it down to play "What Child Is This." A slow, mellow song that often helped me escape the fast-paced bustle of the holiday season.

Christmas lights were blurred behind me. I wasn't wearing a Santa hat or the red dress. I had on a long-sleeved cream shirt and jeans with my favorite cowboy boots, and I was sitting on a stool. My expression was distant. I wasn't looking at my guitar or at anyone else. I had let the music calm the frenzy of the photo shoot, which was one of the tamest of the ones I'd done. Wynter didn't like chaos, and it wasn't Copper Summit's brand. She'd had the drinks already prepared and had played bartender while I'd changed outfits and the photographer had set up the next set.

A band around my chest tightened. I looked sad. Melancholy. Alone. The picture encapsulated how I'd felt for years.

At the same time, it was also the real me. I might've fought Lucy on the level of sex in my brand—gotta attract the men—and which of my songs I would publish, and I'd argued with the record label about my lack of twang and how much skin to show on my album covers, but I hadn't won all the decisions. If it wasn't for my social media following lending me their collective voice, I'd be a blond on stage in Daisy Dukes with my abs showing. Nothing wrong with that, but it wasn't me.

I had an indie vibe. I didn't do overtly sexual. Sometimes, I had bad days. And this image said all that.

Wynter's stare burned into the side of my face.

I straightened, forgetting the image. I had to play the game a little longer. "I can't believe Myles hasn't stolen you for Foster House's marketing."

She crossed her arms. "Their team does just fine. He

hires only the best, and more importantly, he hires people who can work with him."

"He's barely in the office anymore, so that helps." Wynter and Myles lived on the portion of land Daddy had given her. When needed, Myles commuted to the outskirts of Denver, where the Foster House distillery was located. Many times, Wynter and their daughter, Elsa, traveled with him. "But you worked with him just fine."

Her mouth tipped up in a knowing grin. "We worked way too well together at times. Anyway"—she swiveled back to her computer screen—"is there any image you don't want me to use?"

This was one reason I wouldn't let my music career collide with the work I did for Copper Summit. My family had all the freedom and they respected me and the rest of their employees.

How many times had I argued with Lucy about venues I didn't want to play in, artists I didn't want to open for, or images I didn't want posted by the social media manager she'd hired?

Too many fucking times. The respect I'd gotten from working with my family had delayed my breakout by years. The way I stuck to my convictions about how I'd be presented or how I did business was only one of the reasons I'd watched women younger than me rise to fame faster.

I pointed to the image of me playing the guitar. "Don't use that one."

"I didn't realize Kyra was shooting you then." Her tone was apologetic.

"No, it's fine. I like the shot, but it feels personal,

you know? It's not Copper Summit and it's not June Bee." For now.

"Speaking of which—why haven't I seen anything about your sudden departure from Nashville?"

I wrinkled my nose. "I'm not that big of news."

She tapped her fingers on the desktop and stared at me.

I sighed. "For one, I'm not dating anyone, so I'm not as interesting as usual." I let out a derisive snort. "God forbid a girl gets known for her talent in country music."

"It's not fair." Wynter waved her hands. "All of it."

I trailed my fingers through my hair and captured a strand of blue. Lucy had pressed me to dye my hair blonder and ditch the other colors. I hadn't listened. She had claimed I was putting my entire career on the line every time I appeared on stage with an "unnatural" color in my hair. *Since when have you seen a successful country singer with color in her hair?*

Country music lacked a lot of color and not just in hair, so I kept my stylist and ignored Lucy like I should've done when she'd brought up men I should meet.

"People are starting to speculate," she said.

I snapped out of my trance. "What?"

She tapped her phone. "I know you said you're staying away from everything, but people have noticed there've been no real posts."

Right. I had fired my social media manager too. She'd been a Lucy hire. I'd also changed my login info, but I popped in a lot with quick posts and videos. Not every day, but often enough that as I was approaching two weeks since fleeing Nashville, my silence would be noted. "I just can't bring myself to open an app."

If I saw one thing about me and one of my exes, my restraint might break. I didn't want to be linked to those men, but now I would be. Forever. Proof that I could be duped so easily.

Any muse that had returned while working with Wynter had shriveled and turned to dust. My two months were down to a little over seven weeks.

"Want me to talk to Ruby?" Wynter offered.

"Your new social media girl?" Ruby Casteel was a recent hire, and she worked out of the Bozeman distillery, but she came to Bourbon Canyon regularly to film content. I hadn't met her in person yet, but I'd been informed of her hiring during one of our family meetings.

"We have strict NDAs, but you don't even have to tell her why. We can just say that you want some time off and you don't want anyone to worry." She gestured to the computer screen that had gone black. "Kyra gives us video footage from the shoots too. Ruby can use that."

Yes, that would work. I was home for a breather. I'd just come off tour and I was working on the album my fans were excited about. Easy enough—as long as I wasn't the one diving into the social feed.

Wynter spun her chair again and her arms were crossed once more. "You never said how lessons went."

I frowned and went to the small couch in her office. One side was stacked with props she'd used last week— the dress, a Santa hat, and the cream shirt I'd borrowed. My cardigan was draped over the other side. "I told you it was fine."

"Would you let me get away with that answer?"

No, I'd take it as a sign to pester her more. "He

cleared out as soon as I started with the girls. Then we had a piece of coffee cake and I left."

"Coffee cake?"

"He bakes now."

"The guy who barely stays indoors bakes?"

I nodded and shrugged into my cardigan. The drizzle from this morning had quit, but it was probably still chilly out. "He's a dad now. He can't be gone all day."

Wynter tapped her fingertips together. "He fed you?"

"You make it sound scintillating." He'd fed me a lot since I'd arrived. Muffins, sandwiches, coffee cake. "He's civil. So am I." This time, I was the one folding my arms. "There's nothing there anymore."

She narrowed her eyes. I wasn't lying, but a sour flavor stained my tongue.

"He's moved on. We're different people."

That brow lifted again. I stiffened. Was she going to argue about how I hadn't moved on? Or did she agree with how different Rhys and I were now? I was practically a city girl these days and he wore flannel as a way of life.

"I don't think either of you has changed as much as you imagine," she said.

"Then we definitely aren't destined to be together. Since it didn't work the first time. His priority is not me. It's two adorable, lively little girls."

The scar along my heart ached. He had kids. I had fans. Sometimes, the two were completely incompatible.

Not that I was interested. And neither was he. I was sure of it. The emotions rising in me like a wind had kicked them up were nothing more than echoes of the past.

Either way, I was done with the topic. "I need a

break from *all* men. Anyway, I'm going to Mountain Perks. Want to come along?"

I'd been venturing out more and more. My ball cap and sunglasses were a constant. So far, only my old math teacher from high school had recognized me when I'd chatted with Autumn at the bar in the distillery, and he'd never sold me out before.

The coffee shop would be a different story, but the social media talk with Wynter had shown me that I couldn't hide forever. Nor did I have to reveal why I was home. Besides, I was home and I'd be in a coffee shop. Not exactly front-page material.

"I'd love to." Wynter swiveled toward her desk. "But I have to finish up some things. We're going to Denver over Memorial Day weekend and staying for a couple of weeks."

I was not jealous of her little family unit and how they traveled together. Myles had built his empire in another fucking state, but he'd moved to Montana for Wynter. Their home was here. Yet when he had to go to Foster House, she often accompanied him.

What was it like?

How many times had leaving for an appearance or a performance ruined a relationship for me? The infidelity hadn't helped, but neither had the constant distance. The continued separation. Each time I went on tour or my partner left town for their own gig or game was like a proclamation. We had come together temporarily, and our relationship was nothing more than that.

I gave her a hug. On my way out, I stopped by the viewing windows into the main room where the giant round pots sat with bubbling mash. The tall stills were at the other end with their distillation pipes reaching toward the ceiling.

Tenor and Teller were both by a bank of computers on standing desks. Tenor looked up and waved. Teller did the same.

I returned the wave and took off. Summer had left already.

It was only Tuesday, so I didn't stop at the bar. Autumn worked on Wednesdays and the weekends. Wynter often joined her for a few hours here and there, but it was too early for the bar to be open.

This was the most I'd been involved in Copper Summit business for a long time. Usually, I phoned into meetings or read the minutes afterward.

As I walked to my car, I looked back at the old distillery with its large rectangular windows and peaked roof. I was excited as usual to contribute, but this time, I appreciated the opportunity more. The company wasn't full of people who wanted something out of me.

In town, I parked and stared across the street into the coffee shop. People milled around inside. Why was it so busy at this time of day?

Just then, a group of kids left. Teens. I checked the time. School had gotten out an hour ago. I would've spent all my allowance on iced coffees if this place had been around when I'd been their age.

There was a knock on my window. I yelped and spun around.

Bethany waved at me. "Hi!" she said through the closed window.

Rhys glowered behind her, his jaw cracked down like he'd glued his teeth together. Hannah had a hold of his hand. He wasn't happy to see me, where people might witness us talking and some might recognize me, but a thrill ran through my belly.

He had on a grungy black ball cap, and his worn clothing fit him in all the right places. If he were in a country-boy calendar, he'd be June.

I stuffed my own light-blue ball cap on my head. There was cloud cover overhead, but I stuffed my sunglasses on anyway. Then I got out. "Hi!"

Rhys's lips twitched. "Sorry, ma'am. I thought you were someone else."

I gaped at him. Had he just made a joke? I slid my sunglasses down. "It's me, Junie."

The girls giggled and I took my sunglasses off. If I wore them in the coffee shop, I'd stand out more. After tossing them into the car, I tucked my hands into my cardigan pockets. "I'm grabbing a coffee."

"We're going to the coffee shop too!" Hannah said, tugging on her dad's hand.

"Wanna come with?" Bethany asked.

Rhys's jaw flexed. "Wren's meeting us there. She wants to get the girls a lemonade."

"Sparkling," Bethany clarified.

Had he told her I was in town? That I was giving the girls lessons?

"Mommy called today too." Hannah beamed.

"Oh, that's nice." Was that why Rhys looked disgruntled? What did Kirstin think of the lessons?

"We didn't tell her about you," Bethany whispered.

Hannah nodded solemnly. "Your secret's safe with us."

Rhys refused to meet my gaze. More like I was *his* secret.

Disappointment sank heavy inside me. I'd keep my

coffee shop stop a solo endeavor. My days of being seen at Rhys's side were long over. "Thank you, and thank you for the invite, but I won't interfere with Grandma time. Have fun."

I forced a sunny grin and trotted across the street. Bethany fell in step next to me, Hannah on the other side. A wall of moody heat followed me. This wasn't very solo.

"The girls want to surprise Kirstin with a concert next time they see her," Rhys explained.

Oh. My spirits lifted. Rhys probably hadn't wanted to break the news to his ex that a woman was hanging around him and the girls, but the idea of a surprise for their mom was sweet.

Before I reached the entrance, Rhys rushed around me and grabbed the door. We piled in and he crowded in behind me. The move was so familiar. My daddy used to hold doors for Mama and all of us. He'd take us out and show off his family.

That wasn't what was happening here though. My emotions had to settle down. Rhys and I were practically strangers.

The scent of roasted coffee surrounded me. The familiar, eclectic vibe of Mountain Perks was comforting. There were three kids ahead of me in line. Two boys and a girl. The girl and one of the guys were bugging the third about what he wanted to drink.

When the girl looked back at her friend, she did a double take. "June Bee?"

My shoulders tightened. I would not act like a diva who couldn't bother to be recognized. I put on my winning smile. "How's it going?"

I was swarmed by the kids in the shop. I maneuvered

to the side and the crowd followed. Someone shoved a pen in my hand, but I dug my blue Sharpie out of my bag and signed whatever was put in front of me while fielding questions.

The ones from kids were different than press. *What's your favorite song? Are you on vacation? What's the coolest place you've been to? Who's the meanest celebrity you've ever met? The nicest?*

My cheeks were aching from my smile. "The nicest people I've met haven't been celebrities. The stadium crews at the venues I played have all been A-plus."

"What's Finn Calhoun like?" the girl who'd first spotted me asked.

My smile faltered. *He's a self-absorbed prick with nothing but a nice voice and some muscles. And he was selfish in bed!* "He's . . ." I could be professional. "He's, uh . . ."

"He's an asshole who cheated on her," Rhys growled at my side.

The girl's eyes widened. "Did he really? I thought they say that about every breakup."

I gave her a sympathetic smile. It sucked when reality shattered admiration for a celebrity, but it wasn't my fault or the young fan's. The knot in my shoulders loosened now that I didn't have to cover for a cheater, thanks to Rhys. "He's a good singer. But a trash boyfriend."

She wrinkled her nose. "That sucks. Who are you dating now?" Her questioning gaze lifted to Rhys.

He tensed, and I wanted to laugh. Was this the reaction to being seen together he'd been worried about?

"No distractions for me while I work on my next album."

Her face brightened. "You're writing it *here*? In Bourbon Canyon?"

"It's the best place in the world." I meant it with my whole soul.

"But you have, like, three houses."

A house, a condo, two apartments, and the cabin. Five total. "I like to have options, but there's no place like home. I get to see old friends and family." That should put any speculation about Rhys to rest.

The last of the crowd filtered away, except for Rhys and the girls and an older woman with smile lines. Her sun-kissed blond and gray hair was pulled back in a bun.

"Junie," she said, warmth radiating from her expression and her voice.

Rhys's stepmother. Genuine affection warmed the center of my chest. "Hi, Wren."

"I heard you were in town." She pulled me in for a quick hug. "Are you staying after you get your drink?"

Had Rhys told her about me? Doubtful. "I haven't gotten my tea yet, but I didn't plan to stay."

A knowing glint entered her gaze. Was she wondering if it was the crowd or Rhys behind me leaving? "Why don't you order and sit with us until it's ready." She tipped her head. "Maybe you'll decide to stay longer."

I opened my mouth to deny the possibility, but she turned, presenting me with her pristine bun. The girls were already at a table and they waved to us.

I almost ordered a sparkling lemonade, but I stuck with an iced chai with oat milk.

"I didn't know you could milk an oat," Rhys said from behind me.

I liked growly Rhys a whole lot more than I'd ever

thought I would, but he was the same guy who'd always made me laugh when I'd gotten stuck in my head. I turned, saving my eye roll for when he could see. My mouth went dry. A guy should not look that good in blue-and-green flannel and a black T-shirt. His forearms were covered, but I remembered every bulging ridge and vein.

"Milking oats is a hard job," I said. "You can't take days off and the oats need to be hooked up morning and night."

"Good thing I stuck to a cow-calf operation." He stepped around me to order.

I took the out and created distance between us. While I could be on the other side of town and still be acutely aware of that man, seeing his lighter side scrambled my brain. Tempted me to stay, no matter how close to my ultimate dream I was.

Bethany waved me over as if I couldn't find them in a coffee shop that was three times narrower than it was long. Her genuine reaction bolstered my steps. The girls enjoyed being around me. Hanging with them was like being around my sisters. To them, I was no longer June Bee, rising star. I was Junie, their guitar teacher who liked their dad's muffins.

I slid into a chair. The table was smaller than a card table and there were five of us. The empty seat next to me was for Rhys, and I'd practically be in his lap.

I glanced up at his approach. His brows were drawn together and his jaw was tight. He set his drinks down, including mine.

I wrapped my hands around the mug as if I could still feel his touch on the material. I had forgotten to tell them to make my drink to go. "Thank you."

"Welcome." He brushed behind me, his crotch way too close to the back of my head. I should've taken the chair closest to Wren.

When he sat, our thighs were pressed against each other. I couldn't scoot over without falling off and he couldn't slide the opposite direction without pushing Wren out of her seat.

Instead, he slid backward. I wiggled my chair closer to the table. Wren glanced between us, then took a sip of her sparkling lemonade.

I didn't know if we were friends or if I was supposed to act like I hadn't ever seen him naked. Were we just two people who'd gone to high school together? Regardless, we could be civil. Even if my urges around Rhys Kinkade were extremely *not* civil.

Rhys

Her peony scent curled around me like a lover's embrace. She'd changed whatever the hell she used for soap since we'd dated.

I took a hard pull from my lemonade. Between the suction and my grip, the plastic cup almost crumpled. I set the drink down before I spilled the remaining juice and ice onto my pants.

At least a groin full of ice would temper the heat that simmered in that region when June was around.

Sitting back, I brushed against her arm. She'd crossed one leg over the other, giving us a little breathing room.

"It's nice to see you home," Wren said. She'd been delighted to hear that June was in town. Now she was at the coffee shop with us. She must be elated to see me and June speaking again. Wren had hated our breakup and the reason for it, but she'd supported me.

"It's great to be back," June said.

A canned response. I grunted. June shot me a side-eye.

"Are you in between records?" Wren leaned forward. "Is that what they call it? Tours?"

June shrugged, and damn, I had a good view of the rise and fall of her breasts with each breath she took. The damn cardigan hid most of her cleavage.

I tore my gaze away. Annette Prichard entered the coffee shop. She was a couple years younger than me, also divorced, and had a daughter Bethany's age. We often split duties running kids around if our work got in the way.

Sometimes, she hinted at more. Every time, I pretended to be oblivious.

She waved at the girls, her expression brightening. Her gaze landed on me and her smile widened. She veered toward us. Then she spotted June. Her smile faltered. "Oh my. I didn't realize we had a celebrity in the house."

June stiffened. Was it just from being recognized? "Hey, Annette."

"I don't usually hear about you being in town until after you've left." Annette's gaze jumped between me and June. "How nice of you to . . . visit."

"Well, it is my home." The edge in June's smile wasn't noticeable if you didn't know her. I knew her. She was on alert. Over Annette?

Annette's eyes narrowed. "You're back for good?"

"No, I'm still working." June's smile dripped with more syrup than Bethany had added to her pancakes. "Nothing like crisp mountain air to fuel the creative juices."

Impressed at her adept way of ending further inquiries, unless they were regarding her cocksucker of an ex, I reclined in my chair.

"I'm sure." Annette tugged at the purse strap around her shoulder. "It's almost like old times, seeing you two together again."

A zing of alarm shot through me, tensing every muscle it passed. That was what I got for being too relaxed. Annette wasn't going there, was she? Bringing up old news that was best left in the—

"You two were what the kids say are 'hashtag goals' for couples in high school. I mean, you were together *all* of high school."

My stomach hit the heels of my boots. Both of my girls' spines went ramrod straight.

"What?" Bethany screeched.

"A couple?" Hannah's eyes were wide.

Bethany sucked in a strangled breath and pounded the table. Dammit, we were turning into a spectacle. "Are you one of her exes?"

June winced. My face flushed hot, then cold. They did not need to piece the past together in the middle of Mountain Perks in front of witnesses. In front of the girl who'd broken my damn heart.

Hannah gripped her sister and they both leaned over the table.

"Dad," Bethany said as if what was coming out of her

mouth next was life or death. "Are any of those songs about you?"

Silence fell over the table. June dropped her head, a red blush wicking up her face. Surprise filled Annette's face. Everyone probably thought I boasted about my history with country music's latest sweetheart.

Bethany slumped in her chair. The look of disappointment she shot my way was laughable. "I can't believe this," she said dramatically. "My own father."

I had let her watch too much TV.

"People like to speculate about my lyrics," June said carefully, "but I've never confirmed or denied who, or even if, they're about anyone in particular. It is true I take inspiration from the feelings I've felt before."

"Are you 'That Boy'?" Hannah leaned half her body over the table until we were face-to-face. "Did you make her cry all day and night?"

June peeked at me, her lower lip caught between her teeth. Chagrin filled her face. I was that boy. I'd made her cry. I'd given her all the freedom in the world, but I hadn't asked her to stay.

I wasn't getting into this bullshit in public. I had to divert. Yet when I glanced at June again, she was fighting a smile.

I was panicking, my kids were looking at me like I was a villain, and she was trying not to laugh? "You find this funny, June Bug?"

She failed to smother a snicker. "No."

"When you lie, your nose lights up."

She sucked in an indignant breath. "Rhys Conner Kinkade, that's not the part you used to say lit up."

Then her eyes flared like she couldn't believe she'd just said that out loud, and she dissolved into giggles.

I couldn't believe it either, but the familiarity had gotten to me. I caught the divots forming between Annette's brows. Wren watched us with sparkling eyes. What did June and I look like? Reunited lovers?

That wasn't what we were.

Our situation was unique, and I'd let it be just that for a while.

"Sorry to spill the beans." Annette gripped her purse strap. "I didn't realize . . ."

"Annette." June gave a dramatic sigh. "Rhys is so forthcoming. I just can't believe you didn't know."

Annette's laughter burst out of her. "Yes. Very true." She met my gaze and mouthed *sorry* before scurrying away.

"Dad should be the one who's sorry," Bethany grumbled. She stood, knocking her chair back.

I lunged for it, bumping into June. She caught it and shot me an amused look as she righted the chair.

"I've gotta go to the bathroom." She marched off.

"Me too." Hannah scurried behind her.

June scooted her chair over, leaving a few inches between us that might as well be a chasm after feeling her pressed against me. My fingers itched to drag her closer again.

Wren folded her napkin into neat little squares. "I never agreed with the secrecy, but I can understand with how Kirstin was."

I gave Wren a sharp look, and she rolled her lips in, her gaze skating away. What was it with people bringing up shit that wasn't their business?

June's stare burned into the side of my face.

Wren shifted her attention to June. "How is Mae?"

When June's gaze lifted from me, my lungs could finally expand.

"Good." Fondness filled June's eyes. "She loves having Lane and Cruz living there, but I guess Lane is moving to Denver soon. Now that Elsa's born, Myles plans to train Lane in all things Foster House. Cruz might even get in on it later, but he loves working with Tenor."

"Those boys are so nice." Wren folded her hands on the table and continued to pepper June with polite questions about the rest of the Baileys.

I glowered at the top of the table. The girls returned, mutiny in their eyes. I was going to hear about my role in June's heartbreak. The girls were likely to forgive me though.

A lifetime wasn't enough for me to forgive myself.

CHAPTER EIGHT

Rhys

I stood in the middle of the living room and pressed the palms of my hands into my eyes. For the entire week, I'd been hearing about songs and whether June had been singing about me or not.

That was after I'd given them the abridged version of our relationship. I'd arrived in seventh grade. In eighth grade, I'd asked June to the homecoming dance, and we'd been a couple from then until the August after graduation. Their grandpa had gotten sick, I'd stayed behind, and I'd realized my place was in Bourbon Canyon and June's was in Nashville.

They had asked why I couldn't have moved with June. I'd told them Grandpa had needed me. Then Wren. They'd been satisfied with that.

When they'd asked why I'd never told them, I hadn't thrown their mother under the bus and blamed her for wanting zero pictures of June under the roof. No memorabilia, no reminiscing, no mention of my ex. Even June's songs were banned. I couldn't blame Kirstin, and I'd respected her feelings. I'd told them I didn't talk about June because I thought it might be disrespectful to their mom.

I'd also been happy to bury my memories.

June was due in five minutes and the girls had reignited their inquisition about song lyrics.

"Who was she jealous of in 'Emerald Rain'?" Bethany pressed.

It didn't matter how many times I refused to answer. They kept asking. I also hadn't answered whether I was the guy who'd left her boarding a plane, heartbroken and devastated in "Cowboy Wish Me Home."

"Listen, girls, this is the last question I'm going to answer about June's songs." Or I'd lose my fucking mind. "She drove away from Montana, so I doubt that one is me, and I have no clue who she was jealous of." My intuition knew better.

" 'She walks down the aisle to him and my tears fall like emerald rain,' " Bethany quoted. " 'She gets to wear the white gown while I'm in blue jeans. I'm the richest girl in the world because I've cried so many tears.' Do you know why she wrote emeralds? Because they're *green*, like envy."

My collar was chafing the back of my neck. Did Bethany know the whole song by heart? "You'll have to ask June."

Why was I the one under interrogation?

Because you hurt June so bad she made millions of dollars and fell for shitty men who kept her making millions.

No. I'd made the right decision.

The doorbell rang. They sprinted past me to answer it.

I pinched the bridge of my nose and leaned against the wall separating the living room from the kitchen. A dull thud settled at my temples and I blew out a breath.

When I dropped my hand and looked up, June regarded me, concern in her eyes.

I pushed off the wall. I couldn't be in the house while she was inside. I couldn't hear her answer the girls' questions. "I'll be outside. Girls, for God's sake, please don't interrogate your tutor about her teenage years."

My home was no longer a June-free oasis.

Outside, I sucked in fresh air. The closer I got to the barn, the more the livestock smell lingered in the air. Inside the barn, I stared at the stalls full of muck and old straw. I'd be balls deep in cleaning, then I'd have to stop and see June off and make sure the girls got started on cleaning the chicken coop.

The barn could wait. I didn't want to wallow in dirt and manure dust. Instead, I went to the shop and opened the big overhead door. The inside was cool, but the sunlight spewing in helped. Once I got started, I'd heat up quick enough.

My four-wheeler needed new brakes and the spark plugs were due for a cleaning after a sluggish start this morning.

As I worked, my mind played over the lyrics of June's song. I'd suspected some were about me. I was humble enough to know they all weren't. But June's reaction yesterday was confirmation that she'd been singing about me at least some of the time.

The spark plugs were done and I had one of the new

brake pads in place when footsteps sounded behind me. Those weren't the patter of my kids' feet.

When I rose, my gaze landed on long, jean-clad legs. The denim hugged her skin all the way to the neck of the boot. No more boot-cut jeans for her. Did she still wear those when she helped at the ranch? They'd made her legs look impossibly long. Her maroon knit top hung loose over a white long-sleeved shirt. The mix of tight and baggy only amplified the curves I couldn't keep my leering eyes off of.

"Something wrong?" It came out as barely more than a grunt. I went to the sink in the far corner of the shop.

"No, not with lessons." She followed me deeper into the shop. Goddammit, couldn't she keep a whole cement slab of distance between us? I didn't want to smell her peony scent among the grease and metallic odors.

"Then what?"

"I'm sorry. About the songs."

"Not my business." I turned the faucet on and bit back a hiss at the frigid water that shot out.

"It's become your business, and I never meant for that to happen. I talked to the girls about it."

I scrubbed my hands, working the degreaser over my fingers. By the time I rinsed, the water was finally luke-warm, but I missed the shock.

I turned the water off and yanked a towel off the hook on the wall. Curiosity got the best of me. "What'd you tell them?"

She shrugged, and my gaze dropped to her breasts. My mind was a mess and my body's reactions to June Kerrigan were harder to control. I jerked my eyes back up.

Thankfully, she was frowning at the floor by my feet.

"I said I draw inspiration from my life and those around me. A lot of our experiences are so common, and that's why they resonate so much, even with little girls who've heard stories and seen for themselves what heartbreak can do."

I finished drying my hands. She met my gaze, her expression resolute, her brown eyes solemn.

My irritation grew and I aimed a glare at her. "So you gave them a nebulous nonanswer because they're young, and they won't know?" What else had I expected her to do?

Anger brightened the yellow specks in her gaze. "I did not."

" 'I draw inspiration from my life and those around me.' That's as nonspecific as you can get."

"I was trying to help."

"No, you didn't want to be the bad guy—"

"Would you rather I tell them why yes, girls, your dad is *that boy*. He's so much that boy that I could've written another album about him. Because why would a boy stay with you for five years—*five years*, Rhys—why would a boy make the rawest, sweetest, hottest love to you and then walk out of your life forever like you didn't mean a thing? Is that what you want me to say?"

I took two steps closer to her. "Would it have been better for you to write about being a poor rancher's wife who can't go anywhere, especially not during calving season?" I crowded even closer. "Would that stay in the number one spot for two weeks?"

Her eyes narrowed and she planted her hands on her hips. "It was three weeks."

The yellow in her eyes was sparking. Energy poured off of her. This was the June Bug I used to run the pastures with. The June who drove my high school pickup with the stick shift like she was in a Formula One race. The June who didn't hide in her hometown because she was lost and confused.

"Who's the guy you were crying over in 'Emerald Rain'?" I was inches from her. I needed to hear the answer. Had she been jealous of Kirstin? Had I made a mistake when I'd finally decided to let her go and attempt to move on with my life?

She blanched. "That was no one."

"It was very much someone. Was it me? Did you picture me up on that church altar, saying my vows to the woman who'd be the mother of my children?"

Her eyes misted over, and it was a kick in the goddamn gut. "Rhys, don't."

"Who was it, June? Who made you think you were the richest woman in the world crying those emerald tears?"

"Rhys—"

"Yes or no, songbird." I lowered my voice. The smell of peonies hit my nose and my muscles strained against leaning forward, burying my nose in her hair, and inhaling her deep into my lungs. "Was it me?"

"Yes." One word. Barely a whisper.

My world crumpled around me like an aluminum can. So my worst fears were true. She'd hurt as badly as me. It didn't make me feel better.

Old emotions rushed in. That aching emptiness for years after she'd left. The loneliness. The longing to have her in my arms just one more time.

But I'd made the right decision. I had made it for her.

And she was right here. I could take the blue, silky

strands of her hair between my fingers. I could feel those puffy lips under mine once again.

We were still close, our chests nearly touching. Her face was tipped up. A tear escaped the corner of her eye and tracked down her cheek. I swiped it away with a thumb.

How many times had she cried around me since I'd found her on the side of the road? I shouldn't be making this woman feel bad.

I could make her feel good. I dropped my head a few inches. She fisted her hands in the flannel of my shirt, but she didn't stop me. So I closed the distance.

As soon as my lips hit hers, my epically bad mistake was clear. There was nothing I wouldn't do to taste June Kerrigan again.

I licked my tongue out and she opened for me. Her minty flavor filled my mouth and her tongue danced with mine.

We used to make our own music together. Special notes for the two of us. A bourbon harmony.

I gripped her waist and tugged her closer. She circled her arms around my neck and pressed against me. Turning us both, I backed her to a workbench. Once she was wedged against the bench, I could fully devour her.

A moan went through her and right into me. I swallowed the sound and continued to plunder the warm, wet depths of her mouth. This was no bumbling teenage make-out. We knew what we were doing, but the years between us melted away. What had been complicated was now a simple kiss.

A sweltering, hot-as-fuck kiss. One that would keep me up at night until I had to do something to take the edge off the lust that hadn't gone away since I'd seen her looking back at me in the rain.

I ground into her, and she met my movements with a force of her own. She curled a leg around me. I ran my hand down her ass and hitched her leg higher, notching myself between her thighs. Too much damn denim was in the way, but I'd take what she was willing to give me.

Reversing direction, I brushed my hand up her toned thigh to her waist. Her shirt was tucked in. Tempted to rip it to shreds, I started working the material out of her waistband.

"Dad!" Bethany's voice rang from somewhere outside. "Where are you?"

June jerked away with a hiss and flattened her hands on my shoulders. I didn't move. She was stuck between me and the workbench.

"Dad?"

"Go have a snack, and I'll be right in," I called out the open door. Where we were, Bethany wouldn't be able to see us. If she got closer, we'd be busted, but then June would get away and I wasn't ready to let her go yet.

Her chest rose and fell against mine, those full tits marking me like a brand.

The gravel outside crunched with footsteps.

"Bethany, get inside and have a snack and I'll be right in." The steps stopped. "Now."

"Fine." The scrape of gravel against shoe soles faded.

Only then did I ease back. The fullness behind my zipper wasn't going to go away with June pressed against it.

She licked her bottom lip, looking away. "Sorry, I didn't mean for that to hap—"

"I did."

Her gaze flew up to mine.

"Those songs make it sound like I had a ripe fucking time without you. They make it sound like I didn't suffer for years and that my wife didn't doubt my love for her every damn day."

She shrunk in on herself.

"Singing was your dream. What kind of bastard would I have been to stop you?"

"You made the decision for us." She shook her head. "Am I supposed to apologize because I wrote my pain? Am I supposed to wish that it didn't resonate with so many people? Was I supposed to just pour beer at the honky-tonk and hope my ass attracted some record mogul?"

I propped my hands on either side of her, blocking her in. The fire was back in her eyes. "Never apologize for your talent. But I might be a little raw when my two young girls are blaming me for being a villain in your story."

She boldly met my stare, pink dots flushing her cheeks. "I would've come back if you had asked me to."

"Then I really would've been the villain." I pushed away and cool air rushed between us. "And you wouldn't be the voice of this generation's heartbreak." Before I did something stupid like try to kiss her again, I stalked toward the opening. "See you next week."

"It felt like I was nothing to you. You got married to someone else and had the kids we would've had."

I stopped dead in my tracks. I'd wanted my marriage to be untouched by June, but to hear her talk about it, Kirstin had been dead-on with every one of her accusations. "I was twenty-four. We'd been apart for six years."

"And I was still watching my phone, hoping to see

your name pop up. Instead, Summer sent me a picture of your wedding invitation. I wrote 'Emerald Rain' the day of your wedding."

June

His back was to me, his head half turned. "You hated me for getting married?"

My answer was a bitter stain on my tongue. "Yes."

He slowly pivoted on a heel until he faced me. "Do you still?"

I shook my head. This time, the answer came easy. "No, Rhys. My life would be so much easier if I hated you."

He strode toward me, giant steps that ate up the distance between us. In two heartbeats, he towered over me. "Then we agree that our lives would be a lot fucking simpler if we could get over each other."

If we could? He wasn't over me?

He traced a finger down my cheek. "The girls know the whole story now. There's nothing to hide."

"There never was."

He chuckled and his warm breath fluttered my hair. "Oh there was, June Bug. Everyone in town looked at me like they knew I had no idea what the fuck to do with myself after you were gone." He trailed the tip of his finger down my neck and over my collarbone, following the collar of my long-sleeved shirt. "I think that was why Kirstin was so intriguing."

I swallowed hard. Talking about another woman, the

one who'd gotten to walk down the aisle to him, was the last thing I wanted his mouth to be doing.

"For once, I wasn't some lovesick guy who'd had to stay behind to run the family farm. To her, I was a blank slate. I pretended I could start fresh." He feathered his hands through my hair. "So damn soft," he murmured.

My chest rose and fell. I craved more of his touch. If he didn't back away, I would scale him like a mountain to get his mouth right where I wanted it. I was too weak to take a step back, but I could put my own mouth to use. "Are you blaming me for ruining your marriage?"

"No, songbird. In the end, she was a lot like you. She had a dream, and I was in her way."

How could he think that? "She left her kids."

"Yeah," he said quietly. "But it's better for them to have a stable home. Kids shouldn't be raised on the road."

I stiffened. "You weren't concerned about that before." When we'd planned our future family, he'd known I'd be traveling for work and he'd said nothing. Now it was a deal breaker?

"I've always been concerned about that."

"Why didn't you talk to me about this? Is this because of your mom?"

His expression went stony. "I'm not talking about me."

"It feels like this has to do with you."

"I'm not your business anymore."

I recoiled. "You're shutting me out *again*."

He winced.

"Did you talk to Kirstin about your convictions or did you tell her you wanted a divorce and she needed to go be a photographer?"

"Why? Do you want to write a song about it?"

"Actually, yes. I could write about a stubborn ass of a man who denies his feelings until he kisses *the one who got away* senseless. Then he turns around and pushes her away again. I could call it 'Senseless.' " I sucked in a breath and held it. I blew it out in a rush. "That's actually not bad."

The tension between us drained and the corner of his mouth curved up. "Does the songbird have her muse?"

"Maybe?" I smirked. "Only you could upset me so bad I'd write a song about it."

His gaze softened and sadness crept into his eyes. "Then you'd better go write while the inspiration's hot."

If I stayed, I might do something stupid like ask him to give me more inspiration with another kiss.

"See you next Sunday." I did the world's most awkward wave, spun on my heel, and continued toward the door.

"Hey, songbird," he said, his tone light. "If you write that senseless song, do me a solid and give the guy a name that's not mine, or the girls will kill me."

I looked over my shoulder. "Sure. He'll be . . . Conner."

He groaned, and I laughed. I forced myself to continue walking.

Our chemistry was as strong as ever, and our conversations were getting more comfortable. Familiar. But I couldn't start wondering . . . Fantasizing. He didn't want his kids traveling. He wasn't selling me a promise he wouldn't keep. When I left town again, he'd stay right where he was. Just like last time.

CHAPTER NINE

June

"I can get that, Mama." I took the basket of eggs from her in the chicken shed. We'd just washed them all.

"I know." Mama ignored me and continued out of the shed. A mix of speckled and reddish-brown chickens scattered from our path.

Side by side, we walked the dirt trail up the hill to the house. Once we hit the flatter part of our yard, the grass thickened. A light breeze ruffled my ponytail.

I'd gone to bed every night since Sunday letting some of the strands slip through my fingers, imagining it was Rhys's hand and that his other one was—

"You've been quiet today." Mama's chin was lifted in her *I'm not going to pry but I'll just ask a simple question* way.

"I have a call with my lawyer later." The last call I'd had was promising. The contract I had with Lucy wasn't ironclad. Her deception was enough to extract me without penalties.

"Oh, she's good, right?"

"She's why I can still work freely for Copper Summit."

Mom gave an approving grunt as we entered the house. The warmth of the kitchen surrounded me. Pure comfort. "What about hiring a new manager?"

Stress burned down my throat. "I haven't started looking yet." My inbox was filling up. News of the breakup with my manager had reached my professional circle. Soon it'd be public knowledge. Then I'd have managers knocking on my door, promising me the world.

And I'd have to decide who to trust.

Someday, I'd be that person for people. I mentored who I could, but I wasn't yet in a position to offer more than advice and a few scholarships. For all of Lucy's faults, I wouldn't have gotten as far as I was without her network and influence. Once my name made enough money and promised so much more to come, I could open those doors myself for others.

"Want a drink?" Mama asked. I arched a brow and she rolled her eyes. "*Coffee*. It's only ten in the morning."

"Since when has that stopped us?" I started putting eggs into the empty cartons Mama had stocked behind the door.

She smirked and washed her hands. "You sound just like your father."

"I miss him."

"Me too." She gave me another discreet look. "If he were here, what would you talk to him about?"

I knew what she was getting at. I was scheduled to tutor the girls every week. Tomorrow, I'd be over there again. Each day clicked by, slow as molasses, as I watched the calendar for Sunday to appear. And each day, I picked at my guitar, different melodies coming and going.

But I'd written a song. "Senseless."

I'd gone to the bar last Wednesday. Autumn had looked deliriously happy, and Gideon had been on a stool, rocking worn jeans like he'd been born in them, which was true. The smoldering looks between the two of them had driven me home early. And I'd written another song about a rugged country man oblivious of his appeal. A single dad who doted on his daughters and put hearts in the eyes of single moms everywhere. I'd titled it "Call Me Daddy." I'd probably have to change it, but it made me giggle to think of Rhys hearing it and knowing it was him.

I couldn't ride the wave of euphoria from having two whole songs done after months of languishing. I had at least eight more album-worthy songs to write.

If Daddy were alive, I'd talk to him. I'd definitely open up to my sisters. As it was, Wynter had gone to Denver early with Myles and Elsa. Summer and Jonah were on some road trip to find new wood for him to make gorgeous furniture with. The guys would know something was eating at me if I asked to hang out with them, but I didn't want to open up to them. My brothers wanted to solve problems. They were a different dynamic from Daddy but just as perceptive.

When I'd stopped in at the distillery yesterday, Teller had taken one look at me and said, "You're lingering. What's wrong?"

Then I'd asked Tate when Scarlett would be home and he'd said, "Why? What's wrong?"

I didn't want to talk to him about kissing exes. I still hadn't told any of them about my Nashville issues.

Mama always had an ear and she was more ironclad than an NDA. Usually. I'd risk it this time.

When I wasn't penning a song around Rhys, I was thinking about what we'd talked about in the shop. "Do you think I did the right thing? When I moved to Tennessee?"

She paused pouring water into the coffee machine. Then she finished and stuffed the pot under the spout. She wouldn't look at me.

A band around my chest tightened. Back then, if she had thought I was making a mistake, she'd have still supported my ambitions. Seemed to be a theme with the people I loved.

Finally, she turned. "There aren't a lot of mistakes in life. There're mostly should-haves and doubts. You made the decision you made for a reason. To doubt that now is useless. To think about what you should've done is disingenuous. You aren't the same person. You didn't have the luxury of knowing the future and how it'd all turn out."

The pressure didn't ease around my chest. "When'd you get so wise?"

"From all the doubting and should-ing on myself."

I laughed. "I was doubting." I leaned against the counter. "The whole thing with Lucy made me question my motivation. I've had to look at why I'm pursuing the very top, and sometimes, I dunno, I can't help but wonder the opposite. What if."

"What if you'd stayed, contented yourself with playing at the county fair, and become a mom to two little girls like Bethany and Hannah?"

Nailed it. I nodded.

"Then you'd be in my kitchen asking me if you'd made the right decision because you love writing, singing, and performing and you can't do much of it as a ranch wife and mom." She crossed to me and squeezed my hands. "And that ranch wife and mom wouldn't have known that if she had gone, Rhys wouldn't have followed."

I would've never thought that. "Did you know?"

"Not at first. We were all surprised when you told us he wasn't going with you, but with his dad's illness, it made sense. Then he seemed so distant when I saw him. He barely chatted with us, hardly smiled. You expressed your concern. And this old mom put two and two together that he wasn't trying to get to Nashville."

"Why?" I swallowed hard, voicing the real question beneath *what if*. "Why would he just give up like that?"

She rubbed my shoulders. "Only he knows. But you have to remember, he had his own traumas growing up. And that mama of his . . ." She released me. "Well, I didn't know her, not really, so I shouldn't say."

"I looked her up once," I said. I'd never admit to Rhys that I'd gone snooping on Angela Craft. "All I found was her obituary, some announcements, and medi-ocre reviews." At Mama's alarmed look, I shook my head. "I never described them like that to Rhys. I didn't even tell him I'd found them."

"I'm sure he's sensitive. It was just those two for the first twelve years of his life."

"She dragged him all over. I'm sure that's why he got cold feet about moving his kids around."

"Mm." Mama returned to the coffee maker. "You'd have to ask him."

"I did. He won't talk about it. Or her."

"Then you'll have to respect that he chose his path and he's not willing to change it. So you might as well pick that new manager. Unless you want to become a ranch wife and mom."

The idea wasn't terrible. A lot of ranch wives had full-time jobs. The joke went that every successful ranch had one spouse with a full-time job and benefits. There'd be less time to dedicate to singing and performing, but more importantly, it wasn't the life I'd worked so long for. "I'm almost there, Mama. My own *big* tour. You know how long I've dreamed about it?"

"Yes. Just like I know that you're back home, all your sisters are happily wed, and you think you missed your window. Your feelings for Rhys are feeling pretty fresh and adoring those little girls isn't helping."

"I'm only home for another month and a half. I just keep wondering . . ." I massaged my temples. Rhys was hot, then cold, then hot. We talked like we'd known each other most of our lives and then acted like we'd never gotten along. But six weeks could be an eternity when we already had so much between us. What if we kissed again? What if . . .

"Junie, Rhys chose his path in life again and again. Whatever he commits to, he gives his all."

A large lump formed in my throat, cutting off my air.

She nodded like she could see my thoughts scrolling across my forehead. "He committed to his dad. Then the family farm. He committed to his marriage and then the girls. He's committed to his way of life."

What she didn't say rang loud and clear. *But he didn't commit to you.*

Rhys

I worked on the walls on the breezeway between the garage and the house. The physical labor was doing wonders for the near-constant state of arousal I'd been in since kissing June.

How could she taste better than ever? How could her lips feel softer than I remembered? I'd thought I had every minute detail carved into my memory. The real, present-day June blew my memories out of the water.

I stepped back to assess the window I'd just put in place. Wren was inside with the girls, giving me a full day to work on the breezeway without stopping to make meals or referee arguments. Besides, without Wren, the girls would want to help, and while I would teach them construction skills someday, today wasn't that day. They didn't need to deal with a cranky dad who was sore that he couldn't stop kissing the singer they adored.

The front door banged open. Bethany skidded around the side of the house. "Dad! Junie's on the TV."

Probably. She wasn't currently performing, but it wouldn't be out of the ordinary for her to be referenced, especially if they were bringing up one of her dick exes. "Okay?"

"They're saying she's vanished."

Hannah flew out next and slid to a stop in the grass next to Bethany. "Disappeared."

I was moving before I knew it. Inside, I didn't bother to kick my boots off before marching to the living room. Some young reporter's face was frozen on the screen. Wren loved her entertainment shows.

Wren looked at me while aiming the remote and

hitting the play button. The image changed to clips from June's last tour, where she'd been an opening act for that dickwad Finn. A tan cowboy hat rested on her head and the pink-tinged hair she'd had when she'd dated him streamed out from underneath. Her boots were the flashiest part of her outfit. The white blouse and painted-on blue jeans fit her indie country-rock aesthetic. People thought it was a put-on, but she'd always dressed that way growing up, at least when she wasn't chasing cows on horseback.

The reporter's voice overlaid the clips. "News about the release of the next June Bee album might have to wait. Sources say she hasn't been seen for weeks and even missed appointments with notable songwriter Remi Dahl. We reached out to June Bee, but she's declined to comment."

I narrowed my eyes and Wren shut the TV off. What was the point of spreading this news? She'd taken a ton of pictures with young fans in the coffee shop. Hadn't the kids posted them, or was no one interested in a happy June surrounded by people who cared about her?

"Why is that lady saying she's missing?" Hannah asked, blinking her big blue eyes.

"I don't know, peanut."

"Does Junie know?" A line formed between Wren's brows. "Her fans must be so worried."

Fuck her fans. Would any of them even care she'd been used by her fucking manager? They thrived on her heartbreak, fed off it. Logically, I knew they'd care. Righteous anger would light the internet on her behalf. I just wanted June to have the peace she was seeking. "I don't know. She's staying off social media."

Wren held her phone loosely in her hands. "She's

been posting fun clips from her concerts and images of her writing music."

I frowned. This was all news to me.

Wren flashed her screen and I took the phone from her. Scrolling through the images, I scowled. June's fingers working over her guitar as she hummed a few notes to herself. June smiling in front of a camera as she held a bottle of Copper Summit bourbon. June with her face tipped to the sun. **#selfcare** was the caption. The background was full of familiar trees. The same ones crawling up the slopes behind the cabin.

I scrolled up to the image with her posing with the bourbon. The brick wall behind her was familiar too. There was another image nested with it and a short video.

Wynter's voice spilled out of the little phone from a video on her feed. "June Bee and Copper Summit. A match made in Montana heaven."

Only those of us who knew what Wynter sounded like and had been in Copper Summit before would know this image was both recent and taken in Bourbon Canyon. The general public might think the photo shoot was in Bozeman. It was how June usually presented her work with her family business. The company might want tourism, but none of us residents wanted fans stampeding our small town.

She'd done well at concealing where she was. The cabin images could be mistaken for Tennessee, and she had other homes people could snoop around.

A chill washed over me.

What if they tracked her to Bourbon Canyon and people dug up history of us? They might not care about a guy from fifteen years ago, but they'd care about him if he was suddenly in her life again. If he had two kids that she was giving guitar lessons to.

I did not need the girls to get tossed into a media frenzy. A country darling and some normal dude might not attract much attention, but his adorable kids might. June's fans loved her heartache, but they also wanted to see her happy. Each time she was linked to a man, speculation about kids was next.

Dread had clawed over my shoulders and down to my gut each time I had read those posts. Rich, when I was the one who'd gotten married and had kids.

I had to talk to June.

"Wren, can you watch the girls for a little bit? I need to let June know about this." She probably knew if she'd been elbow deep in her socials, except she'd said she was avoiding them. "I can't have it affecting the girls," I said in a low voice.

"Of course." Concern filled her eyes. "Do you think she knows?"

"She has to, and she has to realize speculation will lead people to her hometown. I just need to know how she's going to handle it."

I couldn't be linked as June's happily ever after. It had been hard enough letting her go the first time. I didn't need the world to shove it in her face that I wasn't leaving my home to go with her. Again.

CHAPTER TEN

June

The air was crisp on my cabin porch, but I sat at the edge of my chair, guitar on my lap. I hummed fragments of a melody. I couldn't quite get a lead on a solid clip.

Mostly, I was enjoying the day. No neighbors. Wide-open spaces. Neither I nor any of my sisters liked cramped quarters after the accident. I'd rather fly than travel in a cramped bus that reminded me of traveling from campground to camping spot. Having a small hotel room at the end of a long trip wasn't any better. More memories would flood in. Me and my sisters crammed too many to a bed. Single-file lines for the bathroom. Greedily watching TV while we had access to electronics.

If I nailed this album, I'd get the plane. A bigger hotel room. A suite even. A tour schedule with stops close to my other homes.

I pushed my hoodie sleeves up. I'd gone for comfort

today in a sweater, soft leggings, and a pair of slides. After lunch, I'd come outside to write, hoping the mix of spring and summer would rouse my muse. The damn thing had hung around for two and a half songs and slid back into her cave.

I hummed a few more notes.

Useless.

I closed my eyes. This album had to happen. I had a solid fan base, but fame was fickle. Their ruined expectations would set me back. I was in my thirties, but I was still seen as a starlet. That came with connotations of innocent but also amateur and unpredictable, which somehow led people to question if I had any true talent.

Professionals in my field, and even a lot of fans, never looked at the male singers and said *But can they actually sing? Can they entertain a crowd and deliver a set at the same time? How do they hold up under pressure?*

I would not flake on my release date.

"*Can I hold up under pressure,*" I sang and ran the pick down the strings. "*Or will I be consumed?*"

What a dismal fucking lyric.

Sighing, I set the guitar aside and propped it against the exterior log wall. I scribbled down my new lyric on a fresh page, then gazed at the land around me.

Spring was in the mountains. The land was alive. I'd seen deer run through the valley this morning. My muse might be hiding, but I didn't want to be. I'd been steeped in sad songs for years. Were these songs harder to write when a blue sky soared overhead and birds sang from the trees?

The sound of an engine coming up the hill gave me pause. Summer had said she and Teller were going to stop by and run through the contracts for the next year.

I continued to plan around a tour I wasn't sure would happen.

But the pickup that came into view was Rhys's red Chevy. Flutters erupted in my belly until I spotted his flashing gaze. The hard cut of his bearded jaw was visible through the dappled shadows of leaves on the windshield as he drove under the trees.

I walked to the railing and leaned my elbows on it. The girls weren't with him.

He parked and got out, shutting the door hard. I jumped, the sound echoing against the slopes backing the house.

He stalked toward the porch stairs. "I thought you were hiding up here."

"I am." I folded my arms, the earlier thrill at seeing him gone.

"You're all over the news. Wren showed me your feed. Lots of updates."

I notched a brow up. "At least once a day."

That gave him pause. "This isn't some PR stunt?"

Anger ignited hot in my stomach. "When have I ever done a PR stunt?"

"When your concert bus broke down on the way to a venue, but it turned out you and your crew had already flown to town and were setting up the entire time the news fretted over your safety and whether the concert would get canceled. That sure as fuck got a lot of attention on your tour."

The media had tracked our movements to each town. It had become a game of spotting June Bee and her crew. "We flew because the bus wasn't doing so hot. The driver thought it was fine to make it, but my promoter didn't want to risk it. We had fun with the attention. It was harmless stuff."

"My kids can't be part of your harmless fun."

"What are you talking about?"

He wiggled his phone. The screen was black. "You've been posting every day. Some from Copper Summit."

I gawked at him. "Are you telling me that you have an app on your phone that's not about the weather or market prices?"

His expression turned flat. "I'm not joking."

"Neither am I. You're quick to accuse me of shit when you don't know how it works. Wynter suggested I hire Ruby from the Bozeman location to post about me once a day. I gave her some videos, and at one of the photo shoots, Wynter helped me out. I haven't seen a thing, but as long as Wynter isn't sounding an alarm, I don't care."

His jaw flexed. Between Rhys's size and his good looks, even as a kid, no one had stood up to him. But I was used to three older brothers towering over me. I wasn't intimidated by an irritated Rhys.

What he'd said earlier finally registered. "What do you mean I'm all over the news?"

"Wren saw it. You know how she likes those entertainment shows."

"Just now?" Wren had been all over *Inside Edition, E! News*, and *Entertainment Tonight*. I used to watch a few with her when Rhys and his dad had been working cattle. I could've helped, but his dad was old-fashioned that way. Since I'd been put to work enough at home, I never argued about being housebound at Jonathon and Wren's place.

He nodded. "They said you haven't been seen for

weeks and you even missed your appointments with some fucking guy."

"Remi Dahl?" He was an amazing songwriter and we worked well together. "I canceled with him over a month ago." Confusion infused Rhys's eyes and I waved my hand. He'd know the process if he'd ever come to Nashville. "I write a lot myself. I get the melody and the chords. Then for a lot of songs, I work with him to get the drums, percussion, bass, whatever. Sometimes, I can do it myself, but for the more pop-sounding ones, the crossovers, so to speak, I like to collaborate. It's a really fun environment. Actually, it's one of my favorite things and it's going to be rushed to get this album produced, but my real appointment isn't until the end of June." I was rambling. His gaze was focused on my mouth. Was he hearing my words or just seeing them? The air thickened between us. "It's probably just a slow news day and my name still garners interest. Filler. Why does it bother you so much?"

"The girls."

"What about them? No one knows I'm in Montana, and if they did, they probably wouldn't care. My fans know I come home, and they know I work for the family company."

"They might figure it out."

I shook my head. His reaction still didn't make sense. "And? Don't get me wrong, I'd rather they didn't. I'd rather keep this cabin to myself, but it's been years and they haven't ventured as far as Mama's place. I'm not an actress. I'm not Taylor Swift. Even Dolly Parton gets some privacy. I'm just a news story when things are slow or when I'm connected to a guy other women want."

He flinched. It was subtle, but I caught it.

"Are you worried about you?" I asked.

He rolled his shoulders and averted his gaze. "I'm not a guy other women want."

"Tell that to Annette."

His expression turned perplexed. "Why?"

"*Puh-lease*, Rhys. She wants you."

His eye twitched like he knew exactly what I was talking about. "You're kidding, right?"

I folded my arms and tapped my fingers on my biceps. For some reason, he didn't like me addressing Annette's infatuation. Made me want to poke the bear more. "Did Kirstin have to club you over the head and drag you off?"

He looked away. "I told you. I was ready to move on."

"And now you want to be single?"

His right eye twitched. No. He didn't want to be single, but he wasn't interested in Annette.

A knot inside my belly unraveled. Annette was pretty and kind, and she related to Rhys more than I ever could. But he wasn't interested.

"I have contacts who can help with damage control," I conceded. He was worried, and since my fans would love to know about a sexy single dad I had a history with, his fears weren't unfounded. "I'll make sure you're not dragged into the spotlight."

"It's Bethany and Hannah. They don't need any proximity to fame." Bitterness laced his tone. No one close to me had been dragged in because of my notoriety, but then they'd had their own already.

Why would Rhys be so worked up— "Your mom."

He blanched. "What about her?"

"Did you get dragged into the news about her?" I

thought back to the articles I had read. "I don't recall her getting much press."

"She didn't," he snapped. "A single mom trying to jump from theater to screen while dragging a kid around? She fought an uphill battle she'd never asked for."

He'd never speak of the scenario like that if it was his daughters. "Is that how she phrased it?"

He stalked to the railing. "No, but I'm familiar enough with public life, and I don't want the girls to be involved."

"Just them?"

He turned back to me. "I'm just some guy from a small town. All the apps I have are for weather and market prices."

I wouldn't get more from him, but he wasn't as upset as when he'd arrived. He also didn't want the attention on him. His tense shoulders were all I'd get on the subject. "I bet you have at least one investment app on there."

"Nah, I don't use my phone for financials. I'm old-fashioned that way."

A soft chuckle left me. "You can really run hot and cold." I inched closer to him. "I miss the easygoing Rhys I used to know, but I think I might actually be seeing the real you."

"You've always gotten the real me."

I closed the distance between us and tipped my head back to meet his gaze. "No. I haven't."

His eyes darkened. "How do you keep drawing me in with those big honey eyes?"

"How do we keep ending up this close?" I whispered.

"Why can't I stop myself around you?" he growled

and dropped his head. My mouth was covered by his, and his arms were around me once again.

My ass hit the porch railing. He lifted me until I twined my legs around him. I let out a moan. Finally. I had him back where I'd craved him.

He broke free from my mouth, kissing his way down my neck. "Too many nights since I've had this."

Was he talking about the kiss? Or everything?

There was nothing behind me but a drop to the ground. All that was holding me in place were his hands on my thighs and my feet hooked around his waist.

I arched back to give him more access to the sensitive flesh at my collar. "Rhys, do you know what I did the night after you kissed me in your shop?"

He paused, then another growl left him. "I want every fucking detail."

His lips were back at my neck and he nibbled a path to my ear. Shivers racked my body.

He brushed his hands underneath the hem of my sweater. Another moan left me when the heat of his touch hit the skin of my belly.

"I don't have any toys." I gasped when his fingertips brushed my sensitive nipples. "So I had to do it myself."

"Did you stroke your clit?"

I nodded, unable to speak. He cupped a breast and his fingers were on the bare flesh above my bra.

"Tight little circles, just like you need it?"

"Yes," I breathed.

Through the lace of my bra, he rolled my peaked nipple between his thumb and forefinger.

"Did you push a finger into that tight little pussy?"

"Oh god." His voice was back in my ear, rumbling the naughtiest things. A spark inside me came alive. A happy little glow that didn't want to be extinguished ever again.

His mouth was back on me for a hot second. "Did you come hard?"

"Yes." I let my eyelids fall shut and rubbed myself against the ridge in his pants. Too much was between us. A tiny alarm sounded in the back of my brain.

Should we be doing this?

Did I care?

"With my name on your lips?" he asked roughly.

"Yes," I said on a gasp. He tugged my bra down and the fabric of my sweater grazed against my sensitive nipple. He rolled it under his palm. Damn, he remembered how sensitive I was there.

"How many times have you done that over the years?"

I opened my eyes and caught his gaze. "Too often."

"Fucking right you did." He claimed my mouth again, hard and unyielding. I was paying for all the times I'd come with his name on my lips. When we'd just broken up. When he'd been married. When I'd been alone and thinking of him while dating other men.

Gravel crunched and he pulled away so fast that my feet untangled from behind him.

I cartwheeled my arms. "Shit!"

He pulled me off the railing before I could tumble backward. As soon as my feet hit the floorboards, he careened to the end of the porch and stared into the trees.

I feathered a hand over my hair and looked behind me. Teller's pickup came into view.

I glanced at Rhys's back. His shoulders rose and fell with his breathing.

My cheeks were probably red and my lips kiss-swollen, but I'd have to put on a show. I smiled and waved like I hadn't been kissed senseless, talked dirty to and then abandoned in the space of a chord.

"I can't do that again."

I paused at Rhys's voice.

"It's too hard to let you go, and I will let you go, June. Don't doubt me on that."

The glow from the kiss was effectively extinguished.

"How can I doubt you when I've lived through the proof?" I lifted my chin and smiled at Summer as Teller parked next to Rhys's pickup.

I was back to being a bucket of conflicting emotions around Rhys, but irritation rose to the top. I was tired of getting burned by his heat.

"If that's what you plan to do, you should probably stop kissing me," I said to his back.

He whipped his head around, and I only cocked a brow. Then I danced down the steps. "Howdy." I gave Summer a quick hug. "I'm ready to talk contracts and bourbon."

Teller's brown gaze swung from me to Rhys. "Did we come at a bad time?"

He knew damn well we'd arranged this meeting. He was digging for an explanation of why Rhys was here. If I didn't give him something, he'd keep probing and he wouldn't be the only one. Summer would be relentless.

"Not at all." I waved for them to follow me up the porch. "Rhys came to tell me that my absence from Nashville has been noted."

Annoyance crossed Summer's face. "Why is it anyone's business?"

"On a positive note," I said, "that means there's

interest. Honestly, if no one talked about me, I'd be worried."

Summer continued to frown. "That's not how it should work."

But it did.

"I'll leave you be." Rhys nodded at Teller, then at Summer. He avoided my gaze as he took the stairs down and started for his truck.

"See you Sunday? Or are the girls taking the summer off?" My breathing ceased until he answered. He had his out. Would he take it? I would miss the girls. They were quick and enthusiastic learners and just plain fun to be around.

He stopped before rounding the front of his pickup. "No, they'll want to keep lessons up except for the weeks they're with Wren." This time, he lifted his shuttered gaze to mine. "Until you leave."

His words hit me dead center of my chest. They came out with such certainty but also with a hint of wistfulness like he was just counting down the days until I left him again.

CHAPTER ELEVEN

June

More lyrics poured into my head. "I have the chorus," I muttered as I scribbled. I hummed a tune and repeated the notes on the guitar. "Yes, that's it."

Damn that kiss.

Ever since Rhys had trampled over my heart by telling me I was a threat to his kids' privacy, I'd been filled with inspiration.

I had a third song about star-crossed lovers. They were never in the right place at the right time.

And a fourth about a girl who thinks the guy finally sees her, only to find out that he does and it was exactly why he was walking away.

That was two more songs in a week. A little collaboration with Remi and they'd be ready to record. At this rate, I'd be done with time to spare. Now I was working on a fifth song. This one about a girl returning to her roots to find the one she'd left behind—herself.

My music came from me. I liked to write from the heart. I processed emotions through songwriting, but this one was hitting close to home. Yet I couldn't stop working on it.

My phone buzzed, but I ignored it. "*She sees herself again in his eyes . . .*" I stopped strumming and sighed. Of course, the man had to show up in this song too. But that was a killer lyric.

I wrote it down for later and turned the page. I could write one song that wasn't about heartbreak or rekindling romance, dammit. Sure, those songs spoke to me, and they were still at my center, but I'd also changed. When I looked in the mirror, I didn't see a heartbroken June Kerrigan. I saw a girl who'd kept going thanks to hope. She'd hoped to do her mamas proud. She'd hoped to show her family how much their support meant. She'd hoped the love of her life would come around. But when he hadn't, she'd continued on. To be the hope for others in her place.

I scribbled down ideas and lyrics. The song might be a standout on the album, or it might not be included at all, but I'd write it. For me.

My phone rang again. I didn't know the number, but it was local. I chewed on the inside of my cheek for a second before answering. "Hi, this is Junie."

"Oh, Junie." An older woman's voice cracked on the end of the line. "This is Wilna, from the church."

Bourbon Canyon had four churches and even more bars, but we all knew which one Wilna meant. She was a living legend in town. Well into her golden years, she still ran the bachelor auction fundraiser and bingo nights, and to be honest, she ran the church too. "Hi, Wilna. How's it going?"

"Oh, you know. Listen, we're not holding the auction this year."

"Oh?" The fundraiser had been responsible for getting Tate and Scarlett together. It'd been a Bourbon Canyon staple for at least ten years.

"Unless you can talk Tenor or Teller into putting themselves up, we're seeing diminishing returns." She paused like she was waiting for me to say I'd have my brothers signed up by the end of the day.

Teller would not agree to it. Ever. Tenor would die of mortification if he was ever on the auction block. His skin would catch fire from his blush burning too hot.

"So," she said, a wistful tone in her voice, "I was thinking of trying something else this year, maybe give it a break for a year or two and see if it rebounds. And then I heard you were in town."

Dread churned in my belly.

"It'd be small," she rushed on like she sensed my hesitation. "I thought we could sell seats for a certain number of supporters. You'd have final say, of course."

No, my manager usually would. There'd be negotiations and contracts. I was managerless for the near future but there were plenty of people on my team who'd have opinions about an impromptu performance, and they'd all want their cut.

"If you need to think about it, that's just fine," Wilna continued. "And if you don't want to, don't worry. I understand. You're a good kid and you're so busy. I'm sure so many people are demanding your time."

There had to be another way to help without involving my team and risking word getting out that I was having management issues before an album release and tour. I liked to play music, and I loved watching people listen to it. I adored being heard.

What if that was all it was? "What day is the fundraiser?"

"I was thinking of doing it at the end of June this year."

Crap, maybe this wouldn't work. "I have to return to Nashville at the end of June. I leave on the twenty-eighth."

"The twenty-seventh is a Saturday. A perfect day for a gathering. We can do it in the afternoon."

I didn't have a lot to pack. I just had to drive to Nashville. Alone. "I'll be honest, Wilna, I'm not sure what my team would allow, and I don't want to drag you through negotiations for something that's supposed to raise money." I couldn't let red tape stop me. I hadn't come this far only to fail at helping Wilna for a simple fundraiser. "What about if I just happen to be playing in the park that day?"

"Oh . . . I'm picking up what you're putting down. Yes, we can reserve a shelter at the park, have a bunch of goodies and food and do a freewill donation."

"I don't know if it'll bring in what the bachelor auction would—"

"Yes. It will."

Her confidence was heartening. "I have to ask a favor. Since I'm trying to lie low . . ."

"You don't want to flood our little town with lookie-loos. You just show up and let us hear your pretty voice and we'll let the local news mill do its thing." She lowered her voice to a conspiratorial whisper. "I might make some pointed hints so people'll want to stop by just in case."

After we hashed out some details, I disconnected. Smiling, I picked out the song I'd written for Jonah and Summer's wedding and gazed at the trees and the way the land dipped into the valley.

I had something to look forward to other than seeing the girls and Rhys every Sunday.

I looked forward to seeing the girls tomorrow. Would I see Rhys after that second kiss? Would he come to the performance in the park?

He hadn't seen me play any shows. He'd admitted to spying on my social media, but other than the rookie appearances I'd done around town, he hadn't seen a real show. I used to dream about looking out from the stage and seeing him. I used to fantasize that I'd finish my show and run right into his arms.

It's too hard to let you go, and I will let you go, June. Don't doubt me on that.

I flubbed a note.

Letting out a frustrated growl, I put the guitar down.

I didn't need him, and where my career was concerned, I couldn't count on him. I'd done everything on my own and it would stay that way.

Rhys

I paced inside the shop. The big door was open. June was in the house with the girls for their weekly lesson. Next week would be the last week until the kids were back from Wren's. They were already asking when they could restart. They swore Wren would let them practice at her house, but I couldn't bring myself to give them a response. A yes would mean June was still interacting with my family. I'd hear about it. A no would mean she was done. For good. Unless her car broke down somewhere between my house and town. Until she left for good. Again.

. . . you should probably stop kissing me.

She'd been right. I was the one who'd initiated lip-to-lip contact both times. I was the one who couldn't keep his hands off her. She might've gotten close, but I'd had more control over myself as a kid.

As a kid, she'd been mine.

I rubbed the back of my neck and walked from the barn to the house. Goldie trotted next to me. The dog was in love with June too. She waited by the door when June's car pulled up and got pets and baby talk.

I was jealous of a damn dog.

A knot next to one of my shoulder blades thrummed with my heartbeat. Maybe I needed a massage.

I'd never gotten a massage in my life.

Just as I crested the drive, June emerged from the back door, her guitar case slung over her shoulder. Would she ignore me? Give me a glare or a cool stare?

When she saw me, a saucy smirk curved those pretty pink lips. "Decide to risk getting within a hundred yards of me?"

The tension defused, leaving behind sheepishness. A hundred yards was too fucking far away. "I can yell at you from the barn instead. I've got a pair in there that keeps trying to die on me."

Concern filled her face. "The mama or the calf?"

"Both. Treated the mama first, then she wouldn't let her bull calf drink."

"Did you give her a nice teat massage?" June asked, her tone deceptively innocent.

My body's reaction to her question was not. Her creamy breasts flashed through my mind instead of an engorged udder. "As a matter of fact, I did. The heifers around here are not appreciative of my teat massages."

She nodded knowingly. "They might be used to you trying to kiss them."

"I can one hundred and infinity percent control myself around a cow."

She looked at me from under her lashes. "It's around me you can't?"

The shyness of her question caught me off guard. No, I couldn't control myself around her. It was why I should be at the barn yelling a quick *thanks, see ya* before minding my business. Yet I was within feet of her and it was still too far.

Bethany banged out the door. "Did you hear that she's going to be playing at the bachelor fundraiser?"

Dismay stained my tongue. June was going to hang around a ton of bachelors? Was she going to bid?

She shook her head. "No, not the auction." She held her hands up. "I'm playing in the park for fun, remember?"

Bethany's mouth rounded into an O. "Riiiiight. There're no bachelors."

Hannah charged out. "No batch lores."

June shrugged. "I can't play for money without involving my team, so I'm just gonna play and Wilna's going to get as many people as she can to come and donate money for the goodies she's going to have there."

Many a bachelor had been lured into the auction. Most had donated their time and their muscles and would do a day of work, but I'd heard last year's auction had been a flop. Women had given up on another Bailey stepping onto the block.

"Wilna keeps asking Daddy to do the fundraiser," Bethany said.

June arched a brow at me. "You never participated?"

My cheeks heated. For the last three years, Wilna had asked me what kind of bachelor auction it was when the most eligible bachelors in town didn't participate. No way was I wading into that mess. I wasn't getting some woman's hopes up that I actually had a heart to give. "No. I never did."

"She begged," Hannah announced with utmost authority. Both girls had overheard the conversation in the grocery store when a tiny elderly woman ambushed me in the cereal aisle.

June's light-brown brow quirked. "If only Wilna knew begging wasn't the way to make him say yes."

I narrowed my eyes. What was she getting at?

Her smirk turned sly. "Wilna should've tickled you."

Shit.

Bethany giggled. "Daddy's not ticklish."

"He's so ticklish," June argued.

Shit, shit, shit. I could've gone a lifetime without this secret being unearthed.

"No, Mommy tried." Hannah jumped in to support her sister. They might adore June, but they'd fight her on this.

Confusion filled June's expression as she looked at me. "Did you, like, grow out of it or something?"

"Or something." Any chance that would be a good enough answer?

Bethany crossed her arms and kicked a hip out. "Mommy used to say he's a brick."

Kirstin had meant my emotions, but I kept my mouth shut.

June studied me. In a heartbeat, all three girls were regarding me with crossed arms and cocked hips.

"Which is it, Rhys?" June asked, her tone half-teasing and half-serious. "Are you ticklish or not?"

I worked my jaw back and forth. My mouth would be better staying shut around the girls.

June tapped her fingers against her upper arms. "Because I remember how you used to squeal like a stuck pig when I tickled your armpits. You would jump so high when I touched your sides."

"Daddy used to squeal?" Bethany giggled.

"Jumped so high," Hannah mimicked June's taunting tone.

June would keep goading me and the girls would delight in it. Or . . . I could make June squirm.

"I don't know, June Bug. Why would a teenage boy pretend to be ticklish around a cute girl?"

June's laughter hitched. Her smile died, and I choked on my snicker. I quietly waited for her to put the pieces together.

"You aren't ticklish?"

The scandal in her tone prompted a snort from me.

She sucked in a gasp. "You were faking? We used to wrestle so I could tickle—" She snapped her mouth shut, her gaze darting to my bewildered children.

"And then what?" This time, my tone was deceptively innocent. "What would happen?"

Her cheeks turned pink, and I grinned.

"The audacity," she muttered.

I lost my battle with my laughter. June used to love thinking she got the upper hand by tickling me. Instead, I'd gotten both her hands on me, and she would burrow in close. Those tickle wars had turned steamy more often than not.

Bethany wrinkled her nose. "I'm confused."

June pretended to glare at me, but humor danced in the honeyed depths of her eyes. "Your dad was making me think I was getting what I wanted when he was actually getting what he wanted."

"I like to think we were both benefiting." The lightness inside of me was from laughing with June again. From not dreading the twist of emotions when I saw her. From not avoiding her.

I'd been handling the situation all wrong. June being in Bourbon Canyon wasn't something I should grit my teeth through. It just was. I was me, and she was her, and that was the way it'd always been. We both knew our futures went in different directions. So why not enjoy these moments when they converged?

CHAPTER TWELVE

June

I sat with Scarlett and Autumn in Curly's, our favorite bar and grill. Bourbon Canyon's only bar and grill. Before my voice was on the radio, he'd always seated us in the back, yet my brothers got a table at the front window. My sisters and I were "just" Kerrigans in his eyes, and we didn't have the status of our Bailey brothers. Now that I was June Bee, he'd tried to put me and my sisters front and center, but I'd smiled sweetly and asked for a table in the back. "For privacy," I'd said, enjoying his disgruntled acceptance. Two could play his games, but I really did want privacy.

Curly was old-fashioned in the worst of ways, but he made excellent food and we were on our third basket of buns. We were having an early dinner. What had been a sparsely filled restaurant was now half-full. The Saturday night crowd would start to pour in soon.

People around town were getting used to seeing me.

I'd ventured onto social media platforms and there'd been speculation, but most of my fans had pushed back, insisting I was holed up writing my next greatest hits. They cited the selfies I'd taken with the kids in the coffee shop. After the news clip, the posts had blown up. My supporters guessed I was in town to write and prepare for my release and rumored tour. They wanted the tour announced and didn't want me interrupted.

I loved my fans. But reading those words piled giant boulders onto my chest until I struggled to breathe.

"You're stressing," Autumn said around a mouthful of bun.

I scowled at her. I still had five songs to write. "How can you tell?"

"Your eyes are glazed, and you haven't finished buttering your bun."

Scarlett nodded like it was obvious.

My knife was poised over the bread. Curly made his famous bourbon cinnamon butter from Copper Summit products. I'd let him seat me in the parking lot for that spread, yet I was staring at the wall instead.

Should I tell them that I was worried I wouldn't finish the album? I was, but those thoughts weren't dominating my brain. My mind strayed for a reason that had nothing to do with my career. The reason was six foot two, bearded, and a phenomenal baker.

And I had a month left to be frustrated with him. Yes, I needed some of those boulders lifted from my lungs. "I found out Rhys just let me think he was ticklish the whole time we dated."

Scarlett's eyes widened. "Why would he do that?" She wrinkled her nose. "Never mind. I've had dates pretend worse things."

Autumn patted her arm. "We had to wade through some frogs to get to our princes."

"Except those guys thought I was the frog." Her gaze went dreamy. "I don't have to worry about any of that with Tate."

Gah, I wanted what she had. She was stupid in love, and Tate earned that feeling. She could trust him until the end of time.

"Have you decided yet if that was incredibly sweet or decidedly creepy?" Autumn asked.

"Nothing Rhys does falls into the creepy category. Not with me." He'd done it for me and not his wife. My heart went out to her. How many times had I been in her place, the woman wondering why I wasn't enough for a guy?

I never thought I'd be the why for someone else.

"I can't believe he admitted it." Autumn leaned back while our food was delivered. After the young server left, she scooted closer to the table. "Lessons going okay with Bethany and Hannah?"

I rolled my eyes and dug into my rib eye. "Subtle."

"I thought so," Scarlett agreed. "We're dying to know, but we know it's not our business."

"So we talk about it at work," Autumn said, "but school's out soon. Then what are we going to do?"

"Your husbands," I joked and crunched my rising envy under my boot. I was irritated with them for asking about Rhys. I was jealous they had someone at home.

Scarlett poked at her sweet potato. "The drawback of being a teacher is that if I have a day off, the kids have a day off. Chance does, anyway. The other two are in day care for the school year. But enough about us." Her gaze lifted to behind me and brightened. "The girls can tell me themselves how lessons are going." She smiled and waved.

I whipped my head around and met Rhys's closed-off stare. He cocked a brow. I shrugged. I hadn't known they'd be eating out tonight, not that I would've changed my plans.

Bethany and Hannah were weaving through tables behind their dad. The hostess stopped at a booth, but the girls kept going. Hannah threw herself at me for a hug, then went around the table, embracing everyone else. Bethany did the same after her.

Rhys murmured a few words to the hostess and walked toward us with that rolling gait of his. He'd taken his hat off and finger-combed his dark wavy hair. His beard had been trimmed, and he wore a navy cable-knit sweater instead of flannel tonight.

He could close the distance and give me a hug. I'd stuff my face into that soft shirt and lean against his granite abs. I'd soak up his warmth.

I'd do more than that. I'd get hopelessly turned on, and it was already impossible to go to sleep without fantasizing about him in bed with me.

"Hey," I said. "Fancy meeting you here."

"That's small town for ya." He lifted his chin toward the remnants of the bourbon butter. "Which line?"

"Oldest Summit. The line Daddy made for Tate."

A ghost of a smile played over his lips. "You missed when Curly did June's Summit bourbon butter. He claimed he was kicking off your last tour, but I think he was trying to ride your coattails."

"He wouldn't be Curly if he wasn't capitalizing on the Bailey family."

Autumn cleared her throat. She had an arm around

Hannah. Bethany was between her and Scarlett and they were all watching us.

Rhys dipped his head. "Ladies," he said gruffly.

He and I had been talking like there was no one else in the restaurant, much less at the table.

"I was just asking Junie how lessons were going," Scarlett said, "and then poof—you appeared."

"They're good," he replied.

"I can play all the notes," Bethany said proudly.

"She's working on 'Brown Eyed Girl,' " I answered. She struggled, but she was stubborn, like her dad.

"I didn't like it," Hannah said. "I'm doing 'Row, Row, Row Your Boat.' "

Rhys tapped the back of my chair. "Come on, girls. Their food's getting cold."

I'd forgotten I had a steak waiting for me. "I'll see you tomorrow."

"You can come eat with us," Bethany offered.

"Oh no—"

"I have to go soon," Scarlett blurted out. "In fact, I might have to take this to go."

Kerrigan sisters weren't the only bad liars.

Autumn yawned. "And I told Gideon I'd help him at the house tomorrow."

I'd wager half a concert's revenue that was false. "I thought you hired contractors."

"We did. We need to figure out, you know, the details." She flagged down one of the teen servers rushing past and asked for to-go boxes. "Girls, do you want to help June move her plate?"

Embarrassment cut off my air. I sputtered.

Autumn snapped her fingers. "A ride. Scarlett's chauffeured all of us. Rhys, do you mind seeing June home?"

His expression was deadpan. I'd rub my temples, but that'd only show how tragically badly this was being staged.

"Sure," he said.

The to-go boxes were dropped on the table, and three minutes later, I was seated by Rhys.

***

Rhys

All I'd wanted was a quiet night without figuring out what to make for dinner. No juggling Bethany's hatred of green beans and most other green foods with Hannah's adamant protests that cooked vegetables are awful. They both agreed we had too many hamburger-based meals, except for hamburgers themselves, and while they claimed they liked pork, their actions didn't match their words. Every time I mentioned chicken, they groaned. I was running out of protein sources. Yet if Curly's prepared the same exact thing I would've cooked, the girls loved it.

June's body heat seeped into me. The girls had argued over who got to sit next to June and had compromised; neither of them would get the honor. They'd put her next to me.

She was close, but we weren't touching. Something I'd like to remedy. I'd fought my libido for the entire meal, starting from when June had excitedly chatted with each girl about their favorite thing to eat to now, when I wanted the check to arrive but also hoped it'd take another hour.

"I've gotta go to the bathroom," Hannah said. Both girls scooted out of their side of the booth and hurried off.

"That's twice," June said. "Are they feeling okay?"

"We're lucky to get out with under three bathroom breaks. It depends on how bored they are."

The check came.

The girl who'd waited on us hesitated with her hand on the receipt, her gaze on June. "I, um, didn't know what to do with your meal . . ."

Instead of telling the teenager she could've asked, June smiled her social media special grin. "It's fine. I'm treating everyone tonight."

"No, you're not." I dug out my wallet. "Keep it all together."

June blinked. "I can pay."

"I know." I handed the server my card and she scurried off.

June spun farther in her seat. "I crashed your meal."

"Is that what you call it?"

"It sounds better than my sisters dumped me on you."

I didn't mind June joining us. I liked it too much, as was often the case when it came to her. The why behind her sisters' sudden departure intrigued me. They had seemed like they were spending quality time together.

Did her sisters know something I didn't? Was the chemistry between us so powerful it made people around us hope that we'd become a thing once more? They'd been left wanting once, and I had no desire to repeat history.

Except I had a lot of desire for June. "The girls always enjoy your company."

"I love hanging out with them." She took a long pull from her ice water and glanced around the restaurant. Every table was full, and with the way we were sitting, we looked like we were on a date, cozied up on the same side of the booth.

June had garnered discreet attention all night. People murmured when they saw her, a few had stopped by to tell her they loved her music, and a couple of girls a little older than Bethany had asked for autographs, but otherwise, we'd been left alone.

I was tempted to lean in, chat with her like we used to, as if these booths were the entirety of our world. I kept my ass in place. "Is your writing coming around?"

Her soft smile went straight to my gut. "Yeah, it is. I think it's really going to be a fresh album. Less heartbreak and more . . . appreciation. Hope." Her full lips curved further. "Of course, there's a fair share of missing-him songs. Those sell too well to not include."

While I liked that she'd gotten her muse back, that she was healing from the bullshit caused by her manager, discontent settled hard in my stomach, right next to the ribs and mashed potatoes I'd just eaten. Her album would be a hit. I didn't have to hear a single song to know. "Your tour is going to span the world?"

Excitement lit her eyes. "It's going to be a year long. London, Paris, Sydney. Toronto, of course. So far, I have a few opening acts I've requested. Lucy shot down the ones I've scrolled past in my feed, but I'm going to talk to my new manager about how important it is to me. I shouldn't have to be at the pinnacle of my career to finally have that much of a say."

"But you do?"

She nodded. "It's give and take, but sometimes I feel like I give up a lot more."

The girls emerged from the hall of the bathroom, but they were waylaid by the display case full of specialty muffins and pies. Curly's baked goods were on par with his buns. He pimped Copper Summit bourbon in those too. I kept trying to copy his bourbon butterscotch muffins.

"Do you get to visit all the places you perform in?" I threaded my napkin through my fingers.

She didn't respond right away. "I love performing. The crowd. The connection. It's intoxicating to connect with that many people at once. I never forget that it's their support that makes my job possible. I love it." Her smile mirrored the joy she received on stage, then she looked down and grew serious. "But there's not often time to play tourist. And it does get lonely," she finally said. She leaned on her elbow and faced me, giving us the illusion of more privacy. "It's rare these days that my family can meet me in a city and travel around. Sometimes, I've had someone, but often, if they were on tour with me, they had their own obligations."

I shredded my napkin. Her fucking worthless boyfriends.

"I'm not going to let that stop me this time." She shook her head. "I'll have more say about my schedule than when I joined another performer's tour. I'll be busier, but it'll be an experience of a lifetime. I don't know. Maybe Lucy was onto something, and I have to date my opening act."

"The fuck you do." Anger was a firebrand against my ribs. "You don't need a fucking man to do what you want."

"But it'd be nice to have someone to do things with. I'm surrounded by people on the road and it's lonely. I bought homes, thinking that'd help. I played in Florida a lot and I love the beach, but I hardly get to use it. I think New York City is amazing and so different from Montana or Nashville. Same with LA."

"I hated both those cities."

"Because you were alone too?"

Any response died on my tongue. The topic of my mom was off-limits. Why had I even alluded to my experiences as a kid alone in the city?

The feelings from that time roared back. Alone and scared. Eating out of a can. Mom would sometimes be gone overnight, and I'd be in charge of getting myself to school.

I massaged the middle of my forehead. I'd never leave the girls overnight. They could be eighteen and I'd still feel like shit if I left them.

Eating out of a can?

Acid swelled in my stomach, churning away at my dinner. Bethany and Hannah helped me with meals, but they'd never had to eat alone while wondering when I would get home. They'd never had to go to bed wondering if I'd be there to take them to school in the morning.

I'd blocked out so many individual experiences, I'd forgotten what my childhood had been like. Or the things Mom had said. *If it wasn't for you, I'd be so much further ahead by now.*

"Rhys? Are you all right?" June's warm breath wafted across my cheek.

I shoved those memories to the far recesses of my mind. My kids didn't have to experience what I had because they had a nice, stable home. I made sure of it. "Yeah, I'm fine. I just don't like cities."

Her eyes narrowed on me, but just as she opened her mouth, the girls returned to the table.

I snatched the opportunity for escape. "What was the best-looking muffin?"

CHAPTER THIRTEEN

June

I wandered into Rhys's kitchen. The smell of meatloaf and baked potatoes filled the air. My stomach was growling. I wasn't cooking a lot at the cabin. I'd been going to Mama's for home-cooked meals, but I made sure I didn't do that every night, or she'd worry I wasn't interested in taking care of myself.

I was used to eating on the run, being served lighter food that wouldn't bog me down on tour or make me sleepy, and even trying new places that had the words "fine dining" or "gourmet" in their descriptions. But I missed the food I was raised on. Mostly, I missed sitting at a table surrounded by loved ones.

Tonight, I'd get the experience without worrying Mama. Bethany and Hannah had convinced Rhys to ask me to stay for dinner after lessons because his meatloaf was the best ever.

Rhys's back was to me as he prepared a green salad

to go with dinner. The way he'd shut down last night had left my head spinning. He'd gone from locked in his head to doting dad in a second.

How had I never noticed how he acted when his mom was brought up?

Because I'd been so absorbed in my own trauma and focused on my own dreams. And because he'd let me.

I hovered by the table, unsure of what to do and confused about how I looked back on our time together. "I swear, you don't have to feed me every time you see me."

He shrugged as he chopped a tomato. "I'll tell you a secret."

"What's your secret?" I drifted closer. "Row, Row, Row Your Boat" was getting picked out on a guitar in the living room. The girls wanted to put on a show for Wren when they went to stay there next week.

"I don't mind being around you."

Oh. I rubbed a hand down my arm. "I was prepared for a confession that your meatloaf was store-bought, or that Wren had made it, or that it isn't really that good and the girls want me to be a distraction so they don't have to eat it."

His chuckle rumbled nice and deep. "It's homemade —by me—and it doesn't suck, I promise."

I propped a hip on the counter opposite the sink a few feet away from him, far enough for this moment to not feel so intimate. "I don't mind being around you either. But you always seem to get stuck with me."

He dumped the tomato pieces into the bowl and grabbed the cucumber sitting by the cutting board. "Not feeling stuck with you has been the root issue."

Warmth swirled in my belly. "True." The way Rhys

had always made me feel set him apart from other men. He could warm me up until I felt safe and secure, or he could heat up my insides until I combusted.

Thankfully, that part of us hadn't changed since we were kids. We'd gone from years of avoiding each other to enjoying the other's company. Never mind the kisses. Those had been an anomaly. They didn't fit into our timeline. They stood out. Unforgettable but out of place. Like me in this kitchen.

"You're not so bad when you're not being a grump."

He cocked a brow. "I'm not a grump."

"You're right. I forgot about all the smiling you do around me."

This time, he laughed. "I bet your fans don't know you're a smart-ass."

Some of my humor died. "No, that's not my image. Sweet June Bee with her heart getting broken? They'd never want to hear about the June Bee that told her ex to chew his dick off."

The knife skated against the cutting board. "Was that helpful advice for him?"

"Yes, but I guess that really isn't a good smart-ass example. Maybe the time the hockey player said he hadn't had sex with the naked girl in the picture on his phone, and I told him I wished his brains were as sharp as his blades."

"Oof. That's more snarky than smart-ass."

"He argued that I thought I was smarter than him, I said obviously not, since I'd thought a pro hockey player could be faithful."

"Throwing the whole profession under the bus?"

"I kind of did, but I was justifiably upset. Half his team had known he was fucking around. Bro code."

He tossed the cucumber slices into the bowl. "The only bro code I lived by was treating you right so your brothers wouldn't kill me."

"Was that the only motivation you had?"

"It's still my main motivation."

I playfully shoved at his shoulder. "What can I help with?"

"If you set the table, you'll be the girls' hero forever."

"Sold." I dug out plates and forks. The girls rushed in, poring over plans to serenade Wren next weekend. I finished setting the table and we all sat.

"Are you going to be here for the show?" Bethany asked as we settled around the table.

Next Sunday would've been our normal lesson time, but Rhys was taking them to Wren's on Saturday. "I don't think so."

"You have to be," Hannah said.

"We'll be at Wren's around three," Rhys said. "You're welcome to see the performance. Then she'll want you to stay for dinner."

Another dinner by itself would be hard to pass up. I enjoyed visiting with Wren, and I'd love to see the show the girls put on.

Hannah went ramrod straight and her eyes were bright. "You can sing with us!"

Bethany gasped. "Can you?"

Stunned, I glanced at Rhys first. The girls had worked so hard to master their songs. He lifted a shoulder as if to say it was up to me. "Only if you want—"

"Yes!" they both cried.

I laughed. Performing wasn't going to feel like such a solitary endeavor tomorrow night. "Just one song. I don't want to take over, and I'm not going to play the guitar. We all want to hear you."

They wiggled in their seats and dug into their food.

Bethany heaped a forkful of meatloaf into her mouth. "When do we get to do another lesson?"

Rhys met my gaze, but I could only shrug. I had time, but I didn't, and I didn't want to intrude on their time with Wren.

"June's busy working," he answered. "And she's leaving soon after."

"Two weeks after." I was stuck at five songs and had half a sixth that I'd probably end up scrapping. It was about a lonely boy who grew into a closed-off man. While I stuck to popular themes that resonated with me when I wrote, the song didn't feel like my story. I wasn't familiar enough with the material, though I should have been.

"What about the Sunday before you leave?" Bethany frantically looked between the two of us. Her eyes were watery, like she was devastated to realize today had been our last lesson. Hannah's expression matched hers.

Rhys gave me a noncommittal shrug as if to say it was my decision.

"I'd be happy to," I said. "It'll give us a chance to say goodbye."

Rhys tucked his chin down and concentrated on his meatloaf.

"What if I forget everything until then?" Hannah's eyes were wide.

I smiled. They were very serious about their lessons. "You won't, but I can give you homework. The same as before—keep quizzing each other on counting and notes."

Bethany nodded, her expression intent. "Is that what you do?"

I finished my mouthful, considering the answer. "Practice is always good, but I also like to challenge myself with other things. One of my ex—uh, old friends, used to play drums and he was teaching me."

Rhys's fork thunked on his plate as he sawed a chunk off his meatloaf. Jealous?

I liked the thought way too much. I'd made a lot of money off a song about my jealousy, but penning "Emerald Rain" and singing it was a lot different than seeing a guy feel the same over me. When that guy was Rhys, I might reveal a little more than I should.

"He was also a phenomenal fiddle player." Finn's set included a song he played with his violin. "I got some lessons on that too. I even have a violin now."

Hannah's eyes sparkled. "Cool!"

Rhys chewed his food like he was pulverizing gravel. I caught his eye and grinned. He only narrowed his gaze on me, a promise of retribution in his eyes.

I regretted telling him he'd have to quit kissing me. If I could write a hit song half a country away from him, I'd love to know what I could do when I was within arm's reach.

After the meal was cleaned up, the girls asked me to read them stories. Rhys had run outside to finish up evening chores and close the chicken coop.

He walked into the house and hung his ball cap by the door. I tracked him while Hannah showed off her reading skills with a book about warrior cats. He shrugged out of his green flannel and tossed it into the laundry room. The black T-shirt left behind hugged his broad chest. If I'd hung around for a few more years, would I have ever been able to leave a fully mature and filled-out Rhys?

I was planning to do just that in a month. But we weren't a thing like we'd been then.

He reached behind his head and yanked up his shirt. A strip of his abs was bared and—He caught me staring and released his shirt. A flush wicked up my body.

I gave him a look that said *don't let me stop you*, and he smirked. Adjusting his shoulders so his shirt draped back over those sinful abs, he toed out of his boots.

"Dad, can we watch a movie?" Bethany asked. "June said she hasn't seen the newest Percy Jackson series."

"That's not a movie," he said and leaned against the wall between the kitchen and living room.

Bethany grinned like she knew exactly what she was asking. They'd already hit me up for a movie-and-popcorn night, but I'd deflected, telling them it was up to their dad. I'd absolutely stay, but it also wasn't my place to decide.

Would he be okay with the plan? I hadn't had a movie-and-popcorn night in so long. My sisters and I used to do them when we were all home, but they had their families now.

"Two episodes." He looked at me and the heat from earlier rushed back. "You staying?"

Relief and excitement filled my heart. "I've heard I can't miss it." Just like I couldn't miss the chance he'd change out of his shirt where I could see.

He pushed off the wall. "Go ahead and start the

show. I'll throw some popcorn in and take a quick shower."

By the time he was done, I was flanked on both sides on the couch by the girls as they rattled off Percy Jackson details.

Rhys handed out buckets of popcorn and took a seat on the recliner. He'd slicked back his damp hair, making his cheekbones sharper and his blue eyes more piercing. I had to refrain from glancing at him every five minutes to get an eyeful. The gray sweats and plain white tee he wore didn't help.

Whenever the girls giggled or exchanged excited notes about the storyline, I caught Rhys's eye and smiled. I used to be like them with my sisters when we'd get into the same shows or books. That no longer happened as much, like the movie-and-popcorn nights. My siblings had more going on in their lives than ever, but I wasn't home enough. Wynter had left Montana after school, but she'd eventually returned. Same with Summer. Autumn had never left, and Scarlett had moved to Bourbon Canyon for her job and then married Tate.

Homesickness filled me. But I was home now. Right?

Was the cabin my home?

My house in Nashville?

The condo in Tampa?

I was hardly in New York anymore, and I made more appearances online than in person. I could just as well let my LA lease expire.

By the time the second episode was done, Rhys was dozing in the recliner. I shut the TV off. "Can y'all tiptoe to bed without waking your dad?" I whispered.

Bethany's eyes were pleading. "He always falls asleep, and we get to watch shows until midnight."

"Is it usually a Sunday night right before your last week of school?" I whispered.

She pouted. Hannah scooted to the edge of the couch. When she stood, she turned and draped her little arms around my neck. "Good night, June. Thanks for watching Percy Jackson with us." Her hug got tight for a second, then she trudged off. Another five minutes on the couch and she would've been snoozing like her dad.

Bethany did the same. "Thanks for hanging out with us tonight."

Their little voices in my ear and those sweet hugs caused an ache in my chest, a longing I hadn't thought I'd have. My life wasn't suited to having kids. Lots of singers had kids, they even toured while pregnant, but I'd want a more stable schedule, quicker modes of transportation, and larger spaces to relax.

I walked them to the base of the stairs and waited until they turned at the top to look back and wave. Going all the way to their bedroom felt intrusive. I was a guest. Guitar tutors didn't tuck their clients in. It wasn't appropriate.

I went to the living room. The TV was dark and the one lamp on in the corner cast shadows over Rhys's face. The line across his forehead was gone, his usual hard expression softened by sleep.

As teens, we hadn't been able to sleep together until that last night. Otherwise, we'd stolen little naps here and there. I'd never been able to pull a fast one over Mama and Daddy. If I told them I was sleeping over at a friend's house, they made damn sure I was at that friend's. There'd been no sneaking around together other than some stolen afternoons and evenings at the cabin.

I should just leave and let him doze. He'd wake and head to bed.

My feet started moving before my decision was made. I didn't move toward the door. I stopped beside the recliner. My fingers itched to curve through his hair, to feel the soft strands tickle my palms once again.

"Rhys," I said softly.

His brow furrowed and he snuggled deeper into his seat. It'd be so easy to climb into the chair with him and curl up, my head on his shoulder. I'd done it before, once upon a time.

Enough reminiscing. I tapped him on the shoulder. "Rhys."

He blinked his eyes open. A sleepy smile warmed the denim blue of his irises and the invite was apparent. I could crawl right into that chair with him.

Just as I was about to answer with a smile of my own, he blinked harder and frowned. "Are the girls in bed?"

The moment was gone. I nodded. "Yeah, Hannah barely made it through the second episode. Bethany tried to bargain for more, but I figured you'd want them to get some rest."

He put the footrest down and sat forward. Letting out a breath, he scrubbed his face. "You gotta get home."

Reality smacked me across the back of the head. For a whisper of a moment, I had forgotten that I wasn't where I was supposed to be. "Home. Right. Yes. Sorry I kept them up late."

He cut his hand through the air. "Not your fault. It's the last week of school. I shouldn't have fallen asleep."

"It really was a dad thing to do."

His chuckle gusted out. "Did I snore?"

"So loud. We could hardly hear the TV."

"My songbird's a smart-ass."

I smiled, but the air was charged between us. I would torture myself if I stayed and hoped something would happen. Just like he'd torture himself if I stayed and something did happen.

"It's early yet," he said gruffly.

Yes, it was early-ish for an adult. But I also didn't want to leave. I wasn't sure I could trust myself if he tried something either. Regardless, the words *good* and *bye* weren't on my tongue. "I didn't sleep half the evening."

He rose, towering over me. "Neither did I, smart-ass." He started for the kitchen. "Want a drink?"

My gaze was glued to the globes of his ass flexing under his sweats. I wanted so much more than a drink.

CHAPTER FOURTEEN

Rhys

June's laughter filled the kitchen. Fuck me, having that sound in my home was a pleasure I had never imagined. I'd loved her laugh before. It was as melodic as her singing, always had been. Hearing it now hit differently. She had options and she'd chosen them. I had encouraged her to. But this house was mine, and she was also choosing to be here.

The moment was bittersweet. She wasn't mine, but the days were so much brighter with her than without.

I poured her a vodka and orange juice. "You are not the reason I don't have Copper Summit in the house."

She put her hand on her chest and gasped dramatically. "Are you saying that seeing a bottle of Copper Summit wasn't so torturous that you couldn't have it under the same roof?"

I poured myself the same drink and left the bottle in

the middle of the table with the OJ. "If that was the case, I'd have had to move from Bourbon Canyon."

A beat of sadness went through her eyes before they sharpened. "Kirstin?"

"It would've been disrespectful when you're tied so closely to Copper Summit." Kirstin already had enough to deal with when it came to my baggage. "Now, there's just no good time for a drink. This shit's ten years old."

"Daddy used to say the best spirit is the one you enjoy with family and friends." She took a drink, holding the glass loosely. Her other arm was folded over her belly, and she had her bare feet kicked up on the chair next to her. Long strands of brownish and blue hair hung from the knot she'd tied it in. "So old vodka is the best vodka."

"That's not a saying." How easy would it be to scoot to the chair next to her, lift her feet and put them in my lap? I could rest my hand on her shins and we'd just talk, like we used to.

"We'll make it one."

We. The vodka warmed the cool path the juice had left. The heat went straight to my groin. Waking up to her had been like falling further into a dream that felt so real. I'd woken up to the woman I had thought would be my forever. The last fifteen years had fallen away. For a moment, I was submersed in the fantasy that we'd gotten married. This was our house. She'd tucked our girls in bed.

Somewhere in Costa Rica, Kirstin's eye must be twitching.

I loved my daughters, and I wasn't wishing away my marriage. I just wanted . . . something different. A woman who was mine and who loved those girls more than anything.

She swirled her glass, relaxed in her chair. "So. Tell me about your life."

"You've been seeing it."

"What'd you do . . . after?"

"Worked."

She stared at me, expectant, continuing to rotate her glass.

"Dad's health was a roller coaster until it wasn't. I thought the ranch was doing fine despite a few dry years and shitty market prices, but Wren was worried. The girls came along and I got busier. Then Kirstin left and it got even harder. Wren and I sold the ranch." My life since I was eighteen boiled down to a few dismal sentences.

"And you struck out on your own?"

"The stress was getting to Wren."

"Rhys." She studied the contents of her glass. "You haven't said whether you wanted to sell or not."

"It didn't matter. We had to."

"For Wren?"

"For the girls." I kept my gaze steady, but the urge to fidget like a little boy was strong.

"Mm."

"What's that mean?"

She took a sip and licked a drop off her lips. The sight stabilized my emotions. Being turned on was easier to handle than her questions.

"What was your mom like?"

I jerked like she'd tossed the vodka OJ in my face. "Why?"

"I'm wondering if she started the pattern of you ignoring what you want for the women in your life."

"Jesus, June," I said roughly and set my glass aside. There wasn't enough alcohol in Bourbon Canyon for this conversation. June had asked more about my mom in the last month than she had the entire time we were together. "No, she's not the start. She's the reason I refuse to let down another woman in my life."

"You were a kid, Rhys. You were, like, twelve when you moved to Bourbon Canyon."

"That's when she died." My heart thumped once, initiating a steady, heavy beat.

She put her feet on the floor and leaned forward. "After you moved, right?"

I nodded. "I was actually living with Dad a few weeks before I started school, but Mom got hit by a car when she was on her way to theater rehearsal in New York. She died instantly."

"Oh god, Rhys." She put her fingers to her lips, sympathy spilling into her amber eyes. "I'm so sorry."

I was too, since the whole event was my fault. "Dad had to travel there with me to settle everything. She had no family. No assets. No money. She'd never been able to make a steady living carting me around."

June frowned. "What do you mean? Our professions are fickle. It's hard to make a steady living no matter what."

"You're doing it."

"Yeah, well, I had to work two or three jobs sometimes."

"She couldn't." I let out a scornful laugh. "At least that's what child services told her."

Her expression turned stunned. She blinked. "She tried to leave you home by yourself?"

I shrugged. That drink was looking good after all. I downed the rest. "She tried to support us. I made it hard."

"Rhys—"

I cut a hand through the air. "I don't want to talk about it. You weren't there, June. Can you just trust me?"

She chewed on her bottom lip. "Sorry. It's your business."

I nodded, but the emptiness inside me yawned wider.

"How about we talk about your ex?"

I barked out a laugh, caught off guard. "Any other wounds you want to pry bandages off of?"

Her soft smile was understanding. "Bethany and Hannah are amazing. I think pretty highly of you, but I know they're also part of their mother. What's she like?"

Not like you.

Kirstin wasn't exactly neutral territory, far from it, but June was asking in relation to the girls. Yet my first thought felt like a betrayal of the years I'd been married. Kirstin couldn't carry a tune, her mahogany hair was short and curly, and she would let a room swallow her up instead of charming the occupants into submission with her siren song.

In the end though, she'd been exactly like June.

"She's quiet. Not shy, just in her own head. I used to tease her that she saw the world through a lens and was always trying to figure out the right filter. She always was more comfortable behind a camera."

June smiled. "I know the feeling. The world makes

sense. Or rather, you can make it make sense through your chosen art."

Like June did with music. "The girls are only a little interested in photography. It irritates the hell out of Kirstin when they express an interest in music of any sort."

A line formed between her brows. "Because of me."

"She heard all the stories. Of us."

"That had to be hard. No wonder she wanted to ban everything to do with me."

"It couldn't be helped. Small town. Most people knew better, and your family was great, but you know how it is." I shut all the doors to my past. They could stay closed forever. "Enough about my divorce. Tell me about your journey. Not the douchebags who wasted your time." I refilled my glass. I'd like to chuck the bottle at the damn fiddle-playing singer.

She grabbed the vodka and added a splash to her glass.

I smirked. "Want some OJ with that?"

"Nope." She took a drink and closed her eyes, savoring. Her throat worked over her swallow, and goddamn, my pulse ground to a halt. Illicit memories flung their own doors open with a bang.

If she opened those eyes and looked at me like she used to when she was sucking my dick, I'd have to run to my shower.

I put the glass to my lips. The smart thing to do would be to dump the alcohol down the drain. But I downed another big mouthful instead.

"I worked as a server and a nanny and performed at coffee shops whenever I could. Sometimes I'd play for tips. Hoping to catch the ear of someone important.

Soon the smaller venues got larger and one time I was playing when Lucy was in the crowd. She was impressed that I wrote my own music." She shifted her gaze toward me like she knew I'd scoff at what she'd say next. "She liked my vibe."

"If that was a pickup line, it'd never work."

"It does when you realize it's Lucy Fillmore talking to you. She'd worked with Frankie Ritz."

"Isn't that the singer who got thrown in jail for taking a hit out on her husband? Calvin something?"

She laughed. "Yes, but she hadn't done that yet. Frankie was on the verge of breaking." Her smile froze. "I wonder if Lucy set her up with Calvin." She tossed back the rest of her glass and poured herself another.

I topped mine off too. I wasn't driven to drink, but this was nice. I'd had a nap, and there was no fucking way I'd be able to sleep after waking up to her. "So Lucy sought you out?"

"Yeah, I'd built a nice following. A small audience who liked my music and came to watch me play. Then Lucy signed me, and we peddled songs to record labels. Her name opened a lot of doors. I was making a small name for myself." Her smile grew wide. "I actually played the Opry. It was so surreal."

"I imagine it was." I struggled to draw a breath. The Grand Ole Opry. She'd done it, just like she'd said. I cleared my throat past the lump that had formed.

"I was even getting pitched by brands." She grinned. "I could've been an influencer." She touched the back of her hand to her chin and lifted her gaze to the ceiling. "A cosmetic company wanted me to be the face of their eye cream." She took a sip. "But they wanted me to quit with Copper Summit. So I said thanks but no, thanks. I know my following trends younger, but I wasn't selling alcohol to the eye-cream crowd."

"June Bee is ride or die for her family."

"Yes." She swirled her glass again and watched the contents. "It makes a difference when you've actually had family die in front of you. A lot of execs didn't understand that. It cost me some progress."

"You'd have ten houses by now instead?"

She rolled her eyes. "I have five places to live."

"Is that all?"

"They're not all houses. I don't like to stay in hotels. I don't like to feel like . . ."

"I know, June Bug. You never have to explain it to me." She craved roots. She didn't want to feel transient again—cramped and uncomfortable. Not knowing when the next shower would be. Others might think she was a diva for wanting a sprawling hotel suite, but it was the traumatized kid inside of her.

She nodded. "Tate always gives me a hard time about renting. He says it's a waste of money."

"Did you ever find out how your birth parents lost their home?" I'd thought of June's birth parents a lot over the years. I'd only had two kids, and my parents had been a support system. Wren still was. June's bio parents had been homeless with four little girls and no other family.

"No. They kept all that from us, and Mama never found out why." She swallowed the rest of her drink but didn't refill her glass. "I like this."

I didn't have to ask her what she meant. "I do too."

"It's nice to be us as we are now and not as we were then."

"Closure."

She considered me. "Yes. Closure," she said finally.

The atmosphere grew heavier. No. That would not do. "How's the songwriting coming?"

The light in her eye returned. "Really good. I have the bones of five songs, but I really don't think it'll take much to finish them. I can hear them clearly."

"What gave you your muse back?"

She pulled her lower lip between her teeth. A shot of lust went straight for my dick. I had ideas for that mouth.

She feathered her hand over her hair and glanced around the kitchen. Two spots of pink dotted her cheeks. "Oh, you know, I think I was just tired of writing about heartbreak."

I tapped my finger against my glass. She'd called me out. I would return the favor. "I know when you're evading a question."

"I needed time off."

"You've had time off and you said you couldn't write."

"It's just . . ." Her flush deepened. How far did that pink go down her chest? She pursed her lips, then huffed a breath out. "Those kisses, okay? You kissed me and boom—lyrics came into my head. A theme for a song. Even a melody." She leaned forward and stabbed her fingertip into the table, glaring at me. "I've written so many songs because of two kisses from you."

"I'm your muse?"

She slumped back and eyed the vodka bottle like she wanted to chug it. "I think so."

Huh. I'd been her muse all those years ago. She'd channeled her emotions into her music. Lost love. "I'm glad I can help."

"Yeah, well, I need five more songs, so you'd better not fail me."

"Are you saying you need me to kiss you again?"

Those plump pink lips of hers parted. "Y-you said you can't risk getting involved with me again."

"We're not involved. I'm just a muse."

Interest lit her eyes. Was I really suggesting we . . .

Could I touch June again and keep from believing it was the beginning of forever? Maybe. "Never mind. This is crazy. You've been drinking."

"Rhys Conner Kinkade. Are you doubting that I can make valid decisions after a few drinks when I've been in the world of spirits most of my life? And when I've been living in a glorified honkey-tonk town for almost half my life?"

She hated being treated like she couldn't care for herself. She'd been tasting alcohol since she was sixteen, and while I didn't drink often, I wasn't a lightweight when it came to the stuff.

I gave her one last chance to decide this idea was a mess waiting to happen. "The girls are upstairs."

"It's only a kiss. Right?" Her voice dropped into a purr that went straight to my dick.

Could I put my mouth on her and not fall faster and harder than I ever had?

It was a risk I was willing to take.

June

I giggled as Rhys tumbled us backward onto his bed. His mouth was on mine and I was twined round him like a vine. His sweatpants did not hold back his erection like his jeans.

"Ssh," he said against my cheek. "You can't wake them up."

"It's like hiding from our parents again."

He rocked into me. "Remember what we used to do when they were in the next room?"

We'd had to stay fully dressed and ready to fly apart from each other at the first turn of the doorknob. My sisters would sometimes act as lookout. Other times, they were quiet as church mice, ready for the show if Daddy caught me entwined with Rhys.

He kissed a path to my ear. "I used to do everything I could."

I widened my legs and rocked against his hard cock. Those pants were so in the way and that was how it was going to stay. But god, it felt good.

"I want to touch you," I whispered. The deal was only a kiss. But we hadn't expressly said we'd just stick to kissing.

His groan resonated right through me. "If you touch me, I get to touch you."

I turned my head to flick my tongue against his earlobe. "Deal."

He claimed my mouth again. I was the first to make the move beyond the kiss. As much as I wanted my greedy fingers on that massive erection, I couldn't resist his untucked shirt.

I brushed my hands underneath the material. He lifted himself enough that I could skate the backs of my fingers along his hard abs. Smooth skin and fine hair slid under my fingers. I flattened my hands on his firm pecs. I wish I could see him, but the lights were off and the door was locked.

Maybe later. Next week, when his kids went to Wren's.

Tonight, I'd do everything I could.

I paused my roaming while he plundered my mouth. His heart rate was rapid under my palms, increasing when he flicked the hem of my shirt out of his way. His hot hand seared my skin. He did the same as me and flattened his hand over my heart.

My pulse wasn't racing, but the beats were loud and clear. For a moment, we just kissed and connected. This was dangerous. He was my muse. Syncing our heartbeats was . . . something else.

Curling my fingers, I lightly scored him as I raked down to his waistband. I gasped when my fingertip touched the tip of his hot erection, a drop of precum smearing between our skin. The position we were in had dragged his sweats down and let that impressive bulge find freedom.

Again, he copied my movements. As I shoved the material of his pants down, he wedged his hand into my jeans. The fabric pulled tight, hugging his hand and fingers to me. I could feel every inch of his advance.

"I've dreamed of this for so fucking long," he said against my lips.

"Me too." So many nights had been spent remembering how good it used to be. I wrapped my hand around his cock. He was hard and real in my grip. So familiar, yet so different. This was the first time since that last night with him in the cabin that intimacy felt right.

His progress stalled as a deep groan came from him. "Fuck me, June. I'm afraid to move, or I'll come."

I nipped at his chin and gave him a pump. "Quiet, remember."

He dropped his head to my ear. "Two can play that game, smart-ass." He went straight to my clit and strummed it.

My noisy gasp, followed by a moan, echoed in the room. I tightened my hold on him, more out of reflex. "I don't know if I can stay quiet."

"Scream into me." He kissed a path to my mouth. "Bite me if you have to. Because I'm going to get you off, June. I'm going to feel those pussy walls clamp around my finger and then I'm going to sleep tonight and imagine that happening to my dick."

Yes. I stroked his length. He circled my clit and lifted his hips to give himself more room between us.

Our mouths were fused and our tongues clashed. I bucked against his hand and he thrust into mine. I could continue forever, but it'd been too long since it'd been this good.

He adjusted his hand, almost moving his hips too far away. I rose with him, keeping my strokes steady. When I swirled my thumb over the crown of his erection, he ripped his mouth from mine.

"*Fuck.* That little hand of yours is wicked." He pushed a finger inside me while making tight circles around my clit.

"Oh, god. Rhys." My orgasm was building. Sensual pressure, pushing against all the right places, preparing to explode in a way I hadn't experienced in a long time.

He was taut above me, his hips bucking into my hand while I writhed under him.

"It's been fucking forever, June."

I was panting, so ready to explode. He pulsed in my hand and grunted in my ear. Then we both came, together, in each other's hold. I hit my peak and buried my face in his chest. Ecstasy exploded inside my body until I felt like I was floating, suspended with him in a special place only the two of us together could reach.

Hot cum slicked my grip. His strength, his size, the way he groaned through his climax. Familiar, but new.

He slumped against me and I sagged into the mattress. His weight was a comfort. We caught our breath together.

After a minute of enjoying the comfort of being satiated, he turned his face into me, his breath wafting over my ear. "Does that make any tunes pop into your head?"

I giggled and patted his shoulder. My other hand was still in his pants, but I had let his erection go. He was still big, and if that part hadn't changed, he'd be ready again if I touched him some more, but I held still. "That's not how it works. But yes. I feel lighter. Freer. Creative in a different way."

He slipped his hand out of my pants and I did the same.

"I'll be right back with some towels." He grabbed a new pair of sweats from his dresser on his way out.

Happy I didn't have to wonder if he'd get grumpy again and kick me out of bed, I waited. The thought of going back to being tense and awkward sat on my chest like a stubborn mule.

A couple of minutes later, he was back. I accepted the warm, damp towel. While I wiped myself off, he flung back the covers.

I handed the towel to him and was about to rise.

"Stay." He draped the rag over his hamper. "Just for a little while. It's been fun."

"I'll say."

Even in the shadows, I could see his eyes twinkle. "Not what I meant, but yeah. That was fun too."

"When you said it's been forever . . ." I shouldn't have broached the subject. The air between us would get uncomfortable again. I'd leave on a bad note instead of a blissful glow.

"I don't date much." He flipped the covers. "Get in, June Bug."

The intimacy of his invite rang a faint warning bell. But I gave in to the lure of not being alone for part of the night. I crawled in, fully dressed. He got in with me, keeping his shirt and sweats on. I rolled to my side so he could spoon me.

"You didn't date because of the girls?" I asked.

"Something like that. Some complications I just don't want to deal with. They have a good understanding of their mom. They're accepting in a way I couldn't've hoped for. But if I dated and it didn't work out? Or worse, if I had to keep seeing the woman around? The girls too?"

"You mean like Annette?"

"You keep bringing her up."

"You keep playing obtuse."

He nuzzled his nose in my hair. "We help each other with the kids."

"She'd help you just like I did."

"Does she have songs to write?"

I laughed. "Now who's the smart-ass?"

"I'm not interested in Annette," he said softly.

Pleased, I relaxed. Being in his arms again was a

forbidden treat I'd never thought I'd have again. His breathing evened out and his arm around me was loose. Was he asleep?

I should go.

Fatigue pulled at my eyelids. I'd had a mellow evening, a couple of drinks, and an orgasm, and I was in Rhys's arms. I'd close my eyes, savor the moment, and then I'd leave.

CHAPTER FIFTEEN

Rhys

"Dad!"

Awareness poked at the edges of my consciousness. A soft, warm body was pressed next to me, tempting me to fall back asleep. This was heaven and I hadn't gotten to hold heaven in my arms in a long damn time.

"Dad!"

The doorknob jiggled.

I jolted awake. June. Her moans. Her heat. Cuddling. She was groaning awake, rolling over to face me. Her dreamy smile almost made me forget what a mess we were in. Her hair was tousled. Bed head. *My* bed.

"Dad? Are you even here?" Bethany called from the other side of the door.

June's eyes widened and she gasped.

I put my finger to her lips. "Yeah, I slept in," I called through the door. "Do your chores and—"

"They're done. We're ready for school." The knob jiggled again. "Your door is locked."

Shit. How late was it? I rolled out of bed and frantically searched the room for an extra pair of sweats. Looking down, I blew out a breath. I was wearing the sweats I was looking for.

I met June's alarmed gaze. She was holding the blankets to her chest. Frowning, she glanced down. I wasn't the only fully clothed one. She dropped the blanket.

I smirked at her, and she shot me a glare, then a smile curved her lips.

This was fucking ridiculous. Not even my mom had slept in with a stranger on a school day. The thought was sobering.

Ideas churned in my head. What should I tell the girls? They couldn't know I was messing around with their music idol. The girls wanted June's autograph. I wanted June's climaxes.

Shit. I stuffed a hand through my hair. My obnoxious dick was awake and aware a woman was in my bed.

"I'm sorry," June mouthed.

I shook my head. I'd fallen asleep and she'd done the same.

"Uh, Bethany . . ." What should I do? Plans were coming together as fast as I was brushing them off. I couldn't let the girls see June in my room. That was out of the question. "Wanna get my coffee ready, and . . . and have Hannah start a load of laundry?"

"We're going to be late."

I usually drove them instead of sending them on the bus. Normally, it wasn't an issue. Normally, I wasn't hiding a woman in my bedroom. "I know. I'll call the school. But I need to get ready."

"Okay," she said dubiously. Her footsteps receded down the hall.

I crossed to June's side of the bed. "Here's what we'll do," I said on a whisper. "I'll go use the bathroom, and after I make sure the coast is clear, you sneak to the guest room. I'll tell the girls you slept over because you were so tired."

She nodded and scooted to the edge of the bed. "I'm really sorry," she whispered back.

Without thinking, I leaned down and kissed her, a quick, firm kiss. "I'm not going to make you sneak out the window."

"I never made you—" At my knowing look, she grinned. "It was once."

"And I had to pretend I was taking a late-night walk in my socks. Your dad didn't buy it."

Before I did something foolish and crawled back in bed with her, I crept out. The hallway was clear. The metallic thump of the washing machine lid flying open was loud and clear. Drawers opened and closed in the kitchen. I waved at June.

She snuck behind me down the hall.

"Don't close the door," I said under my breath. "Otherwise Bethany might realize we're lying."

She nodded. "I was awake and getting dressed in the closet."

Almost believable. Good enough. We nodded at each other like we were departing for a mission. A new connection formed. She didn't question why I was keeping her presence from the girls. She understood.

I dipped into the bathroom and cleaned up. When I emerged, I went to the kitchen instead of getting dressed.

The main concern with dating was whether the other party would respect my limits when it came to Bethany and Hannah. June did, without hesitation. But this was temporary for her too.

Bethany was charging out of the kitchen. She stopped when she saw me, confusion twisting her mouth. "Are you sick?"

I was usually up and had my chores done in the morning before I got them up to feed the chickens, goats, the barn cats, and the dog. I never took sick days, but then I was never still in my sweats when school was starting soon.

"No, I'm fine. Listen, June got real tired last night and I told her to crash here."

Excitement lit Bethany's eyes. "June's here?" She frowned. "I didn't see her."

I shrugged. "Maybe she was getting ready." Before Bethany could think too hard about open and closed and locked doors, I stuffed a thumb in the direction of the bedroom. "I'm gonna get dressed. Just, uh, watch TV until we're ready."

When I was rushing down the hall, June emerged. She hung in the doorway.

"I'll be ready in a few," I said, pausing next to her.

"Are we in the clear?"

Not if I didn't get away from her. The urge to push her back and see if she'd let me sneak more of those tantalizing kisses was strong. I ordered my feet to move. "We're clear." Before I turned into my bedroom, I glanced back. "Next weekend?" I'd have the house to myself, and I wouldn't think about my request any harder than that.

Desire filled her gaze. "Next weekend."

June

I was in a chair on the porch, guitar in my lap, a coffee on the little table, and a notepad full of notes.

A sixth full song had poured out of me. From Monday to Thursday, I'd outlined the melody, then the chorus, and filled it all in with lyrics.

I was close to a full album.

Everything I wanted was within my grasp. A potential record-breaking album. Perhaps some chart-toppers. And a world tour.

I was on the cusp.

June Kerrigan, tragic homeless orphan, would headline a world tour. I pressed a hand against my stomach. Nerves were lighting up. Anticipation bloomed in my belly, mushrooming larger until I could vibrate with excitement. Fear was right next to it. Anxiety that the cloud would dissipate and my chances would vanish. The last tour had been . . . a lot. A lot of travel, a lot of work, and thanks to Finn, a lot of drama. But I wanted more. I hated leaving the stage after a handful of songs. I also delighted in hearing that concertgoers had bought tickets for me and not the headliner.

As long as I cranked this album out, I'd be ready.

But I also wanted the man.

How hard would it be to leave him behind?

This wasn't the first time I'd asked myself that question. The answer was taking longer each time.

The morning had dawned beautiful and quiet. High on my writing, I'd queried a few managers. I'd started with the ones Lucy had detested. Two hadn't called me back and one had told me she was full. But now word would be out that I was looking for a manager. People might think I was a diva and had fired Lucy as soon as I thought I was too big for her, but I didn't care.

The longer I was in Montana, the less I cared about the politics in Nashville.

Another weekend was here, and I had a tune in my head for another song. Some lyrics even. Lyrics about secrets.

I had a secret. And he could do the most amazing things with his fingers.

My phone buzzed and Wynter's name popped up.

I answered and put the phone on speaker. The birds wouldn't share our conversation. "Hey, girlie." I set the guitar aside.

"Hey, Junie. Got a minute?"

I tensed. If this was an *I miss you all the way from Denver* call, she wouldn't sound so serious. "What's wrong?"

"Ruby called. She thought you'd rather hear from me."

I pinched the bridge of my nose. "What's wrong?" My blissful social media hiatus was coming to an end.

"A picture of you and Rhys at Curly's has gone viral."

Cold washed over me, leaving behind fragments of panic as the meaning sank in. "What? How? I'm in Bourbon Canyon all the time and no one cares."

"No one cares that you're here to visit family. But when you're cozy in a booth with your high school sweetheart? The public is quite interested."

I groaned. "What are they saying?" I would have to download the apps again. I had to see for myself, read the comments, track the speculation. But Ruby had been correct. I'd rather have my sister, someone who cared about me, spill the dirty details.

"Well, it took a few days from when it was posted."

"I was out with Autumn and Scarlett, and they basically dumped me on Rhys, but the girls were with us." I gasped, horror somersaulting through my bones. "Were the girls photographed?"

"Nothing like that yet, but they're named. A single dad who's an old flame. Everyone's wondering if you're ready to settle down. They're wondering if you're retiring to have a family. Some comments are calling him . . . uh, a hot mountain daddy."

"I can't argue with that." I fiddled with the ends of my hair. It needed a trim and a new color. The blue was fading and I wanted a new tint to put the old times behind me. New tour, new color.

Until then, I had a bigger issue. "So, his face is scattered all over social media?"

"Just that image, from what Ruby could see, and his graduation picture. Weird seeing him again without a beard," she mumbled.

"And the girls weren't in it?"

"No."

That must've been when they had gone to the bathroom. "Good. At least there's that." But their names were out in the world. Rhys was so damn private. This wouldn't go over well, and I couldn't blame him.

"Tell Ruby thank you and to keep an eye on everything for me." Maybe she had some ideas about how to deflect the situation. A just-friends post?

A friend whose dick I'd had my hand around last weekend.

What a mess.

After I hung up with Wynter, I called Rhys. As soon as the call connected, I didn't wait for him to answer. "Did you see the news?"

"That gas prices are going up again? Or that you're having romantic dinners with your high school sweetheart?"

I squeezed my eyes shut. "You saw it."

"I've seen it, songbird." His tone wasn't light, but there was no longer an edge hard enough to crush diamonds.

"When? Why didn't you say anything? Why weren't you hammering on my cabin door, demanding answers?"

"Figured I already did that."

And we'd kissed. But we'd done more together since then.

"The girls came home yesterday beside themselves and asked if we were dating. Then Hannah asked if that's why you slept over—while Annette was trying to ask me about a playdate next weekend."

I could high-five Hannah. I was a little too territorial around Rhys. Except her comment would only create more speculation.

"Don't worry," he continued. "I said that you were tired after they'd invited you to watch a movie. Then they argued that it wasn't a movie and started to discuss whether two episodes of a TV show counted as a movie."

The chill from minutes earlier diminished but didn't recede. "Aren't you upset?"

An exhale blew over the line. "I'm a little worried. Irritated too, but not at you."

"Maybe a little at me?"

"No. Someone posted what should've been a private moment. But whoever it was didn't include the girls."

"Their names are out there. People know you're a single dad in Bourbon Canyon."

"I think the term that they're using is Hot Mountain Daddy Rhys."

Surprised laughter bubbled out of me. "Are you serious? You're okay with this?"

"I'll take Hot Mountain Daddy Rhys if it means Bethany and Hannah's name don't get tossed around. The comments seemed more interested in me than the girls. And I think the town will rally around Bethany and Hannah's privacy like they have with you."

"Wait—what's being said?" So much for inspiration. My muse would pace in the corners of my brain until I scoured the internet for hours to find every comment regarding Rhys and his kids.

"Just some bullshit about you getting sidetracked by a mountain daddy and delaying the album. You know, stuff they wouldn't say about a guy. But I'm used to it. I'm an adult now and I can take it."

The attention was on him and he was thinking of me?

What did he mean he'd been through this before? It likely had something to do with his mom and he wouldn't say. Regardless, he shouldn't have to deal with this nonsense because of me. "I can work with Ruby to mitigate—"

"Let 'em wonder. Any light you shine on us is only going to turn into a floodlight. That's how it goes with you. Your fan base can be kind of rabid."

"How do you know?"

"I'm just a simple rancher, but I might've looked at your feeds a time or two over the years."

I smiled and cradled the phone to my ear. I'd never tire of hearing that I'd been just as hard to forget as he was. "Yeah?"

"I had to make sure you were still living your dream."

CHAPTER SIXTEEN

Rhys

The girls were preparing for their guitar concert at Wren's place.

I sat on a chair in the living room and scrolled through the threads about me and June. Only a couple of days had passed since I'd learned of the online chatter, but the hubbub had been deflected by the announcement of June's album release.

Between yesterday and today, she'd started working with another manager and had announced July 31 as the release date. Had June worked on finding a new manager all week?

Our secret was mostly safe. My kids were forgotten. Only people who'd been out to the cabin would know where she was from her photos.

I should've been bothered. I should've pulled all the way back. Hadn't I cornered June about the risk of dragging the kids and me into the spotlight? But when reality had hit and threatened to ruin what time I had with June, I hadn't fucking cared. Everyone else could eat shit. I had two weeks while the girls were with Wren, and if June wanted me, I was hers.

Then after . . . I'd have to wean myself off her again. I'd have to watch her leave. And I'd be thrilled for her. This time, I knew what to expect.

Movement outside caught my eye. June parked next to my pickup. She had her hair piled on top of her head. The image of pulling her hair band out and dragging my fingers through those silky locks flashed through my head. *Later*.

We hadn't officially discussed any plans. Were we on the same page? As soon as the girls finished their performance, Wren would feed us sloppy joes and then I'd leave her with the girls for a couple of weeks to kick off their summer. I'd go home, and June would hopefully follow.

"Junie's here!" Hannah sprinted through the living room to the front door. She whipped it open before June reached the steps. "Hi! Did you see the picture of you and Dad?"

"Hannah," I cautioned. We'd talked about piling on June as soon as she walked in.

But had June seen the picture? We'd looked intimate, like a real couple. Whoever the photographer was, they had captured us when June had turned into me and our heads were tipped close as we talked.

I had only stared at the image for an hour. A day.

"I did." June put her hands on her hips. "I cannot believe he wasn't smiling."

Hannah laughed at June's teasing tone. I shot June a

promising look. I wasn't a smiley guy. There was a lot more I wanted to do with my mouth around her.

She winked and the sauciness shot straight to my dick.

Bethany tugged on her hand. "We have the stage set up. First, I'm going to do 'Twinkle Twinkle Little Star' and Hannah's going to do 'Row, Row, Row Your Boat.' Then we both want to play guitar while you sing."

June's brows lifted. "You learned a new song?"

Both girls enthusiastically nodded.

June lifted her gaze to mine. "How?"

"We found a video of a guy teaching 'London Bridge Is Falling Down.' " And they had asked me to make sure they practiced every night.

June's lips parted, then she shook her head. "A two-chord song. Good choice. I bet you're going to nail it."

"Are you going to sing?" Bethany asked.

"Absolutely."

"Grandma!" Bethany called.

Wren breezed in from the kitchen. "Sorry! Now I'm ready." She went to June and gave her a quick hug and kiss. "Nice to see you again, Junie."

"Thanks for having me."

Wren beamed. She was in her element with the girls and with June. She sat on the rocking chair, leaving the other end of the couch open. June perched on the far corner. I refrained from scooting closer to her. The girls somehow believed that June had needed to do nothing more than crash at our place last Sunday night. I wouldn't give them a reason to suspect otherwise.

Bethany picked through her song. Wren took pictures. Pride could make my chest explode. The girls loved their music, and I always made sure they could do what they loved.

June whooped and clapped when Bethany was done. "That was amazing!"

Bethany stepped to the side. Hannah worked her way through her song, her tongue shoving into the corner of one cheek. Wren snapped a few photos with her phone. She'd send me the copies and the video, otherwise I'd take my own.

Then it was time for the group performance.

June knelt between both of them. The sight of her with the girls, her face radiating happiness while my kids couldn't look more delighted, hit in the dead center of my chest. This was what I had wanted.

Temporary. I'd keep the word on repeat. I didn't even know if June would want to do more. I'd survived the week thinking I'd get to touch her again, hear her needy little moans, but I didn't know. If I was a smart man, I'd make the decision to leave her alone, to take the full two weeks off and detox from June Kerrigan, but I'd left my intelligence on the table when I'd kissed her that night.

When the guitars started, June sang, her voice soft. She matched her notes with how they played, sometimes slow and halting. My entire focus was on them. A whole band could set up in the house, and I'd notice nothing else.

June sang the last word, then grabbed a girl in each arm for a giant bear hug. "I'm so proud of you two! Ohmigosh. You're rock stars already."

The vise around my chest cinched several notches tighter. She was so damn good with them. Encouraging and present.

If only she'd stay.

But this was my dream, not hers. And I made sure the women I loved could live out their dreams.

June

I was finishing with the dishes at Wren's house. The dishwasher was going and I was washing what didn't fit. Rhys had already directed the girls to wipe the table and sweep.

Wren hung her damp dish towel up. "I can't believe you're back in my house, doing the dishes after dinner." She continued adjusting the towel on the hook. "I, um, have something. I've been going through everything. Rhys?"

He spun around from where he was watching the girls play another round of "London Bridge Is Falling Down." They played a lot smoother when no eyes were on them.

"Yeah?" He stuffed his hands in his pants, standing tall with those broad shoulders wide.

He'd trimmed his beard since last week. For us? For tonight? Would there even be a tonight?

Had he changed his mind?

I crossed my arms. I'd been impossibly horny for the entire week and my nipples were pebbling just looking at him.

Wren lifted a box from the coat closet by the door to the garage and carried it to the dining room table. "I was going through some things and I found this. It's . . . yours."

His expression shuttered and he sucked in a sharp breath.

Wren clasped her hands together. "I know Kirstin didn't want to have it in the house but now that you're in your own place . . ."

Understanding dawned. The memorabilia that included me.

"I thought the girls would get a kick out of it." Wren waved her hands and shrugged. "Since you two aren't a secret anymore."

A jolt of adrenaline went through me. How did she know? Had she seen the image online and believed what was said? Was it the overnight? Rhys shot me a quelling stare, and I calmed my racing heart.

Oh. She meant the kids knew about me and Rhys in high school.

"Sure," he said evenly. "I can bring it home."

"I have a few more things in the office. Articles and such." She rushed from the room. I stayed by the sink. He remained in place. Then he dragged his gaze down my body. I had on a long pleated skirt with a peasant blouse. The days were warm, but the nights could be chilly. I'd been having hot flashes all week when I remembered Rhys's finger working inside me. The chill wouldn't be an issue.

When he brushed his intense stare up my body, a needy wave of desire rippled over my skin.

"Here we go." Wren entered the room. I dropped my eyes to the floor, my cheeks burning like I'd been caught scaling his body.

She set the papers in the box. The girls rushed in from the living room and pushed around Rhys like they sensed formerly forbidden loot.

"What's this?" Bethany pulled out a photo of me and Rhys at our senior prom.

"That's how you did your hair, Dad?" Bethany snickered.

"It was thicker then," he grumbled.

"Helmet hair was the style," I added.

"I did not follow trends," he protested.

I pinched my fingers together. "Maybe a little."

He pointed at the photo. "If I wore my hair like that, it's because you wanted it that way."

Laughing, I drifted closer to the box.

"Look at his face!" Hannah exclaimed. A clean-shaven Rhys scowled at the camera. One would think we'd had an awful night or argued right before the pictures, but that was his normal expression. Serious. He was only slightly softer now, but he hadn't been when I'd first arrived.

For the next hour, we pored over articles Wren had saved for him from the county paper. A few were from the *Bozeman Daily Chronicle*, and she'd printed some Associated Press articles. I checked the years. The clippings stopped after the funeral. When he'd met Kirstin.

The sloppy joes congealed in my belly. This box was a time capsule of us. There was a beginning and there was an end. Not much different than now. There was an end coming. Then I would return to Nashville and Rhys would meet someone else and this box would go back in storage.

CHAPTER SEVENTEEN

Rhys

I entered the house and kicked the screen door shut behind me. My guest was on her way, but I didn't know if she'd bypass the turnoff and keep going. Would she be the smart one?

Just in case we were both leaving our brains behind, I'd parked outside and left the garage door open for her. I didn't need the goddamn mailman noticing her car in my driveway in the morning.

I set the box of old pictures and articles on the table. I stood next to it, humbled that Wren had thought to save it. I'd brought it to her and Dad, unable to explain why I couldn't throw it out when Kirstin had demanded it gone. Wren had taken plenty of pictures from when I was a kid that didn't include June. I'd kept all those and the girls had pored through them over the years.

I tugged at the collar of the long-sleeved shirt I was

wearing, then I just tugged it over my head and draped it over a chair. Damn thing chafed.

Was this really happening?

June's car pulled in.

Fuck yes.

A few moments later, she entered, that skirt swirling around her ankles. "Thanks for giving me the garage." Her gaze raked over my bare chest. "Getting started without me?"

All the lust I'd been keeping a tight lid on bubbled over. Desire flooded my veins and blood went straight for my dick. "You've been a goddamn tease in that skirt all night." I ripped the fly of my jeans open. Lust rippled under my skin, but I wasn't going to jump on her. The pressure would drive me nuts, yet there would be no rushing tonight. I was taking my time with this woman.

"As if your flannel porn is any better." Her bare feet whispered over the floor as she approached me.

I snagged her hand and drew her in. Then my mouth was on hers, and I lifted her. She wrapped her legs around me and I spun us. I plundered her mouth while I carried her into the living room. I couldn't wait for the bedroom.

In front of the couch, I dropped to my knees. June stayed plastered against me. Her mouth was warm and wet, just like I knew her pussy would be, but we had all night.

I palmed her ass cheeks, gripping and rubbing. She ground against me, ripping her mouth from mine to suck in a breath. I kissed down her neck.

"Oh god, Rhys," she groaned.

"You taste so fucking sweet." She was her very own

bourbon cocktail, right on my tongue. I laid her back. Her lips were kiss-swollen and parted. "And I know for a fact where you'll be even sweeter."

I ran my fingers down her legs to her ankles, then slowly reversed direction. Her skin was soft under my touch. As I went, I pushed the fabric of her skirt up, over the curve of her calf, past the crease of her knee. Higher and higher, exposing her thighs. When the skirt was bunched around the place I wanted to uncover the most, I flipped the hem up. Lacy white underwear greeted me.

"How wet are you?" I dragged my finger in a line down the middle of her panties, following her seam. The dampness on the cloth was pure heat against my fingertip.

She rolled her hips. "I don't recall you being this slow."

I planted my hands on her firm thighs and leaned in to place a kiss at the edge of her collarbone. "I'm not a teen anymore and we're not hiding from our parents."

She rocked against me. "I don't think I can wait that long."

"I'll make it worth it." I hooked two fingers over the waistband of her underwear and dragged them down her legs.

She was bare to me. I gently pushed her legs farther open.

"Fuck me, June. Such a pretty pink and so fucking wet." It was like coming home.

I pushed that thought right out of my head. I was home. She wasn't. She'd never been mine. If she had been, she'd have never gotten what she wanted. But this right here? We both wanted it. And I was going to give it to her.

I tucked my arms under her legs and settled low, not caring if I strangled my erection in the opening of my pants.

I spread her lips wide and looked my fill. This wasn't exploratory like when we'd been younger. This was greedy. "Your swollen little clit's begging to be licked."

She threaded her fingers through my hair and tugged my head toward her center. I gladly went.

I traced my tongue around her clit. A ragged moan left her and her fingers twisted against my scalp.

She gasped, her hips undulating. "It's not going to take long." More pants. "I can't believe it." Her hands fell from my head. "Not long at all."

I was supposed to be taking my time, but June was an instrument I'd become an expert of long ago. I'd only needed seconds to reacquaint myself.

We had the whole night and I'd savor her for each second.

I lapped at her needy nub. Her legs fell all the way open and a long groan left her. "Rhys."

She was blistering hot against my tongue, and she rode my face. So fucking close, my greedy little songbird. I would make her come fast and hard the first time and then the second time I'd—

There was pounding at the door.

June made a strangled noise and pulled away. "What the fuck?"

I glared toward the door. Who the fuck would be here—

"Rhys? Girls?" a familiar voice called from the outside.

Shit.

"Who is it?" She pushed her skirt down.

I stuffed my dick into my jeans and wiped my face off against the bottom of her skirt. I was zipping up and praying I didn't catch skin as I rose. "It's—"

The door creaked open. "Hello? I know it's late."

I spotted June's underwear on the floor. I swiped them up and hid them in a pocket.

I lunged inside the kitchen to give June extra time to straighten herself. My shirt was hanging against the chair, but I didn't have time to grab it. "Kirstin. What are you doing here?"

I sounded guilty as hell. This hadn't been her home, but I'd always buffered her from how I'd felt about June. I had owed it to the mother of my children.

Kirstin closed the door behind her. Her dark hair was short in a chic, spiky style. Her black workout leggings disappeared into fluffy boots she wore most of the year and not just in the winter. With her puffy coat, she looked like she should be on a ski slope instead of photographing birds in Costa Rica.

"Oh, hey. There you are." She pushed her suitcase toward the wall. "Listen, I saw something online and figured I needed to come back early—" Her gaze lifted to behind my shoulder. Her jaw went hard as she looked back at me. "I'm interrupting."

I'd say no, but fuck yes she had interrupted. Since she'd spied June, I crossed to the table and grabbed my shirt. "The girls are with Wren. School got out this week." Which she'd know if she were here.

"Right, the girls mentioned that when I called."

I shrugged into my shirt. When my head poked

through, I found June hovering where I'd just been standing.

"Hi, Kirstin," she said quietly.

"June Bee," Kirstin said flatly. "I saw you were in town. Because my kids' names were being thrown around on social media."

Kirstin only followed artists and other photographer accounts. Either she'd been looking at June-related accounts, or the curiosity about June's private life was pervasive.

If Kirstin could get internet for social media, why didn't she call more?

"They didn't get pictures of the kids," I said gruffly and stuffed my hands in my pockets. June's underwear was at the tips of my fingers. My erection almost made a comeback.

Kirstin lifted her chin. "You two were on a date, and they were where?"

"They were in the bathroom. Is there a reason you suddenly don't trust me to keep our girls safe?"

June held her hands up. "I let my guard down and images made it to the internet. I'm sorry." She hugged herself. "I should, uh, probably go. Let you two talk."

Kirstin gave her a *yeah, you should* look and stepped to the side to clear the doorway.

June pushed her feet into her sandals and disappeared out the door. I had to let her go. I had to stay and talk to Kirstin.

This was supposed to be my night. My fucking weekend. Hell, my two weeks, and my ex-wife had swooped into the country to cockblock me.

Kirstin took her coat off and slammed it onto a hook. "What the *hell*, Rhys?"

Was she upset about the girls' names online or June being in my house? We'd been divorced for four years. "The girls are taken care of, and June and I are two consenting adults."

She rolled her eyes and shook her head. "But *her*? I leave the country and you think it's safe to—"

"It wasn't like that, and you don't know what it's like because you aren't here."

She went rigid, and I gritted my teeth. I'd sworn to myself I would not make her feel bad for pursuing her career. I knew how hard it'd been for her to live in June's shadow. After spending time with June, I could admit how not over her I'd been during my marriage.

"Look, we've had an amicable divorce, and I don't want to ruin it. The girls deserve that."

"You're right." Her demeanor softened and she went to the cupboard to withdraw a glass. "I never thought it was over between you and her anyway."

"It was. It is." At her dubious look, I nodded. "She's not in town for long. I'm single. She's single. Full disclosure—the girls love her."

A sigh dragged her shoulders down. "Of course they do. The great and sparkly June Bee Bailey Kerrigan." She tipped her head back. "You said she's not going to be here long. How are Bethany and Hannah handling that? Or do they think America's Country Sweetheart is going to be their new stepmom?"

"We're not telling them or anyone else. It's no one's business."

She smirked. "Until your ex-wife walked in."

"It's a bit of a mood killer."

Her laugh was faint until her gaze landed on the box. My stomach sank as she crossed to it. Would her improved attitude last after she saw I'd never gotten rid of a thing? She poked through it with her fingertip. "I used to kid myself that you'd burned it all."

"She's a big part of my past, Kirstin."

She jerked her hand out of the box like it burned. "Funny. So am I."

Yet both women were in my house. I glanced at her suitcase. When she was in town, she stayed with me or Wren. There'd been nothing sexual between us since the divorce, but for some reason, having her under the same roof as me now felt wrong.

June might not care. Or she might tuck her muse back into the recesses of her brain. "You can stay here tonight and then you mind going to Wren's?"

She snorted. "I'm actually surprised you're letting me stay tonight after what I walked in on. You sure it's just temporary?" Her question was laced with sarcasm. "You're not tied to Bourbon Canyon like you were when she left town."

"Her life isn't here, and it's too public. I'll always do what's best for Bethany and Hannah."

She hummed a noncommittal noise. That sound said a lot. I could run through it all in my head, replay old arguments, but there was somewhere I had to be.

***

June

How cold of a shower was too cold? I kicked off my sandals and trudged toward my bedroom. Energy zinged through my body. The steady beat between my legs hadn't gone completely away. I'd been *so* close to orgasming.

I veered into the kitchen and dug out a glass. Whipping open a cabinet, I deliberated between the wine my sisters had left and the bourbon. I selected the holiday line from last year and poured enough to cover the bottom. Then I tossed it back and swallowed in one gulp.

"Sorry, Daddy." I would've never talked with him about tonight—too mortifying for a dad-and-daughter conversation—but if I had, he'd have given his blessing for shooting good bourbon.

Leaving the glass on the counter, I went to my bedroom. I turned on the light and stepped out of my skirt. The fabric whispered over my skin and I shuddered. I could still feel the scrape of Rhys's beard along my neck.

I rolled my head back and forth and savored the alcohol warming my belly. Change of plans. The shower would have to wait. I'd have to get myself off, then shower, or I'd never get to sleep.

All I had to do was think about Rhys's head between my legs and I could come. A hard shiver rolled through my body. How could I still be so turned on?

Loud knocking at the front door made me jump. My heart pounded and I spun around in my bedroom. I had on my shirt and bra and that was it. I tugged my skirt back up my legs when banging shook the cabin again.

Where was my phone? There was a shotgun in the closet, bear spray in the cabinet, but I should call a brother. I was nearly defenseless in the cabin and alone.

"June!" Rhys shouted from the other side. "It's me."

I rushed to the door and whipped it open. Rain

pelted the ground behind him, but he only had a few drops on his shirt. "You're here." My obvious statement came out breathless.

"She's staying at the house. Didn't think that'd go over well with you."

"I mean, we're not like a thing . . ." A heavy tug on my heart stole the rest of the words.

"But we have something we didn't get to finish."

"And that's what you're here for?" He'd come to the cabin for me. He could've used Kirstin's arrival to talk himself out of something that could be so epically stupid for each of us.

"I'm here to make sure we finish a whole lot."

My lips parted on a puff. I liked the sound of that.

"Gonna let me in, June Bug?"

I wasn't able to finish my step backward. He charged in and swept me off the floor. Then he kicked the door shut and pinned me between him and the slab of wood.

"Your underwear is still in my pocket."

I yanked my skirt out of the way. Too much damn fabric. "And I'm still wet for you."

He reached between us to open the fly of his jeans.

Okay. We were doing this without removing too many clothes, but we were both impatient.

I needed him inside me.

When he freed himself, he slid the blunt crown of his erection through my soaked pussy and notched himself at my entrance. Then he stopped.

"Fuck," he gritted out. "Protection."

I blinked, rocking against him because I couldn't help myself. I was so close to ecstasy. "Um . . ."

"Fuck." He clasped my hips and held me still. "I was

married, so I'm not used to using any." His voice was haggard.

A small portion of my libido took a step back as curiosity rose. "Like you haven't used condoms for years?" It wasn't like Rhys to throw caution to the wind. His sense of responsibility was his strength as well as his biggest weakness.

"Like I haven't been with anyone in years."

"Oh." Now I was impressed. And pleased. He said he hadn't dated, but I hadn't ruled out hookups.

"But before that, I used it religiously, otherwise I wouldn't have thought of it."

My body was screaming at me to cinch my legs tighter and take him inside me. My logical brain was barely on board to find a solution. "I see. So, um . . . I have an IUD and I've got my checkup routine down since I dated shitheads. But I've never not used protection."

His eyes went hooded. "Never?"

I shook my head. "I never trusted anyone enough. Except you, but I wasn't on birth control in high school. I trust you now."

He rolled his hips. The tip of his cock dragged through my wetness. Then he pushed inside.

I let out a gasp as he entered me in one smooth motion. "Oh god."

He filled me so completely I didn't know where I ended and he began. My clit came alive at the pressure, and when he pulled out and thrust back in, the pressure was enough to propel me right back to the top of my orgasm.

I dug my fingers into his thick hair and held on as he pounded into me. I crept higher and higher, my climax imminent. "I can't believe how fast you can make me come."

He grunted and wound his arms around the inside of my thighs. He widened my legs until I was as open as possible. Everything stretched tighter. Every part of my body that was touching him clamped down harder, and oh god, the steady rub of his abdomen against my clit was pure heaven.

Pleasure expanded outward until I couldn't stand it. My heart might stop. I would implode, then explode. I hit the top of my peak and stayed there, suspended, as he plunged into me over and over.

"Rhys!" The explosion happened. Pure pleasure detonated where we were connected and spread outward. My back slid up and down the wall as I shook through my orgasm. He punched into me one more time before he curled around me, a growl ripping from his throat.

"Fuck, June. Fuck, fuck." His hips made small pumps as we finished coming together.

My chest heaved in time with his as we caught our breath.

"It's never been like that," he rasped.

No, it hadn't. I'd come quicker and more powerfully than I ever had. But what had he meant? Never been like this between us before? Never like this for him at all?

Did it matter? We'd both gotten pleasure. He'd ended his dry spell so I could write songs.

Fair trade?

He tipped his forehead against mine. Our breathing was evening out. The threads of a case of nerves were settling in. He'd basically declared us a thing in front of his ex. He hadn't dispelled the notion, and since she was there and he was here, I doubt he'd lied.

What now?

Did I make us a snack? Were things going to get awkward? There was no curfew. No running off to sleep in our own beds. Cuddling?

He pressed a kiss to the curve of my jaw. "I'm going to fuck you all night long."

CHAPTER EIGHTEEN

Rhys

Warm water pounded against my chest. It could be a thousand degrees and I wouldn't notice. June was on her knees in the shower and my dick was in her mouth. Her lips were stretched from my cock, and *fuuuuck*. What a sight.

I wanted to fuck her again, but we'd decided on a shower before we went to bed and did things that would ensure we needed a shower again.

"June, I'm going to fucking explode." I pressed a hand against the shower wall.

She increased the suction and my eyes rolled back in my head.

"You're a wicked girl, you know that?"

She didn't answer. Instead, she hummed, goddamn *hummed*, when I didn't think I could take it anymore.

My climax crashed into me. Lightning raced down

my spine, drew my balls up tight, and then shot out into her willing mouth. She didn't flinch or pull away.

A shower experience so much different than the ones I'd given myself in the last few years. She didn't let up, sucking and licking. I shook until I thought my knees might give out.

I cupped her face. "You're going to kill me."

She released me with a pop. I slumped against the wall but helped her to her feet. I planted my lips on hers.

She raked her fingertips down my chest. "I didn't kill you," she murmured against my mouth.

"It's a miracle I'm standing." I rinsed us both and shut the water off. She retrieved towels from the other side of the curtain, her rounded ass on display.

I traced my hand over a hip, scattering water droplets from her warm, wet skin. My girls were safe, I wasn't keeping June a secret from my ex, and I had the whole night with June.

She handed me a towel. Her gaze dropped down to my half-hard erection, and she arched a brow.

"It doesn't seem to know the meaning of tired around you," I explained. It'd always been that way with her.

She grinned as she dried off. I did the same, then we hung our towels up and I lifted her again, tossing her over my shoulder, her ass in the air.

Her yelp dissolved into a laugh. "You can't keep doing that."

When we were younger, I'd asked her if she minded that I randomly lifted her. She said it made her feel safe.

Had that changed? "I'll stop if you want."

"No. I just meant that you don't have an eighteen-year-old's indestructible back anymore."

"I'll do more stretches." My body would hold out for the next month.

The image of me sweeping her off her feet in my forties rose in my mind. In my fifties. I'd keep trying in my sixties and seventies and beyond.

The swell of emotion behind my sternum almost made me drop her. Instead, I held her tighter. I didn't even have the next month with her. Two weeks.

In the bedroom, I pulled the covers back and gently lowered her to the mattress. She scooted in and I crawled in behind her.

When we were settled, my arm around her and her cheek against my chest, we were quiet for a few moments.

"It's weird, isn't it?" she finally said. "So familiar but so different."

"Yeah." The truth of her words humbled me. She was June. My June. But we'd lived almost half our lives apart. Our bodies were different. Our personalities had matured and changed. I'd never been a happy-go-lucky kid, but after my dad got sick, a lot of humor had left. I'd gone from worrying about how I could spend my life with June without dragging her down to supporting both me and Wren and getting Dad the care he needed. Sometimes, I felt like I faked the good times with the girls because I was too worried about how they were doing. Were they happy? Was I enough for them? Could I be doing more?

June was still the girl who was always creating tunes and lyrics when she wasn't around one of her guitars. She probably still got rowdy with her sisters too, but there was steel lining her back that hadn't been there before.

"I really am sorry if I caused a rift between you and

Kirstin. You two seem to have a good . . . thing . . . going on."

"Thing?" I asked wryly. "You don't want to call it co-parenting?"

"Doesn't seem to fit your situation."

I stared at the dark ceiling. The rain outside had lightened up. "Any rift between me and Kirstin wasn't caused by you. You were having a meal with a friend and his family."

"Are we friends, Rhys?"

"I'm your muse. Besides, I'm friends with your brothers, but I don't fuck them."

She giggled and poked at my chest. "I know, but I knew it was a possibility and I got complacent. I didn't think about how sitting right next to you would look."

"Don't blame yourself. Kirstin was probably worried because she was so far away. She might be dealing with the guilt that comes with her decision to pursue the career she loves."

"It's really hard to leave important people behind." She traced circles on my stomach with her thumb while the rest of her fingers were splayed across my skin. "It's lonely, and you're almost driven more because you don't want your absence to be for no reason. I can't imagine what it's like with kids."

"A lot of people in town want to hate her."

Her damp hair brushed against my skin as she looked up at me. "You defend her, don't you?"

"She's their mother, and it's a little fucked up that I could've left to go do the same and no one would've batted an eye. I'd get cheered on."

"It is a decision though," she said softly. "You have to

choose between the ones you love and what you love to do. The selfishness bothered me, but I also thought that if I had kids . . . I dunno. That I'd do something differently."

"She didn't want . . ." I chomped on the inside of my cheek. The tendency to tell June everything had resurged with a vengeance. "She had kids because she knew they were important to me. But that doesn't mean she doesn't want the girls," I rushed out. "At some level, she knew she'd have to decide between Montana and her job."

June's soft eyelashes brushed my chest as she blinked. "You're a good dad, you know that?"

"I work hard to be, but why are you saying that?"

"You'll never let the girls know how their mom felt about having kids or how she feels now."

"Yeah." I wanted them to see it was important to follow their dreams. If they didn't want a quiet life in a small town at the base of the mountains, then they didn't have to settle for it. Just because they were growing up in a fairly isolated area didn't mean the world was closed to them.

"It's okay though."

"What is?" Did I want to know?

"To want Kirstin to be more involved when it comes to the girls."

"She's involved."

"Okay."

I frowned at the dark ceiling. Kirstin landed in Bourbon Canyon two or three times a year. Last year, she'd stayed with me . . . once. And she'd stayed with Wren . . . Last year had been a busy year. She'd launched an online store for prints and calendars and other merchandise and she'd needed to be in the field for long stretches of time to get a variety of images.

She left messages and called when she could, which wasn't that often. The girls no longer asked as much as they used to about when their mom would call. They had also quit asking why she didn't call very often.

But fieldwork made it difficult.

"Penny for your thoughts." The outlines she drew on me turned to the familiar shapes of musical notes.

Had I been quiet that long? She must be worried I was upset with her about bringing Kirstin up. "I was wondering if you were going to help with chores in the morning."

She laughed and rolled to her belly. "I think I'd better steer clear of your house until your ex moves out."

I rolled her to her back and stretched out on top of her. Arousal floated through my veins and flowed down to my dick. "Then I'll stay here tomorrow night too." I trailed kisses down her belly. "By the way, you've only had one orgasm. I'm a few behind."

"A few?"

I nudged her legs apart. "I'm not a boy anymore, June Bug."

***

June

My body was deliciously sore when I woke up. I stretched and smiled to myself before the quiet of the cabin sank in. I looked at the other side of the bed. Empty.

Frowning, I sat up. The covers fell down. I was naked. Rhys had proven that he was indeed no longer a boy, and he knew how to use his experience.

Then he'd left.

My breath shortened and my chest rose and fell faster. He'd left me again and he wasn't coming back.

I closed my eyes and sucked in a long breath. He was gone, but we were still in the same town. This wasn't the day I'd left Bourbon Canyon for years.

That day was coming soon enough.

My throat tightened. I would return soon. Maybe before I kicked off my tour. There would be time between interviews and appearances and rehearsals.

Right?

I scrubbed the sleep out of my eyes. What Rhys and I were doing wasn't like before. We weren't committed to each other. We liked having sex together. The same, but different.

I got out of bed and dressed in shorts and a Grand Ole Opry T-shirt. I might've bought one or four when I played there. I twisted my hair up into a bun and shuffled to the bathroom.

Was Rhys having regrets? Did he think my job here was done and he'd go on his merry way? I wasn't feeling too inclined to finish the upbeat song I was working on. I could write one about a girl who'd thought she'd turned the corner with an important guy in her life, only to wake up alone after a long night of hot sex.

Actually, that'd make a pretty good song.

I hummed, trying to catch a melody that would work. Lyrics piled into my brain. *"Just when I thought . . ."*

The front door opened and Rhys walked in. He was holding a basket piled high with muffins in one arm and he juggled two Stanley cups in the other hand. The mouthwatering smell of fresh coffee filled the air.

I stopped in the middle of the living room. I'd have to end the song with the guy returning with muffins and coffee, looking rugged as sin with a trimmed beard, a frayed ball cap, and worn jeans that hugged his powerful legs. "I thought you left."

He gave me a look like I'd accused him of going on a crime spree while I slept. "You're on Nashville time, songbird."

"I am not, and they're only an hour ahead."

"You're not on ranch time, then." The corner of his mouth tipped up. "Did you look at your phone? The one that has the time and the text I sent that said I was running home to do chores and I'd bring back coffee and something to eat?"

My cheeks warmed. "I wanted to wake up to you." If I was blushing before, my face had to be beet red now. I hadn't meant to blurt out something so intimate. "I wanted to wake up and know neither one of us had to leave right away."

His brows drew together, and he went to the counter. I should help him with the coffee but embarrassment kept me rooted in place. He set the muffins down and one of the metal cups. The coffee smell was divine. My stomach grumbled.

He handed me the coffee. "I'm sorry." His apology was weighted with the past. He'd been sorry then too, but he hadn't apologized. "Tomorrow morning, I'll make sure to stay in bed until you wake up." He leaned against the counter, took a long sip from his coffee, and raked his gaze down my body. "But we've gotta go to bed earlier, sleepyhead."

Songbird. Sleepyhead. Smart-ass. June Bug was my favorite, but I preened no matter what he called me.

Songbird would be a good title. *His little songbird wanted to soar . . .*

I thrust a finger in the air. "I've gotta write that down."

I rushed to the end table closest to the door. My guitar was propped on the wall by it. I scribbled the ideas that had gathered in my head. "Okay. Done."

"The muse was in action?"

"The muse got a lot of action." I sauntered toward him. "Stress baking?"

He tossed a muffin at me. "That's not the only reason I bake. I threw them in and put the coffee on and ran outside to get some work done."

"I have a coffeepot here." I tore a piece off the muffin and popped it in my mouth. Sweetness burst over my tongue. Damn, these were good.

"Do you have the locally roasted beans sold at Mountain Perks?" When I shook my head and smirked, he shrugged. "You're picky about bourbon; I'm picky about coffee."

I swallowed and inspected the berries in my muffin. "Are these huckleberries?" Mama would make huckleberry muffins every year, but I'd been traveling so much I never got them fresh. She kept a batch frozen for me, but they weren't as good as straight out of the oven.

"Autumn let her class pick them on her land last year. There was a bumper crop."

I took another bite, chomping off half a muffin. "Then they'll probably be sparse this year. I miss going to pick them."

He handed me another muffin and took one for

himself. We ate and drank coffee admittedly better than mine.

"How was Kirstin?" I set my cup down. *Quit prodding, June!*

But if his ex put her foot down about my presence in their kids' lives, I would be ousted. I would respect her wishes around her kids, but I had no wish to learn that Rhys would side with her. He'd be right to do so, but also . . .

Didn't he see that he was letting all the responsibility for his ex's happiness fall on him? He'd done the same for Wren. The ranch had stressed his stepmom out, so he'd acquiesced and sold without even discussing alternate plans first.

Just like he'd left me sleeping on the cabin floor with only a note to show for five years together.

"She was still sleeping," he said. "It's one reason why I went so early." He put his Stanley next to mine.

"What if she doesn't—" I took a fortifying inhale. "What if she doesn't want you and me to be a thing, even if it's only for two weeks?"

"She doesn't run this part of my life." His resolute tone helped ease my tension. "*This* isn't affecting the kids, so she has no say."

Were the kids the excuse he hid behind?

It wasn't my business. Time for a subject change. I lifted my chin toward the coffee mugs. "I didn't picture you as a Stanley guy."

"The girls begged for them for Christmas but Wren got them each one before Thanksgiving. They used them for two weeks and then forgot all about them." He shrugged. "They keep my coffee hot as fuck all day." He crowded me against the island. "I've gotta get back to work."

"No rest for the rancher?" I twined my arms around his neck. The echoes of the hurt from when I was eighteen faded away. I had him in this moment. We had two weeks to wake up together.

"I've got a couple more minutes."

I batted my eyelashes. "Whatever are we going to do with them?"

He tugged my shorts down. "I have some ideas."

CHAPTER NINETEEN

June

I pulled up to Autumn's house. She and Gideon lived in town, but they were cleaning out her place now that renovations had started on the house that was on Gideon's land. Now their land.

She opened the front door and waved to me. Her red hair was piled on top of her head. Like me, she wore linen shorts and a loose, short-sleeved shirt. Where I wore pinks and white, she preferred browns and more neutral tones.

I gave her a quick hug after I stepped inside. "Have you started sorting yet?"

"Yeah, but then Gideon stopped home on the way to another auction with his dad. I didn't get that much boxed."

"More farm equipment?"

The farm and ranch where Gideon had grown up hadn't been in business for years. His dad, Hank, had leased out pastures before he'd sold. My brothers had bought the place, much to Gideon's consternation, but then if my family hadn't gone through with the sale, Gideon and Autumn might not be together.

"Uh, bulls."

"Your casino CEO isn't just a farmer, he's going to ranch too?"

Her lips curved. "Not all the land is good for farming."

"And he crunched the numbers and figured out how to profit and with just how many head of cattle?"

She tipped her head toward the kitchen table. "You want to see his notes? He's quizzed Hank for hours about the years he was gone, market prices, issues with the land, the weather, and costs. I wish I was joking, but I think Hank had to go to an extra AA meeting for a few weeks after."

"Your husband can be intense." I hadn't met him very much, but he reminded me of Myles. Both guys were corporate gods, commanding a staff while keeping to themselves. Their air of authority was catnip to my sisters.

Come to think of it . . . Rhys had the same authoritative persona.

Gah, was I just as bad?

"I think it dredged up all the things Hank couldn't handle," Autumn said as she led me to the spare room. "I told Gideon to reiterate he was gathering data, not making a case for the prosecution. He finally approached his dad a different way that didn't sound like an interrogation."

"Only you like it when Gideon interrogates you."

She sat on an office chair and kicked her feet up on

an already full box. Her expression was unrepentant. "I like it a lot." She folded her arms across her chest. "The girls were talking at school about how they get to spend the next couple of weeks with their grandma. Does that mean Rhys is home alone?"

"Nosy much?"

"Who called me in the middle of the workday to ask about Gideon?"

Fair. My days and nights were mixed up when I was on tour. I leaned against the doorframe. Rhys had left the cabin an hour ago after fucking me in the kitchen. I'd already come twice and it wasn't even noon. I wasn't counting the orgasms after midnight either.

I ran the ends of my hair through my fingers. A black hair tie was around my wrist, but I'd waited to put it up. It'd been kind of nice not to have stage-ready hair at all times. So what if the ends frayed a little? I could trim it before I returned to Nashville.

Autumn was fishing for information on Rhys. I hadn't been around my sisters during my relationships, not since I'd left Bourbon Canyon.

What Rhys and I were doing wasn't a relationship, but I wanted to sort out my thoughts. If Autumn, Summer, or Wynter thought I was making an epic mistake, maybe I should hear it. "We're messing around."

She slammed her feet to the floor and sat up straight. "Shut. Up." Her wide eyes filled with disbelief.

I held my hands up. "It's just messing around. I had like writer's block, then he kissed me a couple of times and the songs started coming. I'm supposed to finish this album by the end of the month, produce it and release it in a month, then start touring. When I came here, I had almost nothing."

"Then he kissed you," she said dryly.

"It got me out of my head. He's agreed to be my muse."

"Uh-huh."

I scowled at her and picked a spot to sit by a half-empty bookshelf. I leaned an elbow on a box labeled *books*. "We're also doing everything we couldn't do then, you know?"

She gave her head a slight shake, confusion filling her green eyes.

"Having sex without worrying about getting busted."

A laugh barked out of her. "You think Mama and Daddy actually bought that you two were abstaining?"

"No, but they didn't make it easy."

"True. I think they liked cockblocking you two as much as possible."

"Our brothers sure did. Remember when they took the snowmobiles to the cabin?" I narrowed my eyes. "Don't think I don't know that was you."

She gasped. "I did not mean to tell them. I said *you* might be at that cabin. I forgot you'd also said you had plans with Rhys."

They'd only interrupted a heavy make-out session. We'd been fifteen and still exploring. The excitement of those times was reminiscent of now. Getting caught nowadays had a lot more levels to it though. "Speaking of getting busted . . . Kirstin came home."

"She's in town?"

"She was at the house. She walked in when . . ." I couldn't finish. The embarrassment was high, but that moment had been so personal. An explosive reconnection. A moment that had waited for fifteen years, and then boom, ex-wife worried I was going to get her kids' images splashed over the internet.

"Oh my god."

"Yeah. He let her stay there and came to the cabin. She's going to be at Wren's for however long she's in town."

"The plot thickens."

"Not really." At her sidelong glance, I shrugged. "It's not serious between us. Kirstin flew home worried my fame was going to drag the girls in front of the camera."

"Did she come home for the girls—or for Rhys?"

"It sounds over between them, but I just hear Rhys's version, which isn't terrible. It was like an echo of us, only they had kids and had to divorce before she left."

"Those are pretty major differences."

"I don't know what to think." Other than I wanted my time with Rhys. I wanted to have sex with him. To store up the way he made me feel before I went back to my career. "We don't want anyone knowing. The girls can't think I'm more than a friend."

"Well . . . they're young. But that picture of you two that came across my feed looked pretty cozy."

"It's your fault for ditching me with him."

Her smile was unrepentant. "Why don't you invite him out next weekend?"

I ran through my brain for what the significance of next weekend was.

Autumn rolled her eyes. "We're working cattle. Tate's doing one of the days on a weekend so we can all help. It's all hands on deck. I, for one, am not missing Gideon on a horse and working cattle."

"I heard you did before."

"I saw him after." Her face got all dreamy, and if I had looked in a mirror when Rhys had entered the cabin with muffins and coffee, I'd have had the same expression.

"I made Wynter take pictures. She and Myles are coming home for that, by the way. Summer's coming because Jonah said he'd give it a shot. He's going to help drive and deliver meals."

Jonah still had a limp from the accident he'd been in when he was younger. According to Summer, he could no longer ride horseback. Walking on uneven ground could be hazardous for him, but there was plenty to do on cattle-working weekends.

"I should send Ruby to take some photos to post for me. Unless she wants to come?"

"She'd either love to or get scared away."

From our online interactions, Ruby seemed like a mix of timid and adventurous. "Any big-sister advice?"

Autumn's expression turned solemn. "You have to keep it at the front of your mind that you're going to walk away again, and he's not going to follow."

Her words were a quick stab to the heart. "I did it before."

"But you thought he'd be coming later. You thought that when his dad got better, he'd run to you."

I swallowed hard. His dad hadn't gotten better. Rhys hadn't run to me. He'd run me off.

"He's already let you go twice, Junie," Autumn said softly. "Unless you're willing to give up everything to be here, all those homes you collected, and your touring, there's going to be a third time."

Twice. She was counting when I had returned for the funeral.

My throat was growing thick. I had come to help pack and load boxes. Instead, she was taking a red pen and circling my insecurities, highlighting them just in case I missed one. "I don't collect homes."

"What about that flat in London?"

I licked my dry lips. "I was only looking." A whole lot of people didn't have one home, but I was looking at a flat for the month I'd be playing in Europe. "What if I want to give it all up?"

"Do you?"

The answer almost burst out of me, but I caught it and mulled her question over. "No. I love performing. I want this." I hugged my knees to myself. "At the same time, it's . . . lonely. I'm tired of the hustle. What if I hit my peak just as my muscles give out?"

"You aren't thinking of quitting for a guy, are you?"

I slid my gaze away. "No."

Autumn got down on the floor with me. "June, you never got over Rhys— Don't give me that look. It was obvious."

It was not. "How?"

"The obvious have names—Clinton, Toby, Finn. You went with guys who were easy on the eyes, convenient, the ones that didn't exude settle-down energy."

I worried my lower lip. I could try to argue that Lucy had used the idea of Finn being ready for commitment to snag me, but Autumn had said settle-down energy. Finn did not have that.

"And Rhys got married." She softened her tone. "He had kids. You and I both can guess how much his dad's ranch sold for and what his cut was. He can go anywhere, but he's not. He bought a place and made a home. Again, in Bourbon Canyon."

I hugged my legs tighter with each point she made. "When I was home for his dad's funeral, he said we were high school stuff."

She shrugged. "You two are attracted to each other, but now you're questioning what you've worked fifteen years for. You've done most of it while not waiting for him. So why now?"

"I want it all." I was at a crossroads. In one direction, I had to sacrifice everything I'd worked for to have the man of my dreams. In the other direction, I'd have to leave my heart behind and forever write songs about missing him.

Autumn cocked her head to study me. "Can you imagine an entire stadium of thirty thousand people cheering?"

A grin tugged at my lips. "I've heard. Just not for me."

"You're so close. If you decide not to walk this path, we'll all support you. But I think you know what you're going to do and you just wish it was different this time."

Nailed it. On the stage, I could inspire others. I could help them *feel*. If I stayed behind, if Rhys and I did try to work on us, what example would I set? For myself. For my future kids. For my young and impressionable fans.

I puffed a lock of hair out of my face. "When did you get so wise?"

"Maybe after you butted into my pity party and made me tell you all about Gideon."

"It's the middle kid inside of us."

She giggled. "The Baileys have a lot of middle kids." A moment of silence passed between us. "Whatever you decide, make sure it's for you."

That was the problem. The right decision for me shouldn't hurt so bad.

Rhys

Bethany ran out to greet me as soon as I pulled up in front of Wren's house. "Daddy! Did you see Mom's here?"

I swooped her up in a hug. "I sure did." Kirstin had left before I'd gotten home after my coffee-and-sex break with June. I hadn't planned to stop at Wren's tonight, but Kirstin's presence changed things and possibly confused the kids.

Hannah streaked out the door next. Bethany wiggled out of my hold so I could hug Hannah.

"She brought me a stuffed macaw," Hannah said. "I named it Mac."

Bethany hopped up and down. "And she got towels with macaws on them and candy!"

"Nice." They towed me into the house, telling me about the pancakes they'd made with Wren this morning.

Wren and Kirstin were in the kitchen. Wren gave me a knowing and concerned smile. Kirstin had her arms crossed, but her expression wasn't hostile.

I leaned against the counter while the girls fluttered around the kitchen, showing me the souvenirs their mother had gotten them and relaying the stories she'd told them already this morning.

"You know how big those birds are, Dad?" Bethany

held her hands farther apart than I thought any macaw would be. "She showed us pictures. And we performed for her. Grandma sang instead of Junie."

"It was a very good performance," Kirstin said. She crossed one leg over the other. Her heel was bobbing.

Shit.

Wren nodded and the girls beamed. An awkward silence fell between all of us.

"Girls," Wren said gently, adding a dash of enthusiasm. She gracefully rose from her chair. "Can you come outside with me? I still have some fencing to put up around my garden to keep those bunnies out."

Once they were outside, Kirstin's smile dipped. "Lessons?"

"They wanted to surprise you."

"What happened to your ban on music?"

"I never banned it." And she knew it.

"You never encouraged it."

"Because I was afraid you'd think I was holding on to June by encouraging them to learn an instrument." My temples throbbed. I knew exactly why I'd made the decisions I had, but I was tired of feeling like the bad guy because of them. "They wanted to surprise you, and I didn't want the headache. I'm sorry."

"Headache." She tsked. "We're not married anymore. You're worried I'd be jealous."

"You used to be."

"Yes. Any wife would've been."

The truth of what she said sat heavy on my shoulders. "I know you put up with a lot. I never meant to make you feel like I didn't love you—"

"I know you did, in your way."

What'd that mean? "I just need to know if you're going to have an issue with me and June now."

She studied me for a moment, then ruffled her short hair off her face. "I know the girls are your priority. Behind them is your ranch." She didn't make it sound like a good thing. "And I know June can't derail that. Just like I couldn't."

"Kirstin." Were we going to rehash arguments from our divorce?

She held up her hands. "I'm just saying. June isn't my business unless the girls think she's going to be a part of their lives forever and have their hearts broken when she leaves."

Wouldn't she have to be in the country to know if June's absence affected the girls? I pushed that question out of my head. I was being unfair.

"Otherwise, I'm an adult, Rhys. I can handle any old feelings she brings up."

I was an adult, and most days, I couldn't face the emotions related to June. "Appreciate it."

"I'm dating too, you know."

Surprise rocked me back on my heels. "Oh." Was I upset? Happy for her? Relieved that we were both navigating these nonrelationship waters? "How's it going?"

"Awkward." She huffed out a laugh. "Fleeting. I travel too much. The last one didn't like that I'm going to Brazil in a month."

Surprise shot through me. "Brazil?"

"I can shoot the Spix's macaw. It was an endangered species, but conservation efforts have reintroduced dozens into the wild. My company is doing an awareness campaign. Anyway, I'm leaving next week."

She'd been in Costa Rica, she had another opportunity to photograph a rare macaw, and she was traveling internationally again in a month. But she'd returned worried about the girls because of June? Disappointment soured the taste in my mouth. If that picture hadn't circulated, would Kirstin have ever visited the kids between international trips? "Is that why you came home?"

A flicker of guilt crossed her expression, but she quashed it and lifted her chin. "I was worried about the kids."

Then why didn't she call more? The headache was making a return. Pursuing this conversation wouldn't help. "What if you meet some photographer guy who has a thing for colorful birds?"

Her mouth curved into a smile and what looked like relief lit her blue eyes. "I might have to lock it down. What about you? What happens when you meet some woman who has young kids and no wish to move out of Bourbon Canyon?"

I had already met her. Our kids carpooled and we planned playdates for the girls. But Annette didn't interest me. She wasn't an amber-eyed songbird with the voice of an angel who could speak for brokenhearted women everywhere.

Her eyes widened. "Did I just describe someone?" She let out a scandalized gasp. "I did—and you're not interested. Oh, Rhys." She rose and went to the door. Shoving her feet into her hiking boots, she shook her head. "When we met, you made me feel like a queen. I could tell you were cautious. I could tell you'd had your heart broken, and eventually, I realized your heart was never really mine."

"Kirstin—"

She held her hand up. "But you went through the motions. You treated me like I was your priority. And you kept it up . . . right until I didn't want to live in Bourbon Canyon anymore. I don't know what hold the dirt in this part of Montana has on you, but it's powerful."

We had argued around this subject before, but she'd never been so direct. "Dad was sick—"

"Then it was Wren. You couldn't leave her. But here's the thing . . . I don't think it would've mattered. I think there's something keeping you here and I don't think it's honor or obligation. I think you're scared, Rhys. But you never opened up to me. I used to believe June knew the reason, but I don't know anymore. It's fucked up, but that makes me feel better. Because it was never me. It wasn't even June." She barked a resentful laugh. "You know the real reason I rushed home? I had this weird feeling I'd get pushed out altogether for June because you'd think it was best for the girls." With that, she pushed out of the door, presumably to join the kids and Wren outside.

CHAPTER TWENTY

June

The birds chirped obnoxiously outside. I adored not hearing traffic outside my window, but the birds and frogs were extra loud in the country. Still, the pleasure of waking up to a warm, strong body behind me was worth it. Even in an empty bed, I'd take wildlife sounds any day of the week.

A strong arm banded around me. I'd gone to sleep in Rhys's arms. The sex had been great as always, but he'd been quiet. Introspective. I'd asked him what was on his mind, but he'd said it was the short night of sleep he'd gotten thanks to the sex.

Didn't he realize I could still tell when he wasn't saying everything? I rarely got the sense he wasn't being transparent, but there were times I *knew*. Usually, it related to his real feelings regarding his dad and especially when he discussed his mom. I usually got the glossed-over version, like he was making his time with her seem better than it had been.

He let out a gentle groan and buried his nose in my neck.

I wiggled my ass against him. "Morning."

He slipped his hand down my belly. All I had on was a nightshirt. No underwear. Mostly for this situation, but I was dying to pry. Why had he been stuck in his head last night? Why wouldn't he talk to me?

Because we weren't in a relationship. We fucked around. This was fucking around. So as he slipped his hand lower, I stuffed all my questions to the back of my mind and widened my legs.

His strong fingers found my clit and an appreciative groan left him. "You're wet for me."

"Mmm." I kept my eyes closed and rode his fingers. This was what I had wanted to experience. A lazy morning of lovemaking. He'd rush off to do chores soon enough, but I was the first thing on his mind. I was the one he reached for as soon as he woke. No schedule came first. No performance. No urgency to return messages, calls, or DMs in every single social media plat-form we could be on.

I'd never had that, yet I'd always known I would've had it with Rhys.

"*Damn*, June." He hitched my leg higher with one of his and wedged his erection at the juncture of my thighs.

I ground into him and he slipped inside.

Nothing but our pants and moans filled the air. Like last night, he was quieter.

The mattress rocked. The wooden headboard banged against the wall. The springs squeaked. He pounded away, thrusting in and out with ruthless precision. His fingertip rested on my clit and the movement alone was enough to stroke me toward my peak.

"Rhys," I said on a long moan. I coasted toward the top and then rolled over. Pleasure coursed through me, reaching a crescendo. I rode the wave, milking him as long as possible.

"Let it all go. Take everything I've got." He punched into me once, twice more, then stiffened. His hot release filled me and I clenched around him as my orgasm continued to ripple through me.

We collapsed on our sides and he pulled out of me. He pressed his forehead against my back, his breathing heating my skin. Did he realize how hard his hand was gripping my hip? The wetness from my climax was sticky between his fingers and me. We'd come together hard and fast, but even in this, he was subdued. Quiet.

A few moments of silence passed before I wiggled out of his hold to the edge of the bed. I rose. The cooler air of the morning wafted over my heated legs. I yanked my nightshirt over my head and tossed it on my pillow.

His hot gaze dipped to my bare breasts, appreciation shining in his dark-blue gaze.

I stole one full-bodied glance at him. His big body was sprawled with his legs cocked apart. Dark hair scattered over his chest and trailed down before dusting over his legs. Heavy ball sack. His erection was growing again. Every inch of this man was desirable.

But I didn't just want his body. Like it or not, I didn't want to just be a sex object to him. We had a connection that couldn't be defined as exes or friends, and lovers was too weak. There was more between us than our hormones.

I squared my shoulders, jutting my breasts up. My

nipples were peaked and the desire from earlier hadn't completely gone away, like his erection. The move drew his gaze.

"I'm going to take a shower," I announced. "Maybe when I come out, you'll be ready to actually open up to me a little. I don't like feeling used."

His brows dropped down, his gaze growing troubled. I left the bedroom and went into the bathroom.

My heart was racing. I didn't want this time between us to end. We had almost the full two weeks before the girls were back with him. Then what little he was willing to risk until I left after the fundraiser.

I don't like feeling used? Where had that come from? Rhys would never use me, and it was up to him who he talked to and what he said. Instead, I'd guilted him into staying the night and then acted like I wouldn't put out again if he didn't bare his soul.

Dammit.

I flipped on the water and waited for it to warm up. When I stepped under it, I tipped my head back. The weight of my wet hair pulled at my scalp. I closed my eyes. I'd messed up. When I was done, I would request that he forget I'd said anything.

The bathroom door cracked open. I opened my eyes and tracked his shadow on the other side of the curtain. He stopped at the sink, riffled through his toiletry bag, and started brushing his teeth.

"I'm sorry," I said, jerking my gaze off him. I smacked the bodywash bottle against my hand to squirt some out. "You are under no obligation to talk to me. I guess . . . it's just hard, you know. I can tell when you're in your head, and I want to be in there with you, but I don't have a claim to that space." I quickly soaped up and rinsed off.

He clicked his toothbrush a few times on the sink.

My nerves crawled under my skin. "Even if we were, like, a *thing*, I wouldn't have a claim to your thoughts." When had ceaseless chatter become a habit? "I'm not withholding sex or anything. That'd be a dick move. We talked about what we're doing and you've been honest. I just wanted you to know that."

The shower curtain flapped open. A naked and very aroused Rhys stood in the opening, his erection straining toward me.

I wrung my wet hair out despite the shower spray staying on me.

"If I talk to you, will you let me in to lick that pretty pink pussy of yours?"

A shot of lust spiked in my veins. "You can do that without opening up to me."

He crowded into the tub and didn't flinch when the shower spray hit the side of his body. My back hit the cool wall.

I traced the drops of water sliding down his face into his damp beard, then ran my finger down the scar cutting through his top lip.

"How about we both open up?" He nudged my legs apart before lowering himself to his knees.

I let my head thump against the wall as he spread me with his thumb and licked his tongue through my folds. "Deal."

•

Rhys

. . .

The smell of eggs and sausage filled the air. June was at the sink, rinsing off fruit for breakfast. I was horribly late for the duties waiting for me at home, but I'd fed them all a little extra last night. The food had probably been gone fifteen minutes after I'd left, but this morning had been worth it.

"Everyone's coming to work cattle next weekend," June said. "My sisters and all their spouses are joining. You and the girls should come."

I rolled up the sleeves of my flannel. "What would that make me?"

"A family friend who can call in a favor from any one of my siblings to help work his own cattle?"

"That's a powerful deal." I went to the skillet and moved around the fluffy eggs and sausage. My stomach rumbled.

I don't like feeling used.

Those words had hit me hard. We had an arrangement to prevent her from getting hurt, but that was something I seemed good at doing. Leaving her bed, telling her we were just some high school stuff, and making her feel unwelcome in my house that first day after she had arrived.

My ex's words had stayed with me, which wasn't unexpected. But I hadn't anticipated the way they'd burrow into my brain. Had I thought some part of this situation with June would manifest into a real future? I'd known what we were getting into. So had she.

But sometimes I wondered . . .

"Kirstin and I talked yesterday." I took the pan off the stove and flicked the knob to off.

She finished, shaking the water off the strawberries and set them on the counter. "Oh?"

I gently spun her around to face me. "We agreed that seeing each other with other people is going to be a little awkward, but she's dating too." The next point had been sitting on my mind too. "She also mentioned she was between assignments. She didn't come home only because she was worried the girls had been exposed. And she thinks I'm too scared to leave Bourbon Canyon."

"Oh." June blinked and shook her head like she was having trouble processing what I'd said. She frowned. "She was on her way to Montana anyway?"

"Who knows. She might've been planning to go somewhere else and rerouted to Bourbon Canyon. She might've bumped up her plans." I didn't tell June about Kirstin's last comment, that she thought I'd cut her out of the kids' life if I thought it best. Did I want my ex to be more attentive? Of course. But I wasn't scaring her off of being with the girls, was I?

June leaned against the counter across from me and crossed her ankles. "And the fear? Why does she say that? You have people to take care of."

"All I ever want to do is the right thing by the people I love." As soon as the words left my mouth, I froze. I couldn't take them back. I'd never fallen out of love with June.

June's expression softened. "I know you do. It seems we both had hard talks with people close to us."

"Which sister? Or was it Mae?"

"Mama's already had her turn." She pushed her hair back. "I might've mentioned to Autumn that I wasn't sure if I wanted the next step. The stress of the album flopping. The hectic touring. I just don't know if that's what I want."

It was. Without a doubt, June was made for performing. Her songs resonated with too many people. She was good on the stage. A natural.

I closed the few feet of distance between us. "You deserve it all."

Her plump lower lip puffed out. "I don't know if I want it all anymore." She closed her eyes and shook her head. "I'm sorry. We're not talking about me."

"Yes, we are. You do deserve it. Just like that little girl you used to be deserved a warm home and a roof over her head when it was storming out. Just like she deserved to be heard when she was terrified in that car wreck."

"My parents tried—"

I put my finger on her lips. She licked my fingertip and lust was quick to pool in my groin. "You keep doing that, we're going to have a repeat of the shower."

"Threats aren't supposed to sound like incentives."

I smiled and caged her against the counter. "You deserve to be successful. You're working for it and you're so damn talented. Holding back would be like . . . trapping a butterfly under a glass for eternity."

Her eyes went liquid. "You always made me feel special."

"Not always." Our run-in at the funeral haunted me, but not nearly as much as her giving up ten yards before the finish line.

"The funeral was an emotional time for you," she said, reading part of my expression. "I almost didn't go."

"I'm glad you did." People here would've held it against her otherwise. My high school sweetheart blowing off my father's death would have dimmed the admiration and protection of the people who knew both of us.

"Me too." Her gaze flickered with indecision and she took a breath before she spoke again. "I thought of staying then, you know. Of never going back, but the trip . . . uh . . . reaffirmed the path I was on."

After I'd told her she'd wasted a plane ticket if she'd thought I was waiting for her. Saying the words had been a knife twist to the goddamn gut, but necessary. I'd seen the indecision in her eyes, the homesickness, and the draw between us had still been there. It'd always be there. I hadn't been strong enough to say no to her if she came to me, if we rekindled what we'd had.

"Good. You needed to stay on that path."

And I would be the man she needed again. When it came time for her to go, I'd tell her that we were over, and I'd make sure she heard me this time.

CHAPTER TWENTY-ONE

Rhys

A horse snuffled as it pulled up next to mine. Teller was astride a mare, the brim of his beige cowboy hat pulled down low. We probably looked like we were having a *who wore it best* competition with our jeans and flannel shirts. Tate was wearing something similar, but Tenor had on a gray long-sleeved shirt. The Foster guys wore the same, but only one of them had a vest. The guys teased Cruz for all the snacks he kept in his pockets.

I had loaded my quarter horse, Butterball, into my trailer this morning and met everyone at Mae's place. No way was I riding with June and fueling speculation. I was a dad with no kids for a couple of weeks and I had time to help out. That was all.

"I was surprised to see you pull up with an empty truck," Teller said.

Empty? I had the trailer with Butterball. "Oh, the girls? June told me they were invited, but it's their time with their grandma. And Kirstin's staying with them too."

He gave me a sidelong look. The horses walked next to each other, their tails swishing. We were meeting Jonah with the horse trailer by the gate. He'd already taken June and Autumn back to their mom's. Summer had stayed behind since she was pregnant and Wynter had joined her so she could help with the kids and the meal. The cattle were all in their respective pasture, and when we returned, Mae had promised us a feast.

"You and June seem to be getting along well," Tate said from my other side.

"We've made amends," I agreed.

His dark gaze glittered. "She didn't have anything to make amends for."

Instead of getting upset, I laughed. Ever since I'd met her, June's brothers had tried to intimidate me when it came to their sister. "True. I was an ass at the funeral."

Tate grunted.

Ahead of us, Tenor was flanked by the three Foster brothers. Had Myles faced the same cold reception when he'd returned to Bourbon Canyon? His brothers had been welcomed in like family. They *were* family now.

I was the outsider. I wasn't a surrogate Bailey, and I wasn't married to a Kerrigan. June wasn't mine.

"Nice to have you moving cattle with us again," Teller said.

"I don't remember it being such a strategic process." The Baileys had a lot of land, but several stretches of fence had been added. Tate had been precise about which cattle went to which pasture, where salt blocks were set in specific locations, and he'd stopped to take pictures of the grasses and shrubbery.

"Dad tried to do right by the land," Teller said, his hands resting on his saddle horn with his reins loose in his grip. "But Tate's leveled it up. Put the stick in his ass to good use."

Tate aimed a glare across me. "I use best grazing practices. We've separated the pastures as best we can when it comes to water and vegetation. I'm anal about salt blocks"—another hard look from Tate to Teller—"because it gets the cattle to move around, spreading the grazing over the pasture—and their manure."

"We've cut back on our hay needs," Teller added. "The pastures have time to regenerate, and in drought years we don't have to supplement as much as before. But anyway, back to you and June."

I bristled. "What about us?"

"I can't ask around her or she'd kill me, but what's going on? I've seen your pickup at her cabin all week."

I gaped at him. "How?"

He smirked and traded a gotcha grin with Tate.

"There was the time I was there," Teller answered. "You just confirmed the rest."

Shit. "She's needed help with . . ."

Tate barked out a laugh that sent Butterball's ears swiveling. "Is that what they're calling it these days?"

"Her songs—"

"We didn't believe your bullshit stories then," Teller cut in. "And we're not buying them now."

I glowered at the back of the riders in front of us, thankfully too far ahead to hear our conversation. "It's just until she leaves. I'm not looking for anything serious and neither is she."

"June's always looking for something serious," Tate

grumbled. "It's why she picks those shit sticks for boyfriends."

If she hadn't told them about her manager, then I wasn't going to. "I'm not a shit stick."

Teller sucked his teeth. "You will be if you break her heart."

Again, I wasn't intimidated. I chuckled. "Have you thought up more threats in the years since she's been gone?"

"Definitely thought of more since the first day I busted you at the cabin with her." Teller lifted his chin toward Tate. "They thought they looked so innocent."

Aw, hell. "Yeah, I did."

Tate snickered. "I thought Dad was going to give himself an aneurysm when he couldn't catch them."

We crested a hill. The pickup with the gooseneck was visible. Jonah leaned against the front of the pickup, his glittering gaze on us. Since he and Summer had gotten together, the guy had cleaned up. He hadn't been dirty before, just rumpled. His beard was a lot shorter, his hair trimmed, and he no longer wore an expression that said *leave me the fuck alone*. And I saw him more often. From what I'd heard the Baileys say, this was one of the first times he'd helped move cattle since the accident.

I glanced at all the brothers. "I hope the girls are all up in your love lives. I know Tate already got the Kerrigan treatment."

Tate grunted again, but a smile played along his lips. "They got in my business all right."

Teller snorted. "Tate has two more kids to show how much in his business they got."

"You were in on it too, Teller," Tate said.

"Yup," Teller replied.

I grinned to myself. It used to be like this. Back then, I would think about how lucky my kids would be. They'd grow up in a big, vibrant family. People would surround them with love and excitement. They'd never feel like a burden. No one would tell them they were the reason for their parents' failures.

But now it was up to just me and Wren. Kirstin's absence made the girls question their worth, but so far, we were making it work. And we would keep making it work as long as I stuck to my plans.

June

When was the last time I'd had this much fun?

Probably not since the last time I'd been with my family, which meant not since I'd been in Montana last.

Mama and my siblings, and Daddy before he'd died, had come to performances over the years, but they had their lives and I had mine. We did little more than meet for a meal.

There'd been nothing like this. Sitting around a firepit. Tate and Scarlett sat side by side, the armrests of their camp chairs nearly overlapping. Tenor sat on a square straw bale. Teller perched on a bale too, but he couldn't leave the fire alone, adding sticks and moving logs around.

Gideon was in a camp chair by Mama. He had his legs stretched out with his boots crossed at the ankle. Autumn was in his lap. I'd barely recognized him when he'd shown up dressed like my brothers, a cowboy hat stuffed low on his head and scruff all over his jaw. No wonder Autumn glowed like she had a Roman candle inside her.

Summer and Jonah were sitting closest to Teller. She wasn't on his lap, but her head was on his shoulder and their hands were entwined.

Kids played in the yard, intermittently running to the picnic table to get a marshmallow. One of the adults would help them roast a marshmallow until eventually my oldest nephew, Chance, took over helping them. He was very serious about his s'mores. The kid reminded me more of his dad every day.

I'd laughed more today than any time over the last year. My brothers cracked jokes. Myles and Jonah had loosened up, which sure was something. I'd been back for their weddings, and the guys had been ecstatic on those days, but they'd never shaken their underlying solemnness.

Only tonight, Myles had been out on horseback all day, he was with his wife and daughter, and he was surrounded by his brothers and in-laws—and all of us in-laws had been his foster family at one time.

As for Lane and Cruz, when they'd first started working for Mama, they'd been slightly older than me when I'd left home and they had the immaturity to show for it. But under Mama's care and my brothers' tutelage —and with my sisters to keep them in a straight line— they'd flourished. Both brothers had Myles's serious nature, but tonight they were as relaxed as the rest of us.

Mama sat on my side. Wynter and Myles's daughter, Elsa, was asleep on her chest. Rhys was sitting on the other side of me. Lane had been peppering him about his ranch and the animals he grew. The guys marveled over Rhys running a one-man operation compared to the comprehensive Bailey ranch.

Lane leaned forward, looking past Rhys to me. "You gonna join us this week?" He feathered his shaggy dark hair out of his face.

Tate planned to continue moving cattle. He usually kept the weekends free, but today had been an exception. We'd had an impromptu family reunion.

"I'll have to start charging my brothers if I do," I said in a snotty tone, a grin pulling at my lips. "And they can't afford me."

"Wanna try that again?" Tate said from across the fire. "Tell me who to make the check out to."

I laughed.

"Equal pay for all of us," Cruz said. "Or else I'll sing."

"No one wants that," Lane said.

"You don't sound bad," Mama said, rocking slowly. Tate had gotten her a special camp chair just so she could rock grandbabies while we hung around outside. "I look forward to hearing your shower performances when I'm working in the kitchen."

A genuine flush crept up Cruz's face, and Lane snickered. Mama shot him a censuring look.

Myles barked out a laugh that earned him a hard stare from Mama and his brothers.

Rhys's phone buzzed. He took a look at the screen and hopped out of his chair. "Excuse me."

I peeked over my shoulder, shamelessly stealing a glimpse of his firm ass as he stalked away. When I turned back to the fire, everyone was smirking at me.

"What?" I hissed.

"Missing your boyfriend already?" Teller asked.

I sat on my hands or I'd flip him off in front of our mother and there wasn't an age I felt safe doing that. "You're not very subtle."

"I don't need to be." His grin sent a whisper of warning over my skin.

Did he know?

The question must've been in my eyes because he nodded.

Brothers sucked.

"What am I missing?" Cruz poked a thumb over his shoulder. "You and him a thing?"

"No."

Summer sat forward. "Haven't you heard the stories?"

Cruz and Lane exchanged a look and shook their head.

"Even I've heard the stories," Myles said. He glanced at Gideon. "You're from here, so you probably saw them in real time."

Gideon's eyes sparkled. Autumn's back was to him, but he must sense how her eyes were twinkling. "I moved away probably about when Rhys came to live in Bourbon Canyon."

"Right." Tenor nodded. "I forget he didn't live here until he was like, what?"

"Twelve," I answered for Rhys.

Tenor narrowed his eyes at my tone but nodded. "Twelve, yeah. Because one day, you came home telling me about this new kid in school."

Wynter straightened on Myles's lap. "Little did we know that she'd never quit talking about him."

This time, I scratched the side of my face opposite Mama with my middle finger.

Wynter sweetened her smile. Her gaze lifted over my shoulder. "We're talking about you. More like we're talking about how much she used to talk about you."

Rhys stopped behind me. "Wren would probably make the same claim." He slid into his seat.

"We were reminiscing with Rhys today," Teller said.

Cold irritation washed through my veins. I loved my brother, but he could be a dick. "I certainly hope you showed Rhys the proper Bailey hospitality and didn't pester him."

"Pester him?" Teller had the audacity to look scandalized. "I just happened to mention that I've been seeing his truck at the cabin a lot."

All eyes were on me. Lane pressed his fist against his mouth, trying not to laugh.

Rhys scratched at his jaw. "I forgot how ruthless you guys are."

All my brothers grinned.

Gideon glanced at Myles. "What's it like not getting run right off?"

Autumn patted his arm. "They couldn't run you off, hon."

"Myles either." Wynter's expression was smug.

"Jonah ran himself off," Summer said and Jonah nodded.

Tate tipped his head, his eyes full of mirth. "I'm still debating about Rhys."

Rhys pointed a finger at him. "You did once. Remember?"

Confusion entered Tate's expression. "No, I don't."

Rhys's eyes got a faraway look. "It was when I was thirteen and I'd just snuck my first kiss with June in the barn, and you walked in. You said I'd better not be up to no good, or you'd bury me under the manure pile."

Tate's laughter rang across the yard. "I was kidding, and I didn't know you two were making out in there."

I peeked at Mama, my face hot. "It was a kiss."

"You were practically an adult, Tate." Humor filled Rhys's voice. "Scared the crap outta me."

"Mama," I said in a mock angry tone. "Aren't you ashamed of your oldest? Not that the others are innocent."

Mama rocked away, a faint smile on her lips. "It was a good way of weeding out the fakes. The ones who stuck around knew my girls were worth it."

The dopey, lovey-dovey looks my sisters gave their spouses made me nauseous. I rolled my eyes toward Rhys in a *can you believe this?* way.

His gaze softened. "You were worth it," he said only loud enough for me to hear. "Always have been."

I melted inside. Absolutely liquid. I could pull him into the barn and finish what we'd started all those years ago.

Conversation continued around us, but Rhys and I were in our own little bubble.

"The girls called," he said.

"They okay?"

"They're worried about missing two weeks of lessons, but I said you're working on the album and preparing for the fundraiser."

The fundraiser was nothing. I would show up and sing what I wanted. A novel occurrence. There was no set list, no warm-up, no interviews or autograph signing. I planned to arrive and sing and enjoy myself. No pressure. I couldn't wait.

"I can give them lessons next Sunday." A week before I left.

He scanned the people around us. "Is it bad that I want to keep you to myself this week?"

"No." I wanted to be selfish too.

"Tonight, June Bug." He glanced around at everyone once more. "Your brothers haven't scared me off yet."

CHAPTER TWENTY-TWO

Rhys

June was hanging out at the Copper Summit bar with Autumn. She had said I could wait at the cabin for her, or if I really wanted to get people talking, I could stop by the bar. According to Autumn and Wynter, Wednesday nights were quiet after nine. The bar closed at eleven.

She'd be at the cabin in an hour, but here I was, walking into the distillery.

The only open door at this time of night went into the bar. The main entry to the merch shop and the viewing windows for the tanks were to my left. The glass door was closed and only the security lights were on beyond the entry.

Neon signs glinted off the wood accents on the walls and the beams going across the ceiling. The large picture window bordering one side of the bar let in the ambient glow from the lights in the parking lot.

A couple of men I didn't recognize were tucked into a round corner table opposite the bar. June was behind the counter, her back to me, stocking bottles on the shelves.

She spotted me in the mirror that ran along the shelf. Once the bottles of bourbon she was arranging were in place, she turned, a wide smile on her face. "I didn't think you were coming."

"It's as close as we're getting to a date night while you're still in town." I slid onto a stool. "Are you working alone?"

"I told Autumn to get going. She's still run down from the school year." June propped her elbows on the bar counter. "I think she's pregnant and not telling anyone."

"Yeah? Congrats to them—if you're right."

"I'm right. I've been gone a long time, but Autumn isn't usually that worn down, and I'm sure she and Gideon would get an A for effort."

A knot cinched in my gut. Instead of picturing June's redheaded sister tenderly rubbing her hands over her swelling stomach, it was June in my head, her curtain of hair framing the loving expression on her face.

I coughed to get the tightness in my chest to loosen.

"Do you need something to drink?" She spun, giving me a full view of her not-pregnant stomach. While I never tired of looking at her ass, I had to avert my gaze. The ache left behind was too disconcerting.

Where the hell had that thought come from? I was a father. I had two amazing kids. Why was I imagining June with my kid? I wasn't a young man like before, picturing a theoretically older June with my baby in her belly. She'd been in my head. As she was now.

A square white napkin with the Copper Summit mountain logo was placed in front of me, and a glass of straight bourbon was set on top.

"I can get you a glass of water too." She pivoted away.

Once her back was to me, I took a long pull of the bourbon. The burn wicked up my sinuses and I started coughing. "Jesus."

Her chuckle was soft as she shoved the glass of water toward me. "Here. Been a while?"

"Yes," I wheezed. I had the vodka on hand for when the rare company came over, usually a contact from the ranch or an old school buddy. "I usually have a cold beer."

"You came to the wrong bar, Hot Mountain Daddy."

I smiled and downed the water. After that, I took another sip, remembering to shut off my sniffer like June had once taught me to. The golden liquid caressed my esophagus, leaving the flavors of vanilla and butterscotch on my tongue.

"Better?" she asked.

"Much."

Her gaze lifted over my shoulder. "Y'all have a good night."

Now we were alone.

I sipped my bourbon while she went to clean up their table. When she returned, she washed their glasses.

"Tourists?" I asked.

"Yes. On their honeymoon. If they weren't so googly-eyed, Autumn wouldn't have left me." She rounded the bar and slid onto the stool next to me. I spun on my seat enough that our legs tangled. "She still wasn't going to leave, but I said that you'd be here."

I arched a brow, uncaring that I'd been that predictable. "Do you tell the future now?"

She flourished her fingers by her face. "When I sing, it comes true."

"Except you sing about the past."

"Not my next album."

"No more heartbreak?"

"I wish," she said quietly. "It won't be manufactured, that's for sure." She slapped her hands on her thighs. "My new manager, Shanita, seems cool. She's so reassuring about the album and supportive, like of course I'm going to drop an excellent work of art. I didn't realize how insidious Lucy was about chipping away at my self-esteem. Shanita has taken the reins and is working with my promotion team. The first concert date has been set."

Dismay dulled the numbing of the bourbon. "That's great."

If she noticed the woodenness in my tone, she ignored it. "I told her I wanted all-female opening acts. I want to be the stepping-stone for them that I didn't have because I didn't play the game, or I didn't look how they wanted, or I didn't act seductively enough."

"You don't have to act."

"You're biased." She took a drink from my bourbon. Her delicate throat worked over the fluid as she swallowed.

I curled my fingers behind her neck and stroked a thumb over her windpipe. "You seduced me by just being you."

She brushed the backs of her fingers over my brow. "It was that tortured look of yours that got to me. So stereotypical of me."

I released her to take another drink. "I was tortured."

"Looking back, I can see how selfish I was. You didn't talk about your mom and I let you just not discuss your feelings. It was all about me."

The liquor burned into my stomach lining, and my water glass was empty. "I wanted it to be all about you."

"Maybe that's why we didn't make it." Her eyes flared. "I mean— I don't blame you—"

"It's okay." I grabbed her hands. "We were young. Eighteen-year-olds who didn't know what life was throwing at us."

"You turned nineteen right after I left."

"Yeah." The shittiest birthday of my life. "You were my everything, June. But if the focus hadn't been on you, I think it would've been the same eventually anyway. My path went one way; yours went the other."

She took another sip from my glass. "Do you think they'll ever converge again?"

"I don't know."

"What if we make sure?"

I'd rather talk about my mom than listen to June give up on her dream. "You're going on that tour."

"I am." She lacked the conviction I wanted to hear.

"You're going to enjoy it."

"I'm going to enjoy being on stage," she clarified.

I spread my hands on her thighs. I couldn't have her second-guessing anything. "June. You're going to rock that tour—"

"I play *country* music."

"I've heard people argue that you're not real country."

Her mouth dropped open and she gasped. Loudly. "Rhys Conner Kinkade, you take that back."

"I'm just saying what I've heard." I was goading her, and I would savor the passion that was about to come.

She rolled her eyes. "I know what you've heard. All genres of music change over time, but somehow people expect country music not to grow or morph. Do I have to sound like Hank Williams Senior—or Junior—to be considered country? Guys don't sound like them nowadays, yet you don't hear *nearly* as much complaining about them." Her hands were flying as she ranted. "And don't get me started on the critiques country gets that dance music doesn't. Do you hear so many people complain about asses getting shaken in rap or pop music? Okay, wrong example, rap gets a lot of shit. Country is a story-based art, like a lot of art, and I just wish more people could see it. Like, I can read a thriller without wanting a serial killer in my life. I can also like bro country. Yes, actually, tell me to get my sugar shaker in the truck. I want to hear those toxic love songs. You just can't win sometimes."

She blew a strand of hair out of her face. Her cheeks were pink with indignation and the fire in her eyes was everything I wanted for her.

I chuckled. "Been storing that up?"

The tension in her shoulders drained. "Yeah. Hazard of the trade. Each genre of music has its battles to fight. Each singer has their own too, I guess."

"What was yours?" I'd missed it all, and I kept asking to hear it, as if that would make me part of her journey. Anger at myself rose in my blood, but I quashed it. There'd been no other choice.

"There are a ton of tiny battles, but one of mine was

early in my career when I was starting to get approached by the big record labels. They didn't like my songs—or rather they did, but they didn't think they'd resonate with the public."

"They were wrong."

She nodded, excitement making the yellow sparks in her eyes glow. "Some of the companies had people who've been around a while. People I was told I should be grateful they'd even give me a few minutes of their time. But they didn't want my songs. They wanted me to sing about two things. Feminism or pining after a guy who cheated on me." She waved her hands in front of her face and pretended to cry. "Why can't he want me when he's with her? Why didn't he pick me?"

I ran some of her lyrics from recent years through my head. Her songs were different, like "Emerald Rain," but I tried to pinpoint how. "And you sing about the emotions of moving on or not wanting to feel that way."

She smiled triumphantly. "Yes. Don't get me wrong, there's a place for those other songs, but the dudes in Nashville think that's all women want from female country singers. The guys can relate too, you know." She took another sip of my bourbon and wiggled the index finger of her free hand in the air. "I don't know if these songs fall under feminism, but the *I'm gonna kill my man* or *burn down his house* songs aren't really my brand. I was approached to record a few of those."

"You never keyed an ex's car?" A shame.

"I could've written about popping the tires of one of Summer's exes, but like I said, it's not my brand."

I'd lost out on all this. The way she talked shop and lit up from the inside when she discussed music. Did she have someone to listen to her? Who shared her joy? Had her cocksucker exes? I wouldn't feel so inclined to burn their fucking houses down if they'd done at least that for her. "You stuck to your principles."

"Another thing that cost me years."

She made it sound as if there were more reasons. Her work for Copper Summit. Her branding. Was there something she wasn't telling me? Had Lucy dragged her down? If June hadn't been nursing heartbreak or getting distracted by man-children, would she have taken off sooner? "Did Lucy hold you back?"

June's vision hadn't been heartbreak songs. She wanted to sing about life and love.

Her irises dimmed. "Yeah. Maybe a little."

That wasn't the full story, but if I pushed it, I might squash her spark. "Lucy can kiss your ass."

"Yeah. You know who can kiss my ass right now since the bar is officially closed?"

•

June

My legs hung off Rhys's arms and my ass was on the end of the tailgate of his pickup. He pumped in and out of me. I'd already been sprawled out in the bed, on the blanket that had once helped keep me warm when he'd picked me up from the side of the road. He'd shoved my skirt up, bunched my shirt over my bare breasts, then kissed his way down and licked me into a frenzy under the stars and then plunged inside of me.

"I love the way you fuck me." I clung to his shoulders and kept pace with his thrusts. Our grunts and moans mingled with the rest of the wildlife at this hidden spot of pasture between the distillery and the cabin.

"You're so fucking tight." He gritted his teeth. The tendons in his neck stood out and I could trace the veins on his forearms with my tongue. "So damn greedy for my cock."

Shamelessly greedy. "Yes. Oh god—yes!" I came apart. Stars dotted the sky above us and behind my eyelids. "Rhys!"

He spread my legs wider and slammed into me once before coming. Hot release filled me while I continued to convulse around him. I collapsed back and splayed my arms over my head.

He stayed inside me but sagged over my body, his head hanging. Soft hair brushed above the hemline of my shirt.

I stuffed my hands into his hair and opened my eyes. The Big Dipper soared overhead. I traced the corner star to the Little Dipper. After I'd closed up the bar, Rhys had followed me to the cabin. I'd dropped off my car and hopped in with him. I'd made a comment on the way home that the stars were pretty tonight and he'd driven us to the pasture we used to hook up in. A copse of trees blocked us from the little-used road.

The only downside was that any vehicle driving by would be my family, but these days, getting busted wasn't a concern.

Despite that, something about tonight felt frantic. Was it me?

I curled my fingers around strands of his hair. He gently pulled out and helped me sit up. I tugged my skirt down and he handed me the underwear he'd stuffed into his pocket.

While we were straightening up, he stayed standing and I got my clothes in the right place and managed not to fall off the tailgate. Rhys would be there to catch me.

The sense that something was off stayed with me. I could ignore it, but I had paid enough attention to Rhys over the years. "Tonight was a lot like before."

"When we were kids?"

A quick fuck in the pasture that had felt like the epitome of romance? Sort of. "Rushed and frantic."

He wedged himself between my legs and propped his hands on either side of my hips. The guy continued to be the reason my pussy was pulsing and he'd just gotten me off. Twice.

"There will never be a time that I won't be ready to blow around you."

I brushed my hands over his broad shoulders. "Flattering, but this was different than the last two weeks."

"We're outside."

I poked him in the chest. "*You're* different."

He touched his forehead to mine. "Yeah. We only have a few more days. Then you'll be the hot guitar teacher that I can't touch."

"Can't or won't?" I knew the answer, but I had to hear him say it. We'd agreed to these two weeks. We hadn't discussed the two weeks before I left. Perhaps because I knew the answer.

"I can't, June," he whispered. "If the girls see us so much as kiss, do you know how much they'll get their hopes up?"

I nodded, crestfallen. They weren't the only ones. My hopes were already floating as high as the stars. Each time I was with Rhys, questions streamed through my head. Why couldn't we be together? Why couldn't we make this work? Why couldn't he try?

My instincts said tonight wasn't the night to talk to him, just like I hadn't told him every reason for my years-long trek to country music stardom. He'd already shut me down, but I was starting to see beyond the Rhys he wanted everyone to see. I used to think that I got the real Rhys. Now I knew better.

If I brought up the future tonight, he'd shut me down. He was going to bed with me. He'd wake up to me and we'd repeat until Sunday, when he brought the girls home. It'd be a week after that when I did lessons with the girls again.

No, I'd wait. I wasn't looking forward to leaving town. Great things were waiting for me. My album was nearly done and every song I'd written was a keeper. I was on fire, but I was also spending every day with the man I loved.

There would be a gap from when he cut me off to when I left town. That was when I'd know if there was any hope for us.

CHAPTER TWENTY-THREE

Rhys

The last two weeks had gone by in the blink of an eye, thanks to my nights buried in June. The only thing that dimmed my time with her was not having the girls around. I would pick them up tomorrow, and I'd finally get to see them every day. But the tradeoff was June.

Then moments like these made me think . . . what if?

June and I were in the kitchen of the cabin. I'd just come inside from grilling steaks and she was finishing at the stove. Fried potatoes and asparagus.

"The girls would love this meal." I inhaled around the band around my chest.

I could picture them setting the table while June finished up the food. We'd all sit down together in the cabin, like we had June's first night here.

I wanted a quiet night at home with the woman I loved, but she wanted to share her music with the world. Tonight was my last night to be selfish with June.

Once she was finished with the potatoes, we sat and ate.

She took a bite and sighed. "I'm going to miss this on the road."

"Don't you have a list of demands that goes ahead of you? Like only green M&M's, Evian water, and a medium-rare filet mignon waiting for you?"

The corner of her mouth lifted. "I'm partial to green Skittles."

"Wait." I flattened my hands on the table. "Who the fuck likes the green Skittles? They should make them all red and purple."

"We can agree on any color but orange and yellow. And if I wanted to be a diva, I'd ask for Perrier."

"Not Dom Perignon?"

She grinned. "Maybe when I'm the headliner."

Once we were done eating and cleaning up, we went to the porch.

She sat on the rocking chair and I took the Adirondack. Her guitar stayed inside. I wanted to hear her new stuff, but I'd wait like the rest of the population. She'd always been private with her music until she wasn't. Then the more ears the better.

I stretched my legs out. The valley spread before us, emerald green with twinkling blue water from the rain runoff earlier this week. "Are you nervous for the fundraiser?"

"No. Yes?" She crossed a leg but kept rocking the chair. "I'm anxious for a different reason."

She had to leave right after if she was going to make her appointment in Nashville with that songwriter she admired. "Aren't you used to that? Do a performance and then take off for the next town?"

"Yes." A simple answer. She didn't elaborate.

Silence settled between us while birdsong filled the air.

"You're going to be there?" she asked. "At the fundraiser."

I had planned to, but that was before I'd started sleeping with her each night and daydreaming about a cozy life together. "I don't know, June."

The rocking ceased, and a furrow formed in her brow. "You're not coming?"

Hadn't I been asking myself that for days? It was time to answer. "It'll be hard for me." Harder for her.

She dropped her gaze to the floorboards. "Oh."

The guilt was building in her eyes, making them a darker brown. She would start second-guessing what we'd done. She might even dwell on how much she'd liked it. I hoped she had, but she couldn't afford to romanticize it. We'd been fucking. We hadn't been playing house. Cooking together tonight was just a way to have a date without some smartphone wielder posting about us.

"June . . . going cold turkey has been the best way for me." A bitter lie on my tongue. Peeking at her profiles and listening to her songs when no one was around was *not* cold turkey. "I know we said we're just messing around, I'm your muse, but it's brought up a lot of feelings. I'll have to detox."

She winced, and yeah, I felt that. A shitty choice of words but necessary. "I see."

"I'll send money with the girls to donate. I'm sure Wren will bring them." If she'd been in a bachelorette auction, I'd have sent my life's saving with the girls.

Whatever would keep June with me forever. But she was priceless.

I'd need the time to fortify myself. For when news broke that she was dating another singer. Or some fucking hockey player. She might not have a Lucy trying to set her up with assholes, but they'd flock to June. She was a beautiful songbird and they were . . . cocks.

More than anything, she couldn't change her mind. It might be arrogant to think my presence would do that, but I couldn't risk it. Guitar lessons with my girls while I said hi and bye to her were different than being in the audience where she could see me. Where she could witness all the fucking love in the world shine from my eyes. Where she might see how goddamn proud I was of her, but also that she was my world. I'd never move on. I had my kids to raise and that would be enough. I was support, not an obstacle.

She started rocking again, slowly, sadness filling her expression and breaking my goddamn heart.

"Hey." I scooted out of my chair and dropped to my knees. I pivoted in front of her and slid my hands up her thighs. "I don't want to be a downer. I'd love to be there." But she couldn't have me around. I couldn't see the indecision on her face again, like at my dad's funeral. She didn't need to be in that position. "But I am glad we'll be parting on better terms than we did before."

She rested her hands on top of mine. "I didn't like the thought that you hated me."

Quite the opposite. "I'd never hate you."

"I know that now. I see a lot more now than I did." She stroked the back of her fingers across my cheek, rubbing them down my beard. "I've wished you there at all my big performances. You're the first one I wanted to call when I got good news, and the only face I looked for in the crowd." She ran her bottom lip through her teeth. "I shouldn't be telling you this."

"No," I said roughly. "I wanted you out there, getting the cheers and screams that you deserve."

She cupped my face and ran her thumb over the scar on my lip. "I missed you at the Opry."

I buried my head in her stomach so she couldn't see my face. I'd missed her too. I'd missed telling her how amazing she was. How proud I was of her. I'd missed being to the side of the stage and catching her in my arms like we'd talked about.

"I was so goddamn proud of you." She'd never know the full truth. How her performance had nearly made my heart burst out of my damn chest. My fingers dug into the soft flesh of her thighs. I loosened my grip and my hand brushed the hem of her shorts. I tugged down. My heart was going to explode anyway if I didn't release some emotion.

She rolled her hips up, giving me room to pull her shorts off all the way. I dragged her underwear down with them too.

"I wanted to be there when you walked off the stage." I kissed one of her thighs. "I wanted to kiss that big smile on your face." I pressed my mouth to her other thigh. "I wanted to celebrate with you that night."

"I thought of you the whole night." She tangled her fingers in my hair as I laid kisses higher, getting close to the pussy my mouth watered for.

I lifted one of her feet and set it on the edge of the seat. Then the other. I pushed her knees to the side.

There it was. Her sweet pussy. Wet and glistening for me. Our chemistry could never be denied, but our dreams were too different.

I charted a path with my mouth toward her slick center and I settled in.

She groaned and I tugged her closer to my mouth. I circled her clit with my tongue the way she liked.

When her needy moans got stronger, I pushed two fingers inside of her.

"Oh god, Rhys." Her ass was at the edge of the chair and she'd put her feet on my shoulders.

I pumped in and out of her, looking up her body to her hooded eyes and her flushed face. "You're going to remember this. Every time you're on stage. Every time you put that microphone close to your mouth, you're going to feel my lips on you." It had killed me when I'd thought she'd moved on and forgotten me. I had moved on, but I'd never forgotten her. No matter how hard I tried, I couldn't.

I put my mouth on her clit and sucked while steadily thrusting in and out. Her walls clamped around my fingers. She was so fucking ready but the urge to come with her washed over me.

I ripped my fly open with my free hand and shoved my pants down. The clasp dug into my flesh, but my erection finally popped out. I rose, pulling her with me.

She twined her arms around me and planted her mouth against mine. I turned and planted my ass on the seat. She straddled me and slid down my length, both of us unwilling to take any more time.

The chair rocked and the back whacked against the cabin, but I didn't fucking care. I had her for tonight and nothing was stopping me from consuming this woman.

June gripped the carved wooden backrest and rode me. Soon enough, we got into a rhythm with the rocking of the chair and her movements up and down.

I yanked her shirt off, then reclaimed her mouth. Her flavor landed on my tongue and I couldn't get enough. I put a hand between us. This wasn't going to take me long and I needed both of us to come together. I couldn't say why. We had the whole fucking night, but it was going too fast. Forever wouldn't be enough with June Kerrigan.

I let my finger rest on her clit while she did the rest. Up and down she rode me.

I broke our kiss. "You're fucking mine. When you leave, I don't care who you move on with, you'll always be mine."

I shouldn't be saying any of this.

She caressed my face, her eyes glassy and full of desire. "Yes. I'm yours. Always have been."

Damn fucking right.

Energy shot all the way down my spine and my orgasm hit hard. I twisted my hand around her long ponytail and held her to me as I came, spilling in her. "Mine."

"Rhys!"

The chair quit slamming into the wall. We'd wedged it so tight against the logs and our pumps had shortened. The place fell quiet around us. The birds had been temporarily silenced with our cries.

She rested her forehead against mine. Our breaths mingled.

Had I gone too far? I'd told her within the span of

minutes that I couldn't be at one single performance, but that she should be forever tied to me. I'd basically ordered her not to move on.

She placed a kiss at the corner of my mouth. "I think we broke the rocking chair and marked up a few logs."

June

My sisters and Scarlett were sprawled in various chairs on the cabin porch. They'd each brought their own and I was sitting on the rocking chair that had survived Rhys and me having sex. All the pregnant or nursing women—including Autumn, who'd finally told us she was expecting—were drinking Scarlett's cherry lemonade. Scarlett and I had a splash of bourbon in ours.

I rocked slowly, each movement a reminder of him growling "mine" in my ear.

"So then what?" Wynter wore a troubled frown. "You just go your separate ways again. Then you start dating some pretty boy who's absolutely awful for you."

"My exes are pretty," I agreed. They were good-looking on and off camera. Flawless. None of them had a scar from cleft lip surgery. The ones with beards didn't let it get a little frizzy each week. None of them had worn flannel.

Summer had her legs stretched out, her hands resting on the rounded portion of her belly, and her head was on the back of her rocking camp chair. "Are you really going to let him let you go again?"

"I don't want to," I finally admitted out loud and to

real people. "But he's determined that we're living two different lives and never shall they intertwine."

Autumn snorted and pushed herself back and forth on her portable hammock chair. "I think there's been some intertwining going on."

"Every day for the past two weeks." Instead of being boastful, my response was melancholy. It'd been three days without him. I couldn't bring myself to meet Autumn at the bar tonight. The memory of last Wednesday was too fresh. My determination to figure out how to keep Rhys, with all those stars as my witness, was fading. "I think it's doable, but he has this thing about letting me go. He's gotta be a martyr for me. For Wren. For his ex-wife. For me again."

"Seems to be a pattern," Scarlett murmured from her camp chair. She had on big sunglasses and her hair was bundled on top of her head.

My sisters all nodded. Yes, the pattern was there. Rhys was more comfortable letting go than trying to hang on.

"But why?" Why wasn't I enough to fight for? "He won't even try."

"Tate wouldn't have pursued me," Scarlett said. "I know you guys pitched in to bid on him for the fundraiser, but beyond that day that I had with him, if Chance hadn't wanted him to be with me, Tate would've backed off."

My nephew had been one of Scarlett's students. She'd mentioned that she had worried about Chance accepting her since she'd been a firm teacher with him when he'd been going through a hard time. But the way my brother loved her was all-consuming. "I don't think Tate would've stayed away for long."

She lifted a shoulder and adjusted her sunglasses. "Maybe. We'll never know, but I guess I'm saying that Rhys has a deep-seated reason too."

Wynter crossed one leg over the other. "Myles kept leaving me. To be fair, he left situations, but somehow I was involved in them. He was afraid his mom would corrupt or hurt someone because of him." She ticked a finger in the air. "The first was when he turned eighteen and left Montana entirely." Another finger. "Then when we were getting close"—a third finger—"and finally when he got in touch with the rest of his family."

Summer sat up in her chair. "Jonah pushed me away because he didn't think he could be a good husband and especially not a good father. He was scared." She smiled and stroked the swell of her stomach. "He's going to be a better dad because of it."

We all looked at Autumn. She took a sip from her lemonade. "I guess it's no secret that Gideon and I were supposed to be divorced months ago. He was an all-or-nothing guy until he ended up with nothing. But he had to lose it all to realize what he really wanted in life."

"Same with Jonah," Summer said. "He got a taste of the life he wanted, and when it was gone, he had to decide if he wanted to work for it or retreat into that cabin and become the old Jonah again."

Except for Tate, my sisters' spouses had lost it all before realizing what they really wanted. "Rhys has already lost it all. When I leave, he's going to gut through it. He might miss me, he might still love me, but he's going to stay right where he's at."

"Do you think he loves you?" Summer asked gently.

I ran a finger through the condensation on my glass.

"I don't know. I'm sure there's some part of him that will always love me."

Wynter put a cool hand on my forearm. "But you're in love with him."

A burn roared behind my eyes. "I don't think I've ever not been in love with him."

"Then you need to talk to him, Junie," Autumn said.

I let out a sardonic laugh. "Don't you think I've tried? He's stubborn and determined and he really believes it's the right thing for me. It's all about me with him. All about me. All about his dad. All about the girls. All about Kirstin. All about Wren."

The breeze ruffled my hair and I stuffed the strands behind my ear. How could he be so generous, so loving, and then hurt me this way because of it?

"Do you have any idea why?" Scarlett asked. "I mean, it's admirable that he puts everyone first, but there has to be a reason why."

Before he'd let me go, he'd committed himself to the ranch. No—to his dad. "He always said that he owed his dad everything. He doesn't talk much about his mom."

"That's weird." Summer set her glass on the end table. "Didn't he move here when he was twelve or something?" At my nod, her face scrunched up. "So over a third of his life was spent with this woman and he doesn't talk about it?"

"She was an aspiring actress, theater mostly, but some screen." My information didn't shed light on anything. "That's honestly about all I know."

We all fell quiet for several moments. Any weight that was lifted thanks to talking to my sisters was replaced by hopelessness. All of my sisters had gotten through to their partners. My brothers-in-law had let them all in, had shared with them what was really important, and they'd all changed their lives to suit my sisters. All in the name of love, trust, and respect.

If Rhys hadn't opened up to me by now, I wasn't sure he would ever do it. And if he didn't talk to me, if he could let me leave for a second time, then maybe I had to accept that I wasn't the one for him.

CHAPTER TWENTY-FOUR

Rhys

"Dad? Dad? Daaaad!"

I yanked my attention off a grazing Butterball at Hannah's voice. "Yeah?"

"I've been calling you forever." She flounced down the hill from the chicken coop.

"Sorry." I'd been in my head a lot all week. They had to call for me at least three times before I answered. What a present dad.

"I think Goldie's sick."

I scrubbed a hand down my face. What the fuck had the dog eaten now? It could be anything—or nothing. "Okay. Let's go look at her."

"She's been horcking. Bethany's with her."

"Horcking?"

"Yeah, you know." She made a heaving sound that really did sound like "horck." Shit.

She took off and I followed. Bethany came into view first. The dog became visible just before I heard the horck get louder and wetter.

"Dad!" Bethany spun and sprinted, stopping when she saw me. "She threw up. It's bloody!"

Aw, hell. The girls had been learning about the circle of life since we'd had our own place, and before that, they'd been exposed to ranch life. But Goldie was a pet. She wasn't being raised to sell or be sold for meat.

The retriever licked her chops and what sounded like a groan or a loud burp echoed from her ribs.

I patted her droopy head and inspected the pile of vomit. It was hard to tell what was under the pink foam, but I spied enough material that didn't look like dog food to think that Goldie had munched on something she shouldn't have. A bad habit she'd had since she was a puppy.

"Did I feed her too late?" Bethany blinked back tears.

I checked my watch. June would arrive soon for the guitar lesson. Maybe I could call her and she'd come earlier. It'd been a long fucking week without her. The first of many long weeks without her in my bed, under the same roof, or even in the same damn state. I'd have to hide like I had the last time she'd played at the Montana State Fair.

I hefted Goldie. She whined. Her tongue lolled out and she panted. Her sides felt hard. Goddamn, I hoped she was okay. The girls were adjusting to saying goodbye to their mom and to June. They didn't need a forever goodbye with the dog.

The girls followed me. Hannah ran into the house to

grab a blanket and Bethany helped me get Goldie situated in the back. She started heaving again. The pickup had seen worse body fluids with the other animals on this farm. A little vomit would be nothing, and the vet might be happy I came with a sample.

I called June once the dog was situated.

"Hey." Her sultry voice filled the line, happy to hear from me.

The punch to my gut was strong. Weening off her wasn't working so well. "Hey. Can you come a little early and hang with the girls? I've gotta get the dog to the vet." After I called Dr. Sanders and got his standard warning about the emergency charge. This wasn't Goldie's first rodeo.

Dad had cared for his animals, but he would've ridden out Goldie's many self-induced stomach issues. I couldn't. The girls loved their dog and seeing her suffer was too much if there was something I could do about it.

"Yeah," June said. "I'll be right there."

She must have been at the cabin. Less than ten minutes later, she pulled in. I drank her in. Her hair was in a long ponytail, the kind I liked to wrap around my hand when I was thrusting into her. She got out and I soaked in her long legs and the way her loose camisole bared her guitar-playing toned arms. Every cell in my body missed her and it'd only been six fucking days since I'd left the cabin for the last time.

She jogged up to me, and I fought my natural inclination to reach for her, to give her a kiss as a greeting, and to tell her that I was worried about my kids and the dog.

"How are the girls?" she asked.

"Scared." I double-checked that the girls were behind me. "Our last retriever got into the neighbor's rat poison."

She grimaced. "Sick pets are so hard on everyone. Daddy always said he still owed working animals his best attempt at help, but he also had a ton of kids watching him."

"Thanks for coming."

"Anytime. Anytime I can," she amended.

This would be the only time. We held our gazes for a heartbeat. I nodded and took off, leaving my girls behind.

June

Bethany hugged her guitar. "I can't believe this is our last lesson."

"Do we have to give the guitars back?" Hannah asked. She wrapped her arms around the body of her instrument like her sister.

"I'll have to talk to your dad. I can't fit these into my car for the drive back, and I doubt my sister wants to hang on to them." I hadn't even checked. I'd bought these guitars for the girls, and I wanted them to stay with the girls. Rhys probably wouldn't mind. When I'd first shown up with them, yes. But not now.

"What are you going to play for the fundraiser?" Bethany put her guitar aside and curled her legs under her on the couch.

"Probably some of my more popular songs. What do you want to hear?"

" 'That Boy,' " Bethany said instantly.

"And 'Emerald Rain.' You're jealous of Mommy in that one," Hannah said.

Alarm detonated inside my rib cage. How'd they know? "Where'd you hear that?"

Bethany elbowed her sister in the ribs. "Hannah."

I could blow it off, but someone had talked to them about the lyrics of that song and clued them in.

"We talked to Mommy about you," Bethany said, guilt making her shoulders drop and her lower lip puff out. "I'm sorry."

All my tension melted away. They didn't need to apologize. I knew my lyrics might affect the real people who inspired them, but the younger me who'd written them hadn't thought I'd have to face a reckoning. I hadn't been insulting to Kirstin. I'd been as embarrassed about my jealousy as I was devastated that I had thought I was losing Rhys forever.

"Don't be. She's your mom. Of course you'd talk with her." If I'd been home to talk to Mama more, I might not have written a song about how Rhys's marriage made me feel. "Yes, I was very envious that your mom got to marry your dad. I was sad it didn't work out for me and him." Two pairs of big eyes blinked at me, so I continued. "I was also happy for him though." I wasn't beneath lying a little bit. None of my feelings had been happiness. "And without your mom and your dad, there wouldn't be Bethany and Hannah, and I happen to think Bethany and Hannah are pretty cool, and I'm glad they're around."

They both grinned. Cool relief eased the knots

around my shoulders. Rhys didn't need to return to two confused girls who were worried they'd insulted a rising country star or were betraying their mother.

"When are you coming back?" Hannah asked.

"I hope I can return after Summer has her baby." The pressure in my skull increased with my heart rate. Would I be able to see my newest niece or nephew? Would Rhys avoid me? Would he let me say hi to the girls or cut me off entirely?

I would return to sneaking in and out of town so I could see my family in peace. Every time I crossed city limits, would I hope my car broke down until I snapped and sabotaged it myself?

Then Lane would know. He'd tell everyone, and they'd all know that I was hopelessly in love with Rhys and I wanted to be with him.

But everyone probably already knew that. Just like we all knew it didn't matter.

"Junie?" Bethany asked, her eyes narrowing. "Are you okay?"

I snapped out of my head. "Yes. Yes, I'm fine. What'd you ask?" Did *I* need an emergency trip to the vet? Was it the leftovers? I rubbed the center of my chest and inhaled a slow breath.

"When's she having her baby?" Hannah asked again.

I let out a long breath. "September sometime. But once the album is ready to release, I'll have to do promotional stuff like interviews and appearances, then the tour will start."

"Where will you go?" Hannah leaned forward like I was getting to the climax of a story.

Fitting. Embarking on the tour would be the climax. Everything afterward would be the denouement. Bigger and longer tours. Maybe even a Las Vegas residency where I could put down roots for a little bit.

I didn't want to live in fucking Vegas.

"All over," I finally answered. "Usually, the shows for tours like these are in the bigger cities of each state."

"You won't play in Bourbon Canyon?" Bethany sounded distraught.

I shook my head and the heartburn flared. "No, sorry. It's the flip side to getting more popular. I have to play in places that can fit more people. It's a good problem to have." My voice pitched up. A good problem. An excellent one I'd been working toward for fifteen years. "And I'll get to travel to some other countries."

Their eyes got big again.

"Whoa," Bethany said. "You're going across the ocean?"

I nodded. I'd fly with my band, try to skip out on the parties, and then go to my hotel room or the bus. "They call it a world tour, but I don't really see much of the world."

"Where will you go?"

"London. Sydney, Australia. I'm sure I'll play in Toronto, Canada."

Hannah shot her hand in the air as if this was a classroom. "Dad said he's been to Canada!"

"Dad says he's traveled a lot." Bethany's smile fell. "He doesn't like to talk about it though."

He never had.

"Dad was the same age as me when he moved to New York." Hannah beamed.

"He hated New York," Bethany said adamantly. "He said he was a little older than me when he moved home."

"I remember when I first saw him." I smiled at the

nostalgia. He'd walked into class, his gaze downcast and his shoulders hunched. The entire class had been interested in him, but I'd pushed to the front of the crowd at lunch and plopped next to him, my sole purpose to make him smile. My incessant questions about his favorite song and singer and what he listened to the most had finally done it.

The girls wiggled, their expressions intent.

Oh. They wanted me to keep talking. "He came in and was introduced. Our teacher wanted us to welcome him, and then told us he'd lived in New York City and Los Angeles, which caused a flurry of discussion." Everyone was asking where he had been, where he'd lived and he'd shut down. It was why he'd finally opened up with me. I leaned forward like we were all in on a secret. "He was shy."

Bethany chortled. "Daddy's not shy."

"He was very quiet in those days." He still was.

They bobbed their heads.

An engine sounded outside. The girls shot off the couch and raced to the back door. I was a few seconds behind them. When I pushed out, Bethany was kneeling on one side of Goldie and Hannah was on the other side. Both had their arms around her neck and their faces buried in her fur. She panted with her tongue lolling out.

Rhys had a hand propped on the side of his pickup. His disgruntled gaze softened when he looked at me. "The good news is that the red wasn't from blood. The vet's best guess was some sort of construction paper, and God knows we have enough of that flowing through the house."

Bethany's head popped up. "We just cleaned out our backpacks."

He nodded. "My guess is something blew out of the garbage. But the paper wasn't the major culprit. The bad news is . . . I paid a helluva emergency vet bill because the cats need a new blanket."

"Goldie ate their blanket?" Hannah was aghast.

"Quite a bit of it, judging by what she puked on the pickup floor. No wonder her stomach hurt." He caught my gaze. "Thanks for staying."

"No problem." I was done here, but my feet wouldn't move.

I got my first good look at the kitchen. I had dived right into lessons to keep the girls' minds off Goldie and had missed the plates of cookies. The basket he'd used to bring me muffins some mornings was by the napkins, filled with a fresh batch. Next to it was a pan of some sort of bars.

He was going to deal with our separation by baking. I'd write songs and make lots of money. Yet neither of us would come out ahead. "I should get going."

His lips turned down, and he worked his jaw like he was going to say something. This would be goodbye for him and me.

"Wait!" Bethany waved her hand. "Can we see you again? Before you leave?"

Sorrow dimmed the pleasant two hours I'd spent with them. "You'll see me at the fundraiser."

"But we won't get to say goodbye." Hannah's eyes shimmered.

"There'll be so many people." Moisture misted over Bethany's gaze.

I opened my mouth, but I didn't know what to say. A quick goodbye seemed so paltry when I'd barely seen them for the last two weeks. "I'll make sure to—"

"Stay for dinner!" Bethany grinned and clapped her hands together. "Can you?"

"Yeah!" Hannah jumped up and down, her ponytail swinging. "We can have a sleepover."

Shock stopped my heart. Sleepover? I'd had two of them so far with the Kinkades. Her suggestion shouldn't be so startling. After talking with my sisters, I wasn't sure if I should give Rhys space that could stretch into forever or try to worm my way into his life somehow. But to do that, I'd have to decide what I could give up.

"Can we, Dad?" Bethany pleaded.

I held my breath as I met Rhys's poleaxed stare.

"A sleepover," he uttered.

The adult thing to do would be to say no. There was too much baggage between us for platonic dinners and sleepovers, but the night wasn't about us. The girls weren't ready to say good night, and after today, the thought of a quick and crowded goodbye at the fundraiser was lackluster at best.

The fundraiser Rhys wasn't going to.

The girls continued their begging while Rhys's expression grew more neutral.

He folded his arms like he was fortifying himself for an argument. "I don't think . . ."

Determination lined my spine. His kids wanted more time with me, and I enjoyed being with them. I needed more time with Rhys to figure out how I felt about getting through to him. I had to know if it was possible, and perhaps it was best to have more time with him, but above that, if this was the end of us, I didn't want a rushed and crowded goodbye with Bethany and Hannah. "It'd be for the girls."

His brow furrowed and suspicion grew in his eyes.

He had every right to say no. My heart was on the line, and his was too. But neither of us wanted to drag two little girls into the mess we'd made of our nonrelationship.

"I'll pull out some hamburgers," he finally said.

CHAPTER TWENTY-FIVE

Rhys

The girls were asleep. They hadn't wanted to miss time with June, so they'd camped out at the base of the couch. They were making June sleep on the actual couch since she was the guest.

After dinner, they had asked her to do their hair. My future might be filled with hair dye. They'd told June she should try orange next since she hadn't done that color yet. Bethany wanted blue and Hannah planned for every color a girl could dream of in her hair.

I should've hidden in the bedroom hours ago, but I hadn't been able to bring myself to leave the party. I'd made myself useful. If they mentioned popcorn, I made some. If they wanted homemade Eggos, I made waffles and put them in the fridge. If they were thirsty, I ran them drinks. Now the girls' mouths hung slack and they were sprawled over the floor, pillows piled around and under them.

June had crunched herself in the corner of the couch opposite me.

"Thank you," I said. The kids didn't stir at my voice.

"You're welcome. I haven't had fun like this since my sisters and I camped in our living room." She ran a hand through her "styled" hair. The girls had each done a braid, then changed their minds and tried to curl June's hair in ringlets. June's hair stuck out of her braid like she'd been in a windstorm and the curls had frizzed. She was beautiful. And the way she'd complimented their efforts left me speechless. Bethany and Hannah had soaked it up like rainwater.

They were missing this kind of interaction with their mom. It was June who gave them the attention they craved.

June peered at me out of the corner of her eye. The princess movie the girls were watching continued to play on the TV, but I'd seen it no less than five times and June had apparently done a good job of feigning interest. "While you were gone, we were talking . . ."

Tension stole back into my shoulders. If my kids had no qualms about asking for a sleepover with an adult woman in front of me, what were they only willing to talk about in private? "About?"

"You don't like to talk about when you traveled with your mom."

I fought back memories that wanted to rise up. "No. I don't."

She nibbled on her lower lip. "I know, but I wonder . . . maybe you should."

The back of my neck grew hot. Sometimes Bethany asked about her grandparents. Kirstin's parents lived across the country and weren't interested in being grandparents, just like Kirstin wasn't interested in being a mom.

That wasn't fair. She was still in town, but she'd been going to state parks to take photos. "There's nothing to talk about."

"Nothing to talk about, but you won't leave Montana? You won't leave Bourbon Canyon? Nothing to talk about, but you want nothing to do with my success—"

"I want you to succeed—"

"Nothing to talk about, but you sold the ranch because Wren was struggling." Pressure built at my temples, but she continued. "Nothing to talk about, but you let Kirstin phone it in as a mom—"

I popped up. Hannah stirred in her blankets.

"Not around them," I whispered and stalked to the kitchen.

Her soft footsteps followed me. "I'm sorry. I do not want them to overhear, but, Rhys, that time in your life clearly defined you and . . . and I think it's keeping you from letting yourself be happy."

"I am happy." I spun. She looked so damn young with her hair flowing over her shoulders and her eyes beseeching me to listen, to understand.

The awful thing was that I did. I knew better than anyone what those years had been like. I knew better than all of them. "It wasn't a good time for me."

"I know. She wasn't a good mom."

"No," I said, immediately defensive. "I got in the way." I ground my teeth together. I'd never admitted that much before. Dad had known some of it.

"How in the world could you have gotten in the way? You were a kid."

The ever-present shame surged through my blood vessels. "I made it hard for her."

"How?" June's expression was dubious. She and her sisters and brothers and even many of her foster siblings hadn't given Mae and Darin Bailey the hard time I had given Angela Craft.

"She had a job." The inclination to defend my mom remained after all these years. No one else had been there. No one else knew what it had been like for my mom. "Her theater practices were demanding, her auditions unpredictable. She had no family to help, and I did nothing but cause her trouble."

"You?" She scoffed.

June only knew the mellow me. The Rhys Conner Kinkade who made sure everyone's lives ran smoothly. She didn't know the boy who'd made his mom's life a living hell. The rebellious shit who hadn't respected the person closest to him.

Maybe I did owe June some of the story. From her point of view, she'd been hurt because of my mom. I had to let her know that it was all me. "If she landed a major role, she'd have more rehearsal. The more I was at a new day care, or with a new nanny, the worse I'd act out."

Sympathy filled her eyes. "You wanted her attention."

"I knew better," I said curtly. "Even at that age."

She studied me, the doubt still in her eyes. "What else?"

Wasn't that enough? "If she had an audition, I'd spill my drink, fall and hurt myself, or even run away. Before she brought me here to live with Dad, I got lost on the New York subway."

Her eyes shot wide. "What?"

"On purpose."

Again, no recrimination. Understanding welled in those big, beautiful amber eyes, understanding I didn't deserve. "Oh, Rhys."

"It was a dick move. I could've been hurt. Mom was finally on Broadway, and she'd missed a critical rehearsal because of me. She almost got fired, but the NYPD had called the theater." I'd known so many details, the police had had no trouble finding her. "I hadn't wanted to stay gone forever. Just enough to . . . fuck up Mom's day."

"You were still a kid, and those were all cries for help."

I sucked in a sharp breath. "There's more." Since I was baring my soul and remembering those disappointed expressions of Mom's, I might as well keep going. "I used to tell her that she couldn't act."

June's lips parted.

"That was our last conversation. After she dropped me off with Dad."

"Rhys," she breathed. "You were so young. Have some grace with yourself." She gestured to the sleeping girls on the floor. "If they called you a horrible father, would you believe them? Or would you think gosh, they must be upset about something, and I need to talk to them?"

I shook my head. She still wasn't getting it. "I did all that on purpose. She had to deal with me being a punk on top of the random bloody noses I used to get and the night terrors. Sometimes, she wouldn't get a wink of sleep because of me."

June's mouth dropped all the way open. "How are you talking about this like any of it is your fault?"

"I was a lot to handle."

"You. Were. A. Kid." She straightened and righteousness lit her eyes. "That's why you're so chill about Kirstin? You let her run off and basically abandon—"

"June." I tipped my head toward the living room. The girls should be asleep, but I couldn't risk them hearing a bad word about their mother.

She slowly inhaled, her nostrils flaring. "If roles were switched, and Bethany and Hannah had gone off with their mom and the same things had happened, what would you say?"

I'd be pissed as hell at Kirstin. "It's not the same—"

"It is too."

"It's not."

"How are you being so obtuse? It sounds like your mom was dealt a hard hand of cards, but she—"

"She's dead because of me."

❧

June

She's dead because of me.

I turned over what Rhys had told me all night. I'd given up on sleep when the sun crested over the horizon enough to pour through the windows.

Angela Craft had dumped her son on his dad and returned to New York for the child-free life she thought she deserved. Then she'd been hit by a taxi on her way to rehearsal.

Rhys blamed himself.

He blamed himself for everything. A kid who'd likely had a narcissistic and neglectful mother.

Why couldn't he see it? He'd never put that sort of pressure on the girls or blame them.

Did his self-recrimination and the flimsy support of his mother make it impossible for us to have a future?

I rolled to my side. Bethany popped her head up and blinked sleep out of her eyes.

"Is it morning?" she asked groggily.

"Yeah, but it's early."

She frowned and peeked at her sister. "Can I cuddle with you?"

Would Rhys mind? Could I say no to that vulnerable request? "Come on up."

She scrambled onto the couch and wiggled between me and the cushions. When she was settled, her head was on my chest and she was snuggled into my side. "I miss having a mommy."

"I'm sure she misses you, but you get to have her around before she leaves again."

"Yeah, but she doesn't cuddle like this. She never really did," she said sadly. "Did your mom?"

"Yes, both of them loved to cuddle."

She frowned at me. "You got two moms?"

"My birth mom, and then Mama Mae adopted me and my sisters."

"Oh. That's nice." She was quiet for several heart-beats. "Did your birth mom leave you too?"

"She couldn't help it," I said gently. "She died in a car accident."

"Oh, I'm sorry."

"Thanks, hon."

She was quiet so long I thought she had fallen asleep. "I used to be really mad at Mommy," she whispered.

Poor girl. "That's understandable."

She lifted her head, her eyes wide and worried. "It is?"

"Yeah. I was mad at my birth mommy and daddy, but as an adult, I know they did the best they could. Sometimes," I said, lowering my voice, "I'd even get mad at Mama Mae."

She giggled. "But Mama Mae didn't leave you."

"No. She didn't. Sometimes she cares a lot and it can be stressful." I rubbed her shoulder. "Have you talked to your daddy about this?"

"No."

"He might need to know you're feeling this way."

"Who's feeling what way?" Rhys's voice broke in.

I found him standing at the end of the hallway. He was wearing the gray sweats from the night we'd almost gotten busted after making out and a loose white shirt that draped over his chest and settled around his hips. His hair was mussed and he was scratching his beard.

The other reason I hadn't been able to sleep was because he wasn't next to me. How spoiled I'd gotten in those two weeks. Waking up next to the one I loved wasn't something I'd ever take for granted. If I ever got to experience it again.

Bethany shrank against me. I didn't want to out her in front of her dad when she'd confided in me about something, but I hoped she'd talk to him soon. "Nothing, just girl talk."

He narrowed his eyes on us. "Sure." He shuffled to the bathroom.

"Thank you," Bethany said in a small voice.

"I really do think you need to talk to your dad about this. Can you think about it?"

"Yeah."

"Maybe if Hannah feels the same way, you can do it together."

"Maybe," she said noncommittally.

I let her rest until the bathroom door opened. Rhys shuffled back out. He didn't say anything, but his gaze went from his daughter to me. "Hungry?" he asked gruffly.

Bethany nodded, her hair scraping against me.

Hannah woke up and stretched. "Morning, Daddy." She scanned the room, and when she spotted her sister, she climbed on top of me too. I hugged both girls to me. Another experience I might never get.

It wasn't too late for me to have kids, but I didn't want them with a guy like Finn. Or Clinton or Toby. They might make good dads, but a shitty husband was still a bad role model.

Damn my standards.

Damn Rhys for his convictions.

The muscles jumped in Rhys's jaw and he cleared his throat. "I'll make some pancakes."

"Thanks, Daddy," the girls said in unison.

We snuggled while Rhys cooked. A girl could get used to this.

A girl might want to wake up like this every morning.

A girl might remember those plans and dreams she'd had with a boy that included a house and kids and a dog just like Goldie. Maybe one that didn't eat random objects and throw up until she had to go to the emergency vet.

Rhys popped back out, spatula in one hand, looking so different than I'd pictured him when we were younger. He was more serious, but now I could see—he was just as withdrawn. He protected himself as much as he protected others from himself.

He made his life about others.

When had others made their lives about him?

He furrowed his brows and shot me a questioning look.

I shook my head.

He lifted his chin in acknowledgment. A silent conversation. "Food's done."

A verbal conversation would have to wait—if we ever had it. A girl could only get rejected so many times by the man she was in love with.

"What are you going to do after we eat, Junie?" Hannah asked. She didn't move from me. Neither did Bethany.

"I'll probably go home and clean up. Then I might see if my sister wants help in the bar at the distillery." It wasn't open on Mondays, but Autumn liked to catch up with inventory and books. Wynter would be at work too. Maybe even Summer.

Bethany sat up. "Can we see the distillery?"

Rhys braced himself as soon as the question was out of her mouth. His jaw clenched and his gaze said *not again*.

I liked when he squirmed. The man ran from some of his problems and he couldn't right now. I enjoyed seeing him uncomfortable.

"That's up to your dad." I smiled brightly and his scowl deepened. I'd love to take them around the distillery, but in true Rhys fashion, he wanted to return to his plan to put distance between us.

He tapped a finger against the spatula handle. "I have to get some work done."

"Later?" Hannah asked. "Can we?"

"Can we, please?" Bethany added. "I've never been there."

This was the time I found his pathological need to please the women in his life useful. The moment he relented to their begging was apparent in the acceptance in his eyes and the loosening of his shoulders. "June?"

I bit back a triumphant grin. "I can give them a tour anytime today if they'd love to smell some yeast farts."

"Yeast farts?" Hannah dissolved into giggles.

Bethany snickered.

I might've said that on purpose. The yeast farts got all the kids.

He grunted. "I'll see what I can get done first."

"Yeah!" The girls jumped off me and ran to the kitchen.

"Don't wait for me. I'm going to clean up quick," I called to Rhys and went to the bathroom. His cedar-and-soap scent hung in the air. I inhaled deeply. This week could not be the last time I was surrounded by the scent of Rhys. It could not be the last time I was part of the girls' lives.

It could not be the end of me and Rhys.

But was I right to keep going down this path? If I wasn't what Rhys ultimately wanted, who was I to question it?

When I was finished in the bathroom, I went into the guest room to put on some fresh clothes. I closed the door and set my toiletry kit on the dresser. The box of memorabilia of me and Rhys was on the edge.

Smiling, I grabbed the image from the top. Our prom picture. I was wearing a dress that had a fitted

skirt that glittered like a mermaid tail. Bethany had said
she wanted her hair dyed to look like that.

Since I'd told them not to wait, I dug farther into the
box, beyond where we'd rummaged through when Wren
had first returned it to Rhys. I found pictures of us from
middle school. Some pictures of us with his 4-H animals.
At the very bottom was a small paper rectangle. A ticket.

I knew that logo.

I pulled the ticket out. The Grand Ole Opry.

When had he—

The date on the ticket was when I'd first performed.
Shortly before Summer had told me that Rhys and
Kirstin were divorcing.

Confusion swirled in my brain. He hadn't been there.
Had he gotten this ticket from someone who was? No,
the only people I knew who'd come that night were my
family, who'd flown out. I hadn't recognized anyone else.

How had he . . .

He'd run me off from the funeral, and then he'd
attended my dream performance?

I wanted to be there when you walked off the stage.

I wanted to kiss that big smile on your face.

My surprise gave way to anger. He'd been there that
night. He'd supported me like he always had, and he'd
hidden it. Like he was a toxic cloud that would taint my
success.

I stuffed the ticket in the pocket of my skirt and
returned all the pictures and article clippings to the box.

I'd always been told that, despite being adopted, I
possessed a lot of Bailey stubbornness. It was time to
find out just how stubborn I could be.

Rhys

I pulled into the parking lot of Copper Summit and parked. Not many cars were in the lot. June had invited us when the main employees were gone.

The building sat in the middle of a stretch of trees. The land behind the place had once been mined for copper and silver. Now it was decorated with grass and trees. One of the Bailey grandparents had started with moonshine in the old mining headquarters and eventually mastered bourbon, turning it into a thriving spirits industry and tourism for the town.

The building itself was a work of art. In high school, June had taken me to Bozeman and shown me the bigger distillery that made much of their popular commercial lines. The facility was large and impressive, but the location in Bourbon Canyon was the apple of Copper Summit's eye. Large windows decorated the front. A portion of them framed Copper Summit neon signs from the bar, but the rest offered a stunning view of the interior, with copper piping and large metal stills arching behind the glass.

I jogged to catch up to the girls, who sprinted toward the door of the distillery. June was standing outside the front door, waving. The breeze caught her long rainbow skirt around her legs and fluttered her loose top high enough that I caught a bare strip of stomach. Instant lust pumped through my veins.

It'd been over a week since I'd been inside her and it was like missing an appendage. I wanted to turn my head while lying in bed and tell her about my day. I thought of texting her pictures of when the goats were standing on random objects in their pen. Or of Goldie when she was eating her dog food with a comment **No blankets consumed today.**

I'd been with her since yesterday, but I missed her. I missed us.

Leaving my bedroom this morning had been the biggest fucking punch in the gut. June had been curled up with Bethany. My daughter had opened up to her about something she hadn't talked to me about. Then Hannah had joined them, and June had accepted her.

What would it be like to wake up to that every morning?

I wanted it so goddamn bad my heart nearly disintegrated in my chest when I thought that maybe . . .

"Hey!" June gave each of the girls a hug like she hadn't just spent the morning with them. "My sisters are so excited to have you. You might see my brothers too. Don't worry, they can look as grumpy as your dad, but they're just as harmless." She shot me a smug grin that made me want to haul her to the closest broom closet.

Fuck, I needed to get control of myself.

The girls rushed inside and went straight for the merchandise displays.

"I want this hat!" Hannah brandished a rust-colored Copper Summit ball cap.

"Ooh, I want the candy." Bethany squished her face against a glass display of bourbon-flavored chocolates.

June nudged my arm. "I hope you brought your wallet, Hot Mountain Daddy."

Wynter appeared around a display of squat glasses. "I hear we're giving a special tour for two special girls."

"We're so excited!" Summer was right behind Wynter. "We love visitors."

The tour started. Hannah slipped her hand into June's, and June led them into the area with the tanks.

"Remember those yeast farts I told you about?" June lifted Hannah to look inside. I did the same with Bethany. A brownish liquid filled the inside and bubbles were scattered across the top. Some were popping and a fruity, bread-like smell filled my nose. "These are the mash tanks, and one way we know the yeast is working is when they create bubbles."

After the girls got their fill and giggled a ton, June led us through the giant copper and steel stills.

Teller rounded a tank and nodded at his sisters and the kids. He stopped by me. "We charge extra for after-hours tours."

"June gave me the family and friends discount."

His expression turned appraising. "You're one of those?"

No, dammit. "Something like that."

Tenor approached us. He hunched his shoulders and stuffed his hands in his jeans. The guy had always been an odd mix of frumpy nerd and rugged cowboy, and most of the time it seemed like each personality was at war with itself. His baggy Copper Summit polo hung off his broad shoulders and fell to past his zipper. Had I ever seen him tuck in a shirt? Even his jeans were looser than most men wore theirs, but the amount of work he did was reflected in his scuffed cowboy boots.

He pushed his dark-framed glasses up his nose. "Hey, Rhys. Glad you could bring the kids."

He was the youngest of the Bailey brothers, but he was also the tallest. His height could be intimidating, but the slouch added an air of harmlessness, although I'd never discounted Tenor's strength.

"Hey, Junie," Teller called, interrupting her discussing how the vapors collect and go through another distillation process. "You gotta take them to the barrelhouse."

"Would you like to lead the tour, Teller?" June asked archly.

"Nah, you're doing fine." He grinned. "If you need a job, we can hire you."

June and her sisters rolled their eyes while the girls giggled.

"All right," June said. "Let's go to the barrelhouse before we go through the packaging area."

"We'll wait in here," Summer said. "Wynter and I want to get a goody package ready for each of them."

"Make Rhys one too," June said, shooting me a sly grin. "He's been a good boy."

I narrowed my eyes on her, but appreciation for June's family filled me like a balloon. My family was tight-knit, but it was small. My kids had friends, but with my job, we were homebound a lot. They had Wren for a grandparent but a mom who was rarely around. No aunts or uncles. Our life was quiet and sometimes I wondered if that was truly the best for them.

June's brothers took the lead, and we wove through the packaging area and out an exit at the far end of the distillery. The comforting smell of warm grain filled the air. They dried the mash behind the distillery before feeding it to their cattle.

Windows broke up the squat, rectangular barrelhouse at regular intervals. Unlike the work of art the distillery had been polished into, the wooden barrelhouse looked like it was made to do nothing but work.

Teller walked backward as he addressed the girls. "You'd never look at this and think there're millions of dollars sitting on racks inside."

Tenor opened the small side door for us and we wandered in. Wooden support beams formed racks from one end of the barrelhouse to the other. There was enough space between the rows to fit a forklift and allow it to maneuver, and each column was stacked four barrels high. The smell of grains was overtaken by the pleasing scent of old wood and musty dry air with a nice undercurrent of bourbon—the angel's share that evaporated out of the oak barrels.

"It's so quiet," Bethany whispered.

"Most of the time." Teller took over the tour, and Tenor followed, answering random questions that Bethany and Hannah asked. "When the forklifts are going and the guys are talking, it can get a little noisy."

June fell in step with me. "I'm glad you brought them."

"I didn't know when they would get the chance otherwise."

My comment landed like an empty barrel between

us. She stopped. I steeled myself and faced her, putting my back to the other four.

"That bothers me for two reasons," she said. "You broke my heart. You didn't even give us a chance, but any time the kids wanted a tour, each one of my family members would've stopped and given them one."

Chagrined, I gritted my teeth. She was right, but I hadn't gone out of my way to keep in contact with the Baileys, knowing I'd hurt June.

"The second reason," she continued, "is that I can't believe you're still determined to end this thing between us after all that's happened between us in the last few weeks." She poked my shoulder. "Since I first stopped in town."

"June." We'd been over this.

"What?" She searched my face. "What, Rhys? You know better? You're going to drag me down? You're no good for me? Didn't we prove otherwise when I started pumping out songs after one kiss?"

An old, clogging fear rose inside me, an emotion that had formed inside me the moment I'd heard my mom would never get to live out her dream. "I'd just get in the way."

She folded her arms. "You're not a kid anymore. And I'd certainly never think of treating Bethany and Hannah, or any other kid, the way your mom treated you."

I recoiled like she'd slapped me. "Jesus, June." Emotions clashed in my chest, making it hard to breathe. June would never speak to a kid like that— My mom hadn't either. I had deserved her hard words. Like my mom had told me, I'd needed a reality check. "You don't know anything about that."

"I know that I can probably commiserate with how hard your mom tried. I can probably even understand the pressure she was under trying to care for you. But what I don't understand is *when* your dad took you in. Didn't Angela ever call him? Did he even know about you? I don't think Jonathon Kinkade turned down custody of his son."

"He knew about me." I didn't know any of the specifics. Dad hadn't talked about Mom. He'd made sure my needs were met, and I'd made sure to behave so I wouldn't lose another parent.

"But you didn't know about him?" She folded her arms, her skirt swirling with the shift in her weight. "What exactly did she say about your dad?"

I ground my teeth again. *Your dad's a single rancher. He can't be a single dad.* Then after Dad and Wren had married. *She won't like you. You'll ruin his marriage.* "June, this doesn't have to do with us."

She flung her arms out. "It has everything to do with us!"

The voices in the background went silent.

"Fuck," I growled and rubbed the tiny cramp forming between my brows. "Can we talk about this later?"

"I don't know, Rhys, is there going to be a later?"

The guys appeared around one of the rows.

Tenor assessed us in that calm demeanor of his. "The girls are bored by nothing but barrels. We'll take them back to finish the tour."

"Thank you," June said, her glare still on me.

The girls were watching us with big eyes. Bethany's mouth pursed like she was chewing the inside of her cheek. I didn't want to worry them. They were in good hands.

"I'll be right there." I forced a smile. "You can each pick out two things from the shop."

June morphed into the stage presence she was adored for. "Y'all go ahead. I need to clear up a few things with your daddy before I leave."

I winced at the subtle stress she put on leave.

Hannah clapped her hands. "I want that hat and a toy." She rushed out the door and Tenor stayed on her heels.

Bethany was older and getting harder to fool. She pinned me with a wise-beyond-her-years gaze before following Hannah.

Teller was the last to leave, but the look he shot me wasn't the warning stare I anticipated. His brown eyes were full of disappointment.

Why was I the goddamn bad guy?

Hadn't I made myself one so June could do what she needed to?

"I love you." Her words slammed into my heart. "I'm in love with you. I always have been, even when you were an asshole at the funeral." She squeezed her eyes shut. "I understand why you did what you did." She opened her eyelids and I was staked in place by the amber blaze. "I understand why you're going to ditch me again. But I'm also enraged. How could you hurt me like that?"

"It's for your own go—"

"Is it?" Her eyes misted over. "It doesn't feel like it. It didn't feel like the best thing for me was to be alone in Nashville. Do you know . . ."

A cloud covered the sun, causing the interior to dim.

"Do I know what, June?" I asked quietly. I wouldn't like what she said.

"Those songs I wrote about us, I kept to myself for years. Then I wrote 'Emerald Rain' after your wedding and I still sat on them." A tear tracked down her cheek. "Then when you and Kirstin had Bethany, I knew I'd lost you."

I lifted my hand to catch the shiny tear, but she stepped out of my reach. I'd never hated myself more.

Wasn't this what I wanted? For her to move on and get everything she wanted?

Her words sank in, one horrifying realization at a time.

She'd held on to the music that had propelled her career? For years?

"Why?"

She sniffled. "How could I sing those if there was a chance for us? So I finally decided to let Lucy listen to them." Her harsh chuckle was swallowed by the large building. "And you know the rest. But you know what no one else can tell? They're different from the songs I wrote after all the other failed relationships. They're better. Because I was so truly in love with you and heartbroken. My other music? It's about superficial love and hurt for no damn reason. And this new album? It's going to be better than anything I've ever put out. So good, I don't know if I can ever top it." She took a step toward the exit. And another. "And you know what else?"

It was pretty clear right now I didn't know a goddamn thing.

She squared her shoulders. "I don't know if I want to top it. I'm at the top and the view is pretty damn lonely. The whole trip has been. Because I don't want fame and money if it means I can't be with the ones I love. If it means I lose the most important person in my life."

Her words were tiny slices along my skin. Little cuts, shredding everything I'd ever thought I knew.

She took a slip of paper out of a hidden pocket in her skirt. "I found this when I got dressed this morning. I should be touched, but it hurts. It really fucking hurts, Rhys."

My stomach dropped when I saw what she held. The ticket to her Grand Ole Opry performance.

"I just wanted to make music that meant something to others, but I'm losing myself in the process." She swiped at her face. "It feels really selfish to say that." Another bitter laugh left her. "I have five addresses!" She shook her head. "Anyway, I've been thinking a lot about what I really want, and I think maybe you need to do the same. Because I think in your case you need to be a little more selfish. You should probably look at how your mom's actions affected you and then wonder what example you're setting for your girls. I know it'd break your heart if they gave up everything for someone else's happiness—and then realized it was all for nothing."

She let the ticket fall to the ground. Then she turned and left me alone. Just like June was. Because of me.

CHAPTER TWENTY-SEVEN

June

I carried the basket of eggs up the hill. Mama walked next to me. Tomorrow I played the fundraiser. My luggage was packed, and in the morning, I'd load my two suitcases and my guitar. And shortly after that, I'd be gone.

She tipped her face to the sun. "I'd be lying if I said it wasn't nice to have you around the last two months."

I hefted the eggs. Twenty from this morning. That was breakfast for just Lane and Cruz. "I've treasured my time here. I need to do this more often."

She held the door to the house open for me. "After the big tour? Or will you have to pump out another album?"

I hadn't gotten that far yet. I didn't want to think about it. "I told the promoter that I couldn't leave for the first concert until after September. I shouldn't miss Summer's baby." I'd missed too many births. Tate's son

Chance with his first wife. Then the two kids he and Scarlett had—Brinley and Darin. Myles and Wynter's daughter, Elsa. I could be around for Summer and Jonah's baby. I'd send a message to my team that I needed dates spaced out around her due date. The promoter had pushed back, but I'd stuck firm.

Mama put her straw hat on a hook. "We'll certainly miss you."

I toed my boots off while Mama grabbed some cartons for the eggs. I set the basket on the counter and stared at it. "Mama?"

"Ah." She put the cartons down and rubbed my back. "It's time for a drink."

In any other family, having a glass of bourbon at nine in the morning might seem dysfunctional, but for the Baileys, it was like our morning tea.

I blinked back tears and sat at the table. Mama dug out a bottle of Summit in June, the line Daddy had created for me, and set it between our chairs at the table. Next she got two glasses out of the cupboard and sat.

I poured for us so she wasn't waiting on me hand and foot. I took a drink. The temperature outside was warm, but the flavor of vanilla and cedar on my tongue had a soothing effect. The warmth of the spirit was reassuring. Familiar.

I licked along my bottom teeth. "I told Rhys his mom wasn't a good mom."

"Mm." She poured more bourbon into her glass. "Your observation didn't go over well?"

"Do you think I'm right? Did you know her?"

"I knew of her. Heard about her and Rhys. That kind of thing. Small towns." She winked. "Anyway, Jonathon met her when she came with a traveling troupe to perform in the park. I also heard she claimed she'd never settle down in a place like Bourbon Canyon. I got the impression the entire state of Montana was too small for her."

"I don't think Rhys grew up in a warm, loving environment."

She nodded. "You could see it in him. The way he hung his head. Jonathon and Wren showered him with attention and he bloomed under their love."

"But he blamed himself for his mom. For everything that went wrong for her."

Mama's expression grew serious. She must've heard everything I didn't say. He blamed himself for his mom's death.

"He broke up with me because he thought he'd be bad for me. He thought he'd hold me back. And he's going to do it again." I took another long sip. The temptation to shoot the rest of the liquid was strong, but Daddy had taught me better than that. *Bourbon's a sipping drink*.

"He's a stubborn boy."

"And I can't out-stubborn him." I added more bourbon to my glass even though it wasn't empty. "I've been able to think a lot for the last two months. I want to dominate the charts with my new album. I want to go on tour and fill stadiums. But after that? There's nothing. More albums. More touring. More work."

"You're ready to transition to a different phase of your life, and there's only one man to do it with."

I nodded, a lump forming in my throat. "But he'll blame himself. He probably won't even give me a chance. He might even meet someone while I'm gone."

"Or you might."

The way my bourbon almost tossed itself right back out of my stomach was a clear indicator that no, I would not. "I can't let my happiness depend on him. But I don't want to just sing songs and only see my family a few times a year."

"Good thing you don't have to worry about that yet."

"What?" It wasn't like Mama to brush off my worries.

"Is he going to the fundraiser tomorrow?"

"Nope." After the barrelhouse, there would be no repeat of the Opry.

"But you were the one to walk away from him this time?"

I nodded, blinking back tears.

"Let's hope that's the kick in the ass he needs."

A tiny thread of hope rose, but I took another drink and let the bourbon smother it. "He ended a five-year relationship and let his ex-wife leave him rather than travel a few times a year or wait for us at home. He sold the ranch for Wren. I can talk his ear off, but he doesn't listen. I might as well play for thousands of people who will."

"It was always important to you to feel heard."

Rhys had given that to me. But I'd never listened to him. If I had, maybe things would be different. Or they'd be exactly the same, but I'd know why. "I guess I'm getting what I want."

"Don't give up yet. Things aren't always clear-cut." Mama held her glass up and studied the fluid inside. "Darin always said this batch was his most complex."

"Daddy said that about all of our batches."

She chuckled. "He said Wynter's was the fruitiest, Summer's was the richest, Autumn's was the sweetest,

Tate's was the boldest, Teller's was the spiciest, and Tenor's was the woodsiest."

Daddy never did pick favorites. "I love Rhys, Mama."

"I know you do, dear. We all do. But he's got to prove that he can't be scared off, even by his own self."

Rhys

"Goddammit!" I tossed the wrench at the workbench. I was supposed to cut hay in a few weeks, but I had guards to replace on my sickle mower. I'd done it a million times, but today I was useless.

"Daddy?" Bethany's voice came from the open door of the shop. "Are you okay?"

By the time I turned, Hannah was only a few feet away. She flung herself into me and wrapped her arms around my waist.

"Aw, hon. Don't worry about me. I'm just grumpy." June used to call me grumpy, and she was fucking right. My irritation notched higher. She was right about a lot.

I patted Hannah's back and Bethany ran to join us in a group hug.

Rain splattered against the ground outside. I inhaled a slow breath. I had to calm the hell down. I was scaring the girls.

"I'm fine. I'm just . . ." Furious at myself. At every damn thing. Except for my kids.

"You're going to miss her?" Hannah hugged me harder.

All the anger drained out of me. I hugged her back. Understatement of the century. "Yeah."

Bethany tipped her head back. "You should come to the fundraiser."

"I . . . can't." I'd spend tomorrow night fixing this damn mower.

I know it'd break your heart if they gave up everything for someone else's happiness—and then realized it was all for nothing.

June's comment had rebounded through my head since she'd left me in the barrelhouse. By the time I had found the girls, June had already given them hugs goodbye and was nowhere to be seen. She'd also told her sisters to put whatever the girls wanted from the gift shop on the house. I'd left Copper Summit with my heart destroyed, two ball caps, every sample of bourbon chocolate the shop had, and a toy whiskey thief and barrel.

My house, which had been a refuge from all things June Kerrigan, was now full of her reminders. Everywhere I looked, I had memories of her. I couldn't even hide while working on the breezeway's construction because it just reminded me of the night Kirstin had walked in on us.

The girls pulled away.

"I wish June could be our mommy," Bethany said.

Shock sent a cold wave through my blood. "But your mom's in town."

She stuck her lower lip out and looked away. Hannah twirled from side to side, her gaze on the floor.

I took off my ball cap, shoved a hand through my hair, and stuffed the cap back on. "You can talk to me."

Bethany twisted her hands together. " 'Member the morning you asked what I said to June?"

The morning I'd woken up to my dream life? Hell yeah, I remembered. "Yes."

"I told her I missed having a mommy."

Hannah nodded along with her.

The words "you have a mommy" stopped at the edge of my tongue.

"I miss Mommy being home and doing stuff with us," Bethany added. "I love Mommy, but she's gone all the time."

Kirstin had been in town for a month and she hadn't spent much of it with the kids. She hadn't even been at Wren's for more than a couple days at a time. She'd gone to Yellowstone to take pictures and then to Banff.

I'd thought she might be steering clear of June, but if I really thought about it, no. Kirstin would've gone off on her own anyway. Her cell signal might suck in the national parks, but not that badly. Not so badly she couldn't call for over a week at a time.

"June travels a lot too." The argument sounded weak. If June had kids, she'd call them every damn day. I didn't have to witness it to know it. She made sure the people in her life felt special. All the rumors of her being spotted in town over the last several years were because she'd come home for her family. That gossip had been circulating during each of her tours.

"June does stuff with us," Hannah said.

"Mommy got mad when I touched her camera," Bethany added.

"You know how protective she is of those." The dejected way they nodded was a knife straight to my conscience.

I know it'd break your heart if they gave up everything for someone else's happiness—and then realized it was all for nothing.

I would want to rampage if I realized my kids were miserable in the name of someone else's happiness.

Had I deluded myself? Was I miserable, and I'd been faking it? I loved my kids. I appreciated everything I had. But there was always the one that got away.

Would I have sold the ranch if I had been with June? Or would I have talked to Wren, persuaded her to sell half, or allow me to make payments no matter how much she fretted over whether I was financially stressing myself?

If I had taken June's hand at my father's funeral and told her that I'd join her as soon as I hired a ranch manager, would I be in Nashville now? Would we have had kids that would've already celebrated her headline world tour?

If I had been with June for either of those, I wouldn't have missed out on it all.

My chest grew tight. All the what-ifs flooded my mind. Overwhelming, but also—a relief. All those questions I'd been afraid to ask, that I'd ignored, were let loose.

The anxiety was fighting to return. I might've gone to Nashville, the new ranch hire might've run my dad's life's work into the ground and cost Wren any chance of retirement—thanks to me.

Kirstin could've walked out of the girls' life forever.

But . . .

June could've hit her milestones sooner. If only I hadn't gotten out of the way.

Fuck me.

"Let's go to the house and make some cookies while we talk."

CHAPTER TWENTY-EIGHT

June

People milled around me. I was in the middle of a stage on a small amphitheater where kids put on plays and local organizations put on shows for parties and other events. The first summer after my sisters and I had come to live with the Baileys, Mama and Daddy had taken us to see a band from Butte. It was where I'd confessed to Mama I wanted to be a singer. I'd told her that I used to sing on empty stages like this at the campgrounds we stayed at with my parents before they died. Mama Starr would help me imagine a crowd full of people coming to watch.

Today, I had no band. The performance was me on a stool with my favorite guitar. Wilna had managed to secure a microphone and speakers. I was singing a new song I had written last night, one that wouldn't be on the album.

It was about a girl who walked away from the only

guy she'd ever dreamed of. A girl who realized her worth, but was still heartbroken over the guy who didn't realize it in himself. I'd titled it "Get Out of Your Way."

A teen girl in the front row dabbed her eyes.

The song could be a hit, but it was too personal. I would sing it today, as a goodbye. To my town. To my family. To Rhys.

Wren was on a picnic table several yards from the stage. I'd been playing for hours. I'd sing, then talk with people and sign autographs. Then I'd sing again. Repeat.

I was tired, and I probably shouldn't drive after a long day like this, but I couldn't pass the turnoff to Rhys's place one more time. I couldn't be so close to him and know that he hadn't chosen me again.

I'd been looking for him all day, hoping that just like the Grand Ole Opry, he'd be hiding in the crowd. But just like that day, I'd seen my brothers and sisters and their spouses. Mama. Lane and Cruz. But no Rhys.

I let the last note for the song fade away before resting my hand across the strings of the guitar. "Thank you, everyone." My voice carried across the park. "Thank you so much for coming and listening to me and for your generous donations. The community of Bourbon Canyon thanks you, and I thank you. This town and everyone in it is special to me."

One man and two little kids more than others.

Kids laughed on the playground on the opposite end of the park. Families had come and gone, packed picnic materials or donated even more money to eat the hot dogs and chips that the grocery store had provided. Wilna had lockboxes set all over the park, darn near by every tree, for collections.

Every citizen in town had to have stopped by, and

while I no longer knew everyone in Bourbon Canyon, I suspected many out-of-towners had joined us. Loads of unfamiliar people roamed, staring in awe at the small-town park that held one of country music's biggest rising stars.

I switched the microphone off and moved the stand to the side.

Wilna rushed the stage with some more folks who held notebooks or shirts.

As I signed what was thrust in front of me, Wilna rattled on about the success. She'd deployed a team of elderly but tenacious ladies to empty the collection boxes and tally money. Another team had run the money to the bank, and the bank's president had stayed on call to make the regular deposits.

". . . and then Sheila added her total and I think, by gosh, we've outdone the year Tate was a bachelor."

I grinned. My siblings had made sure of it, and I'd given Tate money to drop in a box for me. "I'm glad it worked."

"It more than worked." She leaned close and her strong floral perfume surrounded me. "Between you and me, I really hope we can do the bachelor auction again. It's just too fun. This was really special though. But if I can ever get one of your single brothers to step up on the auction block . . ." She squinted at me, her pale-blue eyes sharper than a pin. "You think Lane or Cruz would advertise themselves?"

"I'm going to stay all the way out of that, but good luck. If I can ever help again, please call me."

She winked. "If your phone number doesn't change again."

"Yet you always manage to get it." Mama was behind

that, but she always asked me before giving my number out.

More people approached with items for me to sign.

Wilna enveloped me in a big hug with surprisingly strong arms. "I'll let you finish up here. Take care of yourself, dear. You're pretty special to us."

My heart melted. I returned her hug, then smiled at the little girl holding her stuffed bear and a blue marker for me to sign.

I spent an additional hour chatting and auto-graphing.

My brothers started herding the crowd away from the stage. Their years of moving cattle were coming in handy. The day was growing late and I hoped to drive farther than Billings tonight.

I finished tucking my guitar in its case. Tenor had already packed away the microphone and speakers.

The park was back to normal. Another glance at what was left of the crowd and the trees didn't reveal a hot mountain daddy. I had surreptitiously looked for him all day, and I'd deliberately searched the most obscure places, hoping he was hiding from me and my family.

I'd seen the girls dancing with Wren, but they hadn't approached me. Had Wren told them to let others have a chance since they'd had me to themselves several times over the last two months? Or was it easier for them to let me go than it was for me to leave them?

Rhys and I might be done, but could I continue sending them recorded guitar lessons and souvenirs?

The hollowed-out feeling in my chest would stick around for a while. At least I had some activities to keep me busy. To keep my mind off weekly guitar lessons, yummy homemade pancakes, and the man who loved me so much he was willing to devastate both of us.

I pushed my hair behind me. My car was a bit of a walk.

"Drive safe," Tate said and crushed me in a bear hug that reminded me of Daddy.

"Take care of everyone," I said. "I know you will."

Tenor was next. He was gentler, much more aware of his size and that he could crack all my ribs in a heart-beat. "Call if you need anything. Lane's on standby if you have car trouble."

"Thank you." I turned to Teller.

Not only did he hug me, he gave me a soft noogie. "You're gonna be a big star."

"I already am," I joked.

He didn't laugh. "I know, but don't be a stranger. It's been nice seeing you around."

"It's been nice being home." The truth rang crystal clear. I loved being home. My house in Nashville did not feel like this. Nor did the condo in Florida that I'd only been to twice in the last five years. The apartment in New York was stifling and I really shouldn't renew my lease. Same with the place in LA. It was handy, but I had fewer friends in that part of the world than anywhere else.

But I'd figure out my plan after the tour. I'd sell my car, just like before. And I'd buy a new one—one that wouldn't break down and lead me right into another broken heart.

I looked around the park again. No tall, bearded man in flannel.

Sadness echoed in my empty chest but I forced a

cheery smile. "Well. It's time to go." I'd done what I came here to do.

I'd done a lot more and that was why it was hard to leave.

He moved to grab my guitar case, but I clenched my hand around the handle. "Nah, I've got it. You're needed here."

Teller scowled. "I'm trying to dodge Wilna's bribes to be one of her bachelors."

I looked over his shoulder. "She's chatting up Tenor right now." My other brother was fidgeting with his glasses and more hunched than normal, like he was extra nervous around such a tiny woman.

"God help him," Teller muttered, a rare look of fear in his brown eyes. "I've gotta go . . . somewhere." He gave me another quick hug and rushed in the opposite direction of Tenor and Wilna.

My grin faded as soon as I'd walked far enough that my back was to everyone. The moment had arrived. I was leaving.

My stay had turned out so much differently than I had thought when I'd left Nashville, distraught and betrayed. I had thought I'd spend my time at the cabin, healing and writing. And I had, but that part had been such a small portion of my time.

I'd done extra photo shoots with Wynter. We had the Christmas campaign done, images and voice-overs for the next year, and I'd gotten a lot of extra time at Copper Summit. I loved that place as much as I adored the cabin.

My entire family was in one spot, and I'd spent time with all of them. I'd gotten to be a cowgirl again for a weekend too.

And then there was Rhys. Bethany and Hannah. Those two months would stay with me longer than the five years I'd had with Rhys as kids.

Now it was over.

I could return after my tour. Semi-retire and make a home. But I couldn't fully relax until I got over Rhys. I might as well keep writing and keep singing until no one cared anymore.

Would Rhys stop caring one day? Would we be able to live in the same zip code and not be star-crossed lovers?

I'd have to try not to cry every time I sang that song.

I kept my head down and took the walking path that would lead to my car. Large cottonwoods blocked out the still strong rays of the summer sun. This morning, I had known I would need the time to clear my head, and I hadn't wanted to clog up spaces closer to the amphitheater.

"June!" Bethany shouted.

I jerked my head up. My heart did a leap and fluttered behind my sternum.

Bethany and Hannah were next to Wren. Her small red hybrid was parked in front of my car.

"Hey!" I let my joy at seeing them radiate out. "I hoped I'd see you again."

They ran to me for hugs. Wren came close enough to join in.

"You did so good," Bethany said, and her encouragement meant more than any critic's review.

"Thank you. I was so glad to see you—"

"We have to go," Hannah announced. "Because Daddy has to tell you something."

My pulse stopped midbeat. Rhys was here?

Wren squeezed my hand. "Whatever happens, just know you'll always be a part of our lives." She released me and started for her car. "Come on, girls. Let's let them talk."

Without arguing, they abruptly left me and loaded up in Wren's car. They all waved as they drove away.

Let me talk with who? I saw no one.

"Bye, Daddy!" one of them hollered through a cracked window.

I spun and pressed my fingers to my mouth.

Rhys was leaning against a tree that must've concealed him from me. He wasn't wearing a cap of any sort and his rich brown hair was neatly combed to the side. His blue eyes glowed lighter under the evening sun, and his jeans weren't one of the worn pairs he usually worked in. At his feet was a suitcase.

"Rhys?"

He slipped the Grand Ole Opry ticket out of his back pocket. He held it in the air pinched between his middle and index finger. "It was hard as hell to keep you or your family from seeing me. But there was no fucking way I was going to miss your big debut." He stuffed the ticket back into his pocket. "After your show, when I wasn't the one waiting offstage to give you the biggest hug and kiss, I admitted that I hadn't moved on. I finally told Kirstin to go live her dreams because it wasn't fair to her to be married to me. Even then, I still had no clue that moving on from you was impossible."

He crossed to me and gently took the guitar case out of my hand. Then he tipped my chin up, his touch light but firm. My gaze turned watery. What was he going to say? What wasn't he going to say?

I couldn't get my hopes up again.

"I love you, June. I always have. I won't ever forgive myself for breaking your heart. I can't forget the amount of time we lost, but I sure as fuck have realized that I don't want to waste one second more."

"What are you saying?" I whispered.

"I'm saying that I talked to Wren about my mom and what she knew." He clenched his jaw. "Turned out it was a whole damn lot, and she'd been waiting for me to be ready to hear it." He stroked his hand down to my shoulder. "I also talked to Kirstin. I told her that the girls wanted her around. That she didn't have to be like Wren to be the mom they needed. I said she needed to try harder and that I didn't give a fuck about her travel schedule. I'd need her help with the girls while you're on tour." His smile was tentative, with a thread of trepidation. "We won't be able to be on the road with you the whole time, but if you'll give me a chance, I'll sure as hell make this work between us."

Nothing was making sense. The fear was too strong inside me. "You said you were going to come with me once before and you lied."

"I lied to us both and I'm so damn sorry. I truly thought it'd be the best for you. But when I picked you up in the rain, it was the universe's way of telling me I'd been a dumbass. I don't know how I got lucky enough to get a second chance, but I'm not ready to throw it away yet." He towered over me. "Can you trust me one more time? Can you let me prove that I'll never, ever let you down?"

Could I? He'd resisted a reconnection for two months. He'd broken my heart, but he also had the key to putting it back together and he'd never used it. "I don't know . . ."

"Can you think about it while I drive?"

While he drove? My gaze landed on the suitcase. "You're coming with me?"

"Am I, June?" He feathered a thumb over the pulse point in my throat.

My breathing quickened. This was happening so fast. I had to be dreaming. "What about the girls?"

"They'll stay with Wren. I'll have to come back fairly often for long stretches of time when they're in school, but on vacations, they can fly out with me. Otherwise, I can juggle the schedule with Kirstin."

"What did she—" I shook my head. His ex was none of my business.

"She said it was about time I quit living in a shell. She'd also like to take the girls with her too, and try to bond with them a little more, but she was afraid to ask. She was afraid I'd lock them away." His smile was sad. "I needed a lot of real talk from a lot of women who really care about me."

"You're important to more than just me."

"Kirstin said she'll even get her own place. It's been hard for her to return to Bourbon Canyon and feel like a stranger."

Everything about that sounded amazing. Except I couldn't buy the too-good-to-be-true quality of it. "Your ranch?" He didn't have employees. The whole thing depended on him.

"I can't be gone for long at a time, but I was told once I could call in a favor for helping work cattle with Bailey Beef."

"My brothers know about this?"

"I only talked to Tate, but he said whatever I needed,

whenever I needed it." He continued the steady strokes of his thumb along the base of my neck.

As much as I wanted to sink into him, the young girl inside me remembered waking up alone. Only weeks ago, I'd woken up without him and thought he'd left for good. "I don't know if I can trust you'll stay with me."

"I know, June." His whisper was ragged and he pressed a kiss to my forehead. "I fucked up over and over again. You paid for it. I want to spend my life making you happy. You want to tour for the next twenty years? We'll do it. You want to retire immediately? I don't care. I'm just going to be there for you, no matter what."

"Rhys." I blinked up at him and tears rolled down my cheeks. I was one more adrenaline pump away from shaking. "I'm scared."

"Me too. I want to run, to hide in my small farmhouse and let you go so I'm not a detriment to your career, but I keep telling myself that I've done that. Just because I was out of the picture didn't mean it was smooth sailing for you. After talking to Wren . . . it makes sense. You were right about my mom and I should've seen it years ago, as soon as I became a dad. But then I would've had to admit that I'd let the most important person in my life get away because of a selfish woman who never really cared about me. She was siphoning money from Dad, and after he married Wren, my mom was even more controlling when it came to me."

"Oh, Rhys. I'm so sorry."

"No. I'm the sorry son of a bitch who let you go." He placed a kiss at the corner of my mouth. "I have no business asking you to give me a chance. But if you're willing, I'm here, and I'll drive."

The difference between then and now was that I had a choice. No, I'd always had a choice and Rhys had made sure giving up wasn't one of them. He was doing it again, but this time, he was offering a path that included him.

Would I forever be wondering if he'd fly back to Montana and stay? Yes, probably. But if he was serious, he would work infinitely harder to let me know that though we might be apart, we still had each other. He was a dad. He had other considerations. But I would still be one of his priorities.

So my choices were to leave him behind, to endure the heartbreak for decades more and try to heal.

Or let him drive.

June

Summer and Jonah's cabin had signs of baby everywhere. A little portable bassinet stood by the big picture windows. How many babies got to nap with the view of a wide, sloping valley? A swing and changing table were by the wall. Down the hallway and to the left was a new addition that included the nursery Summer had done up with pictures of wildlife and mountains.

My sister was curled up in the corner of the couch while I rocked in a handmade rocking chair. A Jonah special. I'd have to order one for the cabin, but I had time. My tour would last for almost an entire year. I was leaving after my visit here. The first concert was in four days and it was crunch time for my team.

"I'm so glad you could make it," Summer said. She'd trimmed her hair recently. All the old blond highlights were gone, leaving her natural strawberry-blond tresses.

"Me too. I told my team that no matter what, I was getting here to see you and little Eli."

"I wasn't sure, but I wouldn't have held it against you. Your album is going bonkers."

I grinned. *Canyon Confessions* was on its way to double platinum. The cover photo I'd used was the one taken at Copper Summit, the one I'd asked Wynter not to use in the promotion. My album had topped both the country and pop charts in the first two months, and three of my songs were in the Billboard Hot 100 at the moment. "It's been wild."

My audience was devouring the songs. They speculated about them and which ones had to do with Hot Mountain Daddy. Many of them had concluded that all the songs were about me and Rhys. They were right.

My most successful single to date was the one I'd written for myself about myself and what I could do with the love and support of my family. I had titled it "Don't Wait for Me." The song still sat at number one, but it was about to get bumped out by "Senseless," which had just released. I never did name the man in the song who had pushed me away only to kiss me senseless.

The press and the picture from months ago had started circulating again, along with the story of our high school relationship, and it was fueling interest. More people were buying the album, streaming the songs, and it was hard to scroll through any social media without hearing snippets.

"My favorite part," I said while gazing adoringly at the little sleeping face of my newest nephew, "is how many people have messaged and posted that these songs speak for them."

"Everyone can hear you now."

"Yeah." Only my sisters knew what that meant for me. In a way, we were all still in the same car together. But we'd all survived and now we were all succeeding.

She pushed up the sleeves of her loose, long-sleeved shirt. "So? How often are we going to see you over the next year?"

"I'm figuring all that out." I danced my fingers along Eli's scalp, brushing his superfine hair back. "The first half of the tour will be pretty hot and heavy." My amazing new manager and my promoter had been enthusiastic about scheduling venues, but when I had returned to Nashville and met with them, I'd slowed things down. I'd still have a heavy travel schedule through the end of the year, but I'd also have longer breaks too, and the venues were grouped to decrease the sheer amount of travel.

The good news was that I had graduated from a bus artist to a plane artist. I could fly from city to city instead of spending so much time on the road on a bus. Being able to take planes eased my anxiety about having the girls travel on the road a lot, and it helped with Bethany's motion sickness. She still didn't feel good, but the travel was shorter and she was so thrilled to fly that she didn't care.

Muffled voices carried in from the kitchen, on the other side of the door to the garage.

Bethany and Hannah spilled in. Both of them had ponytails with orange clip-in hair pieces to add color streaks like I had in my hair. The play extensions were our compromise. Kirstin and I didn't want to permanently dye their hair and temporary color didn't show well in their darker tresses.

"It was so cool," Bethany said. Her gaze landed on

Eli, and she shushed her sister who wasn't talking, then made the same motion to Rhys and Jonah behind her.

Jonah's mouth tipped up, but he nodded. "Quiet down, Rhys."

"I'll try." Rhys grinned, but his warm gaze was on me instead of the baby.

The girls surrounded me. They'd been enthralled by Eli since we'd arrived.

"Can I hold him?" Hannah asked.

"Absolutely." Summer got up and took Eli.

While she helped each kid hold the newborn, Rhys squatted next to me. "Somehow, I got talked into ordering two tables, one for each bedroom." He smirked. "They even talked Jonah into making some frames for the Yellowstone pictures they took with Kirstin."

Instead of having Kirstin get stressed about the girls around her lenses that cost as much as a decent used car, Rhys had bought each girl their own camera. Kirstin had told him what to get and he'd bought it.

Co-parenting with Kirstin was going surprisingly well. She'd been quiet when we'd first talked. But her guarded demeanor had eventually dropped and she'd gotten more comfortable around me and Rhys while traveling for and loving her job. She didn't feel like she had to hide it, and she was delighted that Rhys was finally open to letting the girls travel with her. Once he saw how excited the girls and their mom were, he couldn't deny them the opportunity.

The more he divorced himself from the notions his mom had planted, the easier planning became.

During one of the jaunts when Rhys was in Nashville with me, the girls had gone on a trip to Wyoming with their mom. Their pictures had turned out gorgeous.

"Ready to go?" he asked quietly.

"No." I had to return to Nashville. I had rehearsals and meetings and one more big interview before my first sold-out concert. Nerves rippled through my belly. "No. But yes."

"I'll be there when the girls have their first three-day weekend."

I inhaled a fortifying breath. He'd been flying back and forth for months, but each time he left, anxiety chewed a hole through my belly. "Then Christmas in LA."

I rubbed a hand over my other forearm. Rhys had bad memories of LA. He'd been to Nashville. He'd met me in Denver when I'd had an appearance on a morning show. But he hadn't returned to the towns that had given him the worst memories of his time with his mom.

He covered my hand with his. "Christmas *and* New Year's. Tenor said he and Lane and Cruz would handle my animals. I think Goldie likes Cruz more than me."

"Cruz always has snacks." My stomach settled down just a little bit and I chuckled. The girls were cooing over Eli, and Summer was taking pictures. "It doesn't have to be LA. I know how—"

"You have an apartment there, and it's time I rewrite those memories with happy ones. I'm looking forward to the kids having wonderful memories of the city."

"To be fair, it'll be Disneyland they'll love the most."

"To be fair, I'm a little excited about that too." He enveloped my hand in his. "Time to get you to the airport. Three weeks. Then I'll be there, waiting for you to run offstage and into my arms."

Rhys

The organized chaos of the concert never failed to amaze me. Neither did the way June could connect with tens of thousands of screaming fans. Not just them. She laughed and joked with her band and her crew.

"Thank you, Tampa!" She raised her arms and the sound was deafening. I needed to add noise-canceling headphones to my list.

She rushed offstage and right into my arms. I swooped her up and spun her around.

"You're amazing, June Bug," I said into her ear, unsure if she could hear me over the roar.

She grinned, radiant, but she let me support her while her team surrounded her, coaching her on how the rest of the night would go, when our ride to her condo would arrive, and when they'd connect with her for the next show.

Hours later, we were entering her condo. The smell of flowers filled the air. One of June's assistants had arranged for the condo to be cleaned and ready. A bouquet of roses sat on the table.

The floor plan of the place wasn't much smaller than the main floor of my house. With two bedrooms and two baths, it was more than enough for June and a nice getaway for a couple, but also big enough for the kids. They'd love the view of the water. Not to mention the pool in the back. June had mentioned letting go of all her places, but I'd encouraged her to wait and see. She didn't need to shrink her world for me; I was expanding mine for her.

June took her boots off. "Ugh. I need a shower and to sleep in."

She took my hand and tried to drag me to the bathroom, but I tugged her toward the floor-to-ceiling windows. It was nice, but lights dotted the view and reflected off the water. So different than what I was used to, but not at all bad. Not when I was with June, and my kids were having a nice long weekend with their grandma.

I lifted a little velvet box I'd asked June's assistant to place by a vase on a table by the window.

June's lips parted and a small gasp escaped her.

I slowly knelt while watching the shock play over her face. Her jaw dropped farther open and she put her hands in front of her mouth.

The question played in my mind. I wanted to make her mine in every way possible. I wanted her to know I was committed. I knew she feared the travel would wear on me and that the memories of my youth in LA would scare me away. Nothing would keep me from this woman ever again. I wouldn't keep myself from her, and I needed her to know. I needed her to be mine.

"June, will you marry me?"

She looked from the ring to my face and back to the ring. Then she dropped to her knees and flung her arms around me. "Yes!"

Laughing, I hugged her back.

She cried against my shoulder. "You don't have to—"

"June Bug, you'd better not finish that sentence. I want you. You're mine."

She sniffled and pulled back, a wide smile on her

face. I removed the square-cut diamond with delicate smaller diamonds encrusting the band. It was a style she'd talked about in one interview years ago. *Simple but fancy because even country girls liked diamonds.*

I slipped the ring on her finger. A perfect fit.

She held her hand toward the window. The ring sparkled. Her mouth dropped open. "I described this ring once. How did you know?"

"I might've done more than check up on you. I'm a man obsessed. And I'm so damn grateful to be with you." I swooped her into my arms.

She laughed and clung to me. I took us to the palatial bathroom—fanciest one I'd ever been in—started the water and stripped her down. When I was undressed, I led her into the shower.

We took our time soaping each other up, and I used extra care on her, admiring the slope of her belly, the curve of her thigh, and those plump tits.

"Rhys, if you don't get inside me, I'm going to come just from the wicked things you're doing with the washcloth."

I tossed the cloth on the little shower bench and crowded June toward the wall. "Can't have that."

Water pounded us from six different angles. I hitched her legs around my waist and plunged into her. I had the whole weekend to take my time with her, but this was the first time in our long history together that I'd been inside of her while my ring was on her finger.

She tucked her fingers into my wet hair and tightened her legs. "I can't believe I'm going to be June Kinkade."

That gave me pause. "You're going to change your name?"

She wiggled her hips to encourage me to continue. "Two *K* last names would get confusing for our kids. If you want to have more."

I didn't resume thrusting. "Do you?"

"I've always dreamed of having kids of my own, and you seem to make really awesome ones."

Humbled that our dream from so long ago still held firm, I pumped into her. "I want everything you'll give me." I kissed a path from the base of her neck to her mouth. "I told you once to fly free, songbird, but I take it back. You're going to be tied to me forever, and I'll make sure you get to where you want to go."

Her climax was building. She was wide open to me and each thrust made her clit scrape against me.

Water ran down her face and dripped off my beard. Steam billowed around us. My orgasm pushed at the barriers I had containing it until June was ready to go.

"I want to go wherever you are, Rhys Kinkade."

"We're already here. So come for me, baby."

She exploded around me, her walls clenching and rippling over my cock. With a growl, I let my release go. Every time with her was more powerful than the last.

Several minutes later, we were dried off and tucked in a bed plusher than I'd ever slept in before. June was nestled in the crook of my shoulder and her breathing was already even.

I let sleep claim me, knowing that for the rest of my life if I had to leave June's bed, I'd always know I was coming back.

June

Bethany streaked into the apartment. We'd just finished a whirlwind day at Disneyland. "This is even more fun than last year!"

Hannah danced into the place, her arms full of stuffed animals and her mouse ears still on her head. "I wanna swim!"

Rhys wrapped an arm around my waist. "Can't they just pass out for a two-hour nap like last year?"

I laughed. "They built up stamina."

Last year, Rhys and the girls had met me on the Southern California leg of my tour. They'd stayed for most of the Christmas and New Year's break. I'd upgraded apartments since then. This one overlooked the city with a wall of windows like the place I'd just sold in Tampa, and it had a pool on one of the lower levels for tenants.

During my big tour, I'd made new memories of New

York City with Rhys. We'd visited Broadway, and he'd opened up more about what he remembered of his time there. Then we'd placed flowers on the corner where his mom had died. After the trip, I'd let my apartment there go. The urge to be home more and travel less was stronger than ever.

My tour was done. Even though breaks had been planned between major city jumps, I had been exhausted by the time it was over. The international travel had gone smoothly but had seriously hampered the time I could spend with Rhys and the girls. They'd been able to meet me in Toronto over the summer, but any other international travel would be done on our time, without the frenzy of a stadium event.

I'd been in Bourbon Canyon for the last two months, recuperating and enjoying getting to know the girls even better. I wasn't going to retire, but I was going to slow down. A lot. I'd write and release albums and feed my fans via social media.

Rhys and I had had a small fall wedding at our place. Then we'd enjoyed our own little honeymoon over Thanksgiving weekend while the girls were with their mom in Bozeman. She'd gotten a small house so she had a home base and could be just a mom when she had the kids instead of a traveling photographer mom.

Things were going really well.

And they were about to get busy.

"Hey, I have some news," I said.

Rhys gave me a questioning look. I smiled and slipped my hand in his. He pulled me into him and wrapped his arms around my waist.

"Okay?" Bethany was digging out a fresh swim towel. She had her goggles in one hand and her swimsuit over her shoulder. They'd been swimming every day since we'd arrived.

"Do we get to go to London yet?" Hannah asked. She'd been devastated that she couldn't visit every country I had played in.

"Um, no. We might have to put London on hold next summer." I took each of Rhys's hands and moved them down to my lower belly. "We're going to be busy with something else."

His hold on me tightened. "Are you serious?"

Hannah scratched the side of her head and looked around, probably for the swimsuit hanging up in the bathroom behind her. "Why are we going to be busy? Daddy hired a guy to cut hay."

That had been Cruz, but no. We'd be home to cut hay next year. "We're having a baby."

The girls stopped, their eyes wide.

Rhys buried his nose at my nape and inhaled. "I love you so fucking much."

I held my breath. I was thrilled. The last two months of domestic life had been so many dreams come true, and I was already so incredibly humbled that I'd already had pie-in-the-sky dreams unfold. But I wanted the girls to be comfortable with everything that was happening too.

Bethany sucked in a big breath. "A baby?"

"I'm going to be a big sister?" Hannah asked in awe.

"Is that okay?" Rhys asked.

Cheers broke out and they tackled us. A giant group hug was all I needed to erase the anxiety. "I'm so happy that you're both happy."

"I can't wait." Bethany's expression grew serious. "Now can we go swimming?"

"Go get ready, you two," Rhys said, but he didn't let me go. "I've gotta talk to June."

When they disappeared into their bedroom, he twirled me around and cupped my face. "Are you ready for this?"

We'd talked about kids and when I'd go off birth control, but Rhys never quit doing check-ins, making sure he was doing what I needed out of him and that I was content.

I turned my face into his big, warm palm. "I am. Are you?"

The love that filled his eyes was staggering. "I'm always ready to fly right next to you, songbird."

———

Ruby only meant to pick up some shifts working in the tasting room at Copper Summit. She didn't mean to corner one of her bosses into going to a wedding with her as a plus one to show her ex she wasn't hung up on him. But Tenor agrees to a little fake dating relationship to sell the whole image. Then he shows her how low she's set the bar for her dating life. The arrangement was only ever meant to be fake. So why does it feel so real? Read Ruby and Tenor's story in Bourbon Summer.

Find out what Junie and Rhys name their next collaboration (it's a baby!) in a special bonus epilogue. Sign up at my website walkerrosebooks.com.

ABOUT THE AUTHOR

I live the dream in my own slice of paradise where I get to enjoy colorful sunsets from my rocking chair while I'm working. I have my very own romance hero with Mr. Rose and there's more than a few little rose buds running around. A couple aren't so little anymore! We keep things interesting with cats and a dog and the critters that roam though the yard (fingers crossed the mountain lions stay away).

walkerrosebooks.com

ALSO BY WALKER ROSE